PRIEST AND PARIAHS

Centauri Survivors Second Chance Chronicles, Book Three

J. Alan Veerkamp

A NineStar Press Publication

Published by NineStar Press
P.O. Box 91792,
Albuquerque, New Mexico, 87199 USA.
www.ninestarpress.com

Priest and Pariahs

Printed in the USA
First Edition
September, 2018

Print ISBN: 978-1-949340-80-8

Also available in eBook, ISBN: 978-1-949340-76-1

Warning: This book contains sexually explicit content, which may only be suitable for mature readers.

Chapter One

THE DARKNESS REMINDED him somehow of being an unborn child—as if one could remember such a thing—floating weightless, enveloped by warmth. What would anyone give to fall back into such a simple existence, removed of all need beyond instinctual thought? What a fortunate nine months it would be. A wonderful life, sleeping and cared for inside the womb, never requiring a voice. All before anyone could teach a soul to love or hate, or something or someone was unwanted.

Is that what was happening here? Had he somehow regressed back before his own infancy? The pangs of jealousy he was experiencing told him no. Sadly, no.

He felt like he'd been slumbering for such a long time, and very, very gradually he started to wake. Threads of logical coherence tickled his thoughts in the dark. It was not a welcome sensation, and he fought to avoid it. Why couldn't he go back into the lovely silence?

Envy for the ignorance of the unborn rolled through him. How unfair it was to have the innocence of being sequestered and never hearing the taunts of children or comprehending the cries of the intolerant taken away from him. If only he had never heard slurs of hatred or understood what defined a second-class citizen.

What was that sound? Could it be a faint heartbeat in the distant void? It sounded brash and unnatural, refusing to lull him back to sleep like the soothing cadence of a mother's pulse.

Like a child, he wanted nothing more than to stay safe and warm, but like in every instance, someone always forced a person into the painful light and cold of reality. The darkness parted above him with a soft mechanical hiss. The warmth bled away, making him want to cry.

Daring to open his foggy eyes, he squinted in the artificial light. A woman in a white coat hovered over him.

"Welcome back to the real world. Can you tell me your name?"

His voice was dry and raspy, and he had to concentrate to answer her correctly. "Costa...Costa McQuillen."

"Good. Your stats are looking healthy." A warm smile graced the young woman as she read over the flat scanner in her hand.

Focusing was becoming easier. He found himself undressed, lying back in comfort, some kind of foam bedding molded around him. It held him effortlessly, but its touch was delicate, tricking his senses into thinking he was floating. Several small pieces of equipment were attached to his body, taunting him with their hidden binary code. She touched one piece of technology and looked back to the miniature screen she carried.

"Are you a doctor?" Costa asked.

"Yes, I am." A small frisson of panic lanced him. He wasn't about to lie back and allow her to poke and prod him. The doctor placed a hand on Costa's shoulder as he started to rise, holding him in place with little effort. "Hold on. Don't sit up right away. You'll be a little disoriented for a bit. That's normal for a five-year hypersleep."

Costa groaned, trying to sort himself as the doctor's caring tone diffused his anxiety. "Where am I?"

"You're on board the *Mayflower Ark*."

"The *Mayflower Ark*?"

The doctor nodded. "Yes. You booked passage from Earth to Alpha Centauri Prime."

"I did?"

"Yes. Just like everyone else on board."

"I'm sorry. I'm a little confused."

The doctor's smile was sweet with understanding. "It's all right. I have this conversation with most of the passengers. We'll be arriving on Alpha Centauri Prime within twenty-four hours. We're in the process of waking all of the Earth immigrants."

Costa looked around and found himself inside an enormous medical bay filled with mechanical wombs, just like the one in which he lay. Men and women in lab coats drifted from capsule to capsule, setting free the dazed people inside. Some were more awake than others, with men, women, and children milling about the vast room as they dressed. The more he saw, the more the cloud over his thoughts lifted.

"This is odd." The doctor squinted at her handheld display.

"What?"

"There are a few anomalies in your bio-scan."

"That's ridiculous. Your tech must be faulty." Costa granted the device in her hand a vicious stare. "Look again."

The doctor's forehead creased as she blinked in confusion. "Oh. Wait. It's normal now. Must have been an error."

"Yes, it must have been. May I get dressed now?"

With a simple touch, the doctor removed each of the devices attached to Costa's arms and legs. "You seem coherent enough to move around safely. The muscle stimulators kept your body from atrophying during the long sleep, but you may still be a little weak. Be careful until you get settled. If you find yourself feeling lightheaded, I want you to sit down immediately."

"Thank you, Doctor."

She might have been genuine and helpful, but she couldn't go away fast enough for his tastes.

Once she left, Costa took on the slow task of sitting upright and retrieved his clothing from the bin alongside the bed. After he was dressed and found his footing, Costa wandered over to the observation decks located next to the hypersleep room. He couldn't bear to keep looking at the rows of chambers. Even with all the living people inside, each capsule reminded him too much of a coffin, and with so many clustered together, the errant idea morphed itself into some kind of perverse morgue. He couldn't bear to spend time entertaining the image. It sparked far too many horrific memories.

The view into space through the three-story-tall view ports lining the wall pushed back the recollections. Alpha Centauri Prime grew larger as they approached, looking similar to his homeworld with its land masses and blue waters, even if the continents didn't match. He had to look more than once to convince himself the world before him was not actually Earth. Costa had no intention of ever setting foot on that planet again.

It was difficult to find some space from the small crowds forming near the giant windows. Being around so many strangers made him uneasy. Growing up on the fringes of society, he knew the burn of hate which always made him an outcast. With his slight size, he'd always appeared physically vulnerable, which only emboldened the taunts. As he grew older, he had maneuvered his way into a comfortable existence, but in his experience, there weren't many men and women who could be trusted. Hopefully, a new setting would change things, but Costa remained skeptical.

A saccharine voiceover chimed from the observation deck's audio array, announcing the vessel's history. The *Mayflower* was one of a series of migration arks comprising the five-year journey, with trips every year to bring people and their families between the planetary cluster surrounding the Alpha Centauri binary star system and Earth. Everyone had the chance to begin again, with as many as fifteen settled worlds to choose from, depending on what life they wanted to lead.

Costa scoffed at the whitewashed presentation. Few ever made the journey back to Earth, which was just as well. The planet had been corrupted and poisoned long ago.

A dull pressure radiated behind his eyes, making him wish for the silence of the hypersleep once again. His meds were in his storage cube, but he couldn't access them right now. Even so, he only had barely enough with careful dosing to last to the end of his journey. Plus, the other pilgrims might not appreciate his medication efforts—he hadn't been fortunate enough to acquire legal prescriptions.

It would be all right. He could wait. He had held out this long. Several more hours would be no problem.

"Are you okay?"

Costa turned to the young boy standing next to him. Perhaps barely thirteen years old, the tween looked at him with curiosity and a touch of revulsion only a teenager could muster.

"I'm fine. Why do you ask?"

The boy shrugged. "I don't know. You keep rubbing your temples. Got a headache?"

"Yes. I do. It becomes worse in the presence of children."

"You sound kinda British."

"I was born just outside of New London, in the UK continent."

The boy's accent was easily North American, but Costa didn't care enough to extend the conversation. He turned his attention to the planet outside the ship, but couldn't help noticing, out of the corner of his eye, the furtive glances coming from the young man. Shifting his weight aimlessly, the boy kept peeking in Costa's direction and averting his gaze at the last second. Costa held back the urge to roll his eyes. He knew the signs of young desire all too well.

Five years in hypersleep and the first person to look his way was little more than a child—how typical. Costa knew his slender build and youthful features made many men and women question his age, but he had never wanted anyone underage, even when he was underage. Now at thirty-seven, Costa barely stood taller than the boy. He would have to make a point not to encourage him. There was nothing worse than quashing the genuine interest of someone who was in all ways incompatible.

Perhaps if he ignored him...

"This whole thing sucks."

Costa sighed to himself. "What thing?"

"Alpha-fucking-Centauri." The boy snarled, filled with derision.

"You don't want to move to Alpha Centauri?"

The boy shrugged with a disgusted sneer. "Why would I?"

"Then why are you?"

Shoving his hands into his pockets, the boy stared at the ground, kicking at nonexistent debris on the spacecraft flooring. "Dad needs a better job. There's not much left these days, I guess. He says Earth turned into a total shithole after all the pariahs revolted and got themselves killed."

Costa cringed, yet restrained his tone. "Para-humans."

"What?"

"Para-humans. Pariah is a vulgar term."

The boy shook his head, his face twisted in disbelief. "Whatever. That's what my dad calls them."

"In that case, your father is an ignorant bigot. Even if he is right about Earth being a shithole."

"It's not a big deal. They were genetic freaks. It's not like they were even human."

With the pressure behind his eyes, Costa found it hard to contain his annoyance. Every word enunciated itself without his conscious effort. "However they came to be, para-humans had powers that made them capable of feats that others were not. They were more than human, not less. Human beings were scared of them, so they made them slaves."

"But people took care of them. Why did they start a war?"

It was a question only a child could ask, because it was so immature and stupid. Costa had to resist the urge to completely berate the poor boy as he sought to educate him.

"How long would you leave a collar on if you were stronger than the one holding the lead?"

The boy's forehead creased in thought and he shrugged again. It appeared to be the only gesture he knew. "I don't know. I guess it doesn't matter. They're all dead now anyways."

"Yes...yes they are."

Umbrage defused into melancholy, and Costa decided to drop the conversation. It was only a gateway to things better left forgotten. Ignoring the boy once again became the best course of action.

"That's a cool tattoo on your cheek. Do the patterns mean anything?"

Costa closed his eyes and took a deep breath. "They're just decorative. They cover up the ones that were there before."

"I want to get one around my eye."

"Why don't you?" He knew the question wasn't exactly setting the best example, but Costa found himself not caring much. And, quite frankly, the more the boy spoke, the less he found himself in the mood to be helpful.

"Mom says I'm not old enough, and Dad says only pariah freaks get them on their faces."

A spike of offense strengthened Costa's growing headache at the sound of the slur. "I repeat what I said earlier about your father."

A long minute passed as the boy looked around with a nervous eye, clearly trying to find what to say next. Costa hoped the little bastard would stay quiet.

"Did it hurt having it done?"

"Yes, it did."

"Did it hurt really bad?"

The sad, dark smirk curling Costa's lips was more for himself than the boy. "You might even say that getting it bloody well killed me."

"You're kind of a freak."

Once again, there was the proof the boy had been groomed with a lack of tolerance and discretion. Costa could have spent hours teaching the young man how skewed his view of others could be, but he was too exhausted to take the time. In the end, his irritation won out.

"You should get back to your bigoted little family." With a wave, he dismissed the boy. "Run along. We all have new lives to start."

THE GOGGLES OVER Priest's eyes displayed all the pertinent flight data as he piloted the *Santa Claus* into Alpha Centauri Prime's atmosphere. The ship's size should have made for a rough ride, but he knew how to handle this craft. The *Santa Claus* was a decommissioned military transport vessel Captain Danverse had repurposed into a freight liner after the Centauri Civil War. Built for function, not for style, the ship could be a handful during takeoffs and landings, but Priest knew how to manage the beast.

Priest loved his life aboard the *Santa Claus* as they shipped cargo, and occasionally passengers, between the fifteen worlds in the Cluster. Trips between worlds could take weeks at a time, so thirty-two men currently made the cargo vessel their home. Everyone on board was male and non-hetero, which sometimes made for a great deal of fun during the long voyages.

Three pilots traded shifts while off planet, but Priest preferred the launches and landings—they were far more fun. Piloting in space was kind of boring, but necessary. Sure there were moments when they had to maneuver around random debris and objects floating in the dark, but he made a point to be the man on call for his favorite shifts.

Captain Danverse called out from his post behind the pilots at the center of the bridge. "How are we doing, Priest?"

"Just fine, Captain. I'll get us in smooth as usual."

"That's why you're in that seat."

Priest grinned. "Tommy, are we good?"

The long-haired navigator sitting next to him checked his console and nodded, making his ponytail bob. "Centauri Station has us cleared. You should be receiving flight path data any time now."

Priest's fingers danced over the controls, pulling up the telemetry inside his goggles. The holographic display would be easy enough to follow. The ship passed through the outer layers of the atmosphere and they were moments from approaching the planetary jet stream. Their flight path ran right into it and would make for a hard ride.

He couldn't wait for what would come next.

The ship shuddered as high winds buffeted the large vessel. Typically a craft this size would park in orbit and the crew would take a separate schooner to the surface, but this ship didn't come with a shuttle. Not that it mattered. The *Santa Claus* was more than sturdy enough. Still, pushing through a planet's atmosphere did make the takeoffs and landings a little problematic at times.

From the corner of his eye, Priest watched Tommy grip his armrest hard as the shaking intensified. Priest could feel the rattle all the way through his teeth, and he loved every moment of it.

"You crash my ship and I'll kick your ass, Priest." Danverse was the last person to admit to weakness, but Priest could hear a subtle unease in the alpha male's voice.

Priest took a firm grip on the controls and throttle. "Trade winds are smacking us around. Don't worry, Captain. I'll get us through smooth, just like always."

Pushing the control forward, he forced the ship to dive against the current of the air stream, making the quaking even more severe. The whole ship developed a growing echo in protest.

Tommy groaned, his knuckles turning white. "Oh, fuck me."

Priest couldn't help but whoop in excitement over the noise. "Almost there! I just need to get him in the sweet spot!"

He could feel the gravity well pulling them down like the best carnival ride. It was the sensation of harsh freefall that made him want to be a pilot in the first place. Nothing topped the thrill. Except for maybe seducing an attractive man who played hard to get.

Keeping an eye on the sensor reading, he could see the tremors were creeping to the top of the *Santa Claus*'s structural stress limits, beyond which actual damage could result. All entertainment aside, it was time to be a hero.

Reaching over to the console, Priest tweaked the control on the often-forgotten inertial dampener. The devices were built throughout the vessel to absorb the G-forces from travel within an atmosphere. However, no one ever appeared to remember you could turn up the power on the system. He pushed the slider upward with a surreptitious little finger and the ship began to settle.

"There we go." The shaking became little more than a soft rumble. "That's the sweet spot."

Priest leveled the ship on course and eased back into his seat, the dampeners removing all the difficulty out of the flight path. An ache persisted in each of his cheeks from the fierce grin he couldn't wash away.

"Thank you, Priest." The relief in the captain's voice was clear.

He shook his head. "Not a problem. You just have to know how to ease him down."

"I wish the other pilots could land the ship as smoothly."

Priest shrugged. "Don't worry, Captain. You know I'm happy to take us up and set us down each time."

Priest made a mental note to return the dampener control back to its previous setting once they landed. He only used that trick every few times to keep others from getting suspicious. The other men were just as skilled. No need to give away his trade secrets if it meant he kept his position as head pilot.

Once the ship was safely in port, Priest raced back to his quarters to grab his bag. The whole crew would be off-ship for four days before leaving to complete the next leg of their contract.

He unzipped his luggage and took a quick inventory. Clothes, toiletries, and a few simple odds and ends were accounted for to keep him occupied. From the outer pouch, he pulled out a deck of cards with their metal holder and a matching flat cylinder small enough to fit into the palm of his hand.

From the deck case, he extracted a few cards as the holographic surfaces became a five of spades and a six of hearts. Pressing his thumb to the button on the cylinder changed the cards to a king and queen of hearts. The remote and card deck were working perfectly.

He acquired the infamous deck on the ship's last trip to Luxorian when he caught a bar owner using them to cheat in a high-stakes game. For promising not to narc him out, he gave up the deck to Priest. The irony was Priest himself got caught trying to use them in a game of poker on board when the new cook, Erron, joined the crew, but no one back on Alpha Centauri knew about it. This little deck of cards had a special use on this trip.

After shutting down the deck, he stowed it and the remote in his bag and dashed for the exit. His vacation was about to start.

BLOWING OUT THROUGH his pursed lips, Arbor Kittering scrubbed his undersized hands on his pant legs. His palms refused to stay dry. He was so nervous. This job interview was too important. No other employer had been willing to return his application requests and his currency was dwindling. Despite his exceptional tech-coding skills, the mistakes he'd made in the recent past had smeared his reputation. All he needed was a fresh opportunity and he'd have the chance to undo the damage.

Reaching into his shoulder bag—that always appeared too large for his size—he pulled out a small metal rectangle. With a flick of his wrist, it snapped out, expanding into a small step stool. Climbing on top of it in the middle of the men's restroom gave him a better vantage point in the mirror. Without it, if he stretched out to the tips of his toes, his chin would barely reach the standard counter height, and he had no intention of doing anything of the sort. He had some small amount of pride left.

Such was the life of a dwarf in a universe full of normals.

Arbor was accustomed to the odd stares of folks trying not to be obvious. Some were fine, but others treated his condition as something communicable. As if achondroplasia was catching. If it were, he would run rampant through crowds in public transports, touching everyone he could reach, in a millisecond.

He was fortunate not to be more disfigured. A disheveled thatch of mud-brown hair helped reduce the appearance of his pronounced forehead. Thankfully, his head was not grotesquely large. His limbs were short in proportion to his torso, but the possible spinal curvature was minimal. Growing up, his research brought him a battery of medical images with conditions beyond his ability to stomach. It made him thank whatever gods he didn't believe in. His life could have been much worse, but it had also been far from easy.

Occasionally, he would meet a person who was fascinated by his unusual stature. It was often exhausting, but he couldn't blame their morbid curiosity at times. How could you not gawk at something so abnormal, which barely existed beyond obscure medical histories in the last few centuries? From his Subspace Link research, only four cases of dwarfism were cataloged in the last fifty years. It wasn't surprising. Medical technologies were more than capable of detecting and correcting the birth defect well before a child was born.

After checking the time on his handheld pad, he smoothed down his clothing with his stubby fingers as best he could, trying not to grimace at the juvenile style. Hopefully, no one would notice. With his funds so low, he was forced to shop at secondhand stores in the husky children's departments. There was no currency to spare for custom-altered garments anymore. The fact did nothing to reinforce his self-confidence.

Damn, he really needed this job.

Hopping down, Arbor collapsed and collected his step stool, then stowed it in his bag. He shook himself to bolster his courage and headed for the door.

Space Station Alpha was alive with activity. Travelers crowded the walkways between businesses, and Arbor dodged person after person in an attempt not to be trampled. He refused to watch their facial reactions as they leapt to one side. Looks of surprise never got easier with time.

Galaxy Diner was only a few shops away but felt like kilometers. It was a simple little restaurant chosen for the interview. At this time of day, it would be quiet enough to talk, and their pricing was cheap enough he could afford to eat.

Ignoring the odd stare from the host, he spied his party. The man sitting at the booth was large, imposing, and ruggedly attractive. The tight, dirty-blond hair and face matched the holos he'd been sent of Captain Marc Danverse of the *Santa Claus*. The man sitting next to him was stocky and muscular, yet smaller than the captain. This was Mac Smith, looking way too young to be the ship's head tech.

Arbor waved to the pair to get their attention and pretended not to notice how the captain's expression flattened. Mac smiled and beckoned him forward. He took a deep breath and said a silent prayer.

After climbing into the chair opposite them, he received a different vibe from each man. Mac appeared delighted to meet him, which was fortunate, because he was very easy on the eyes. Danverse appeared uncomfortable when Arbor had to nearly crawl across the table to shake his hand, but was polite regardless.

The next half hour was something standard. Questions and answers of a normal variety went back and forth easily enough. Danverse and Mac spoke of how the *Santa Claus* was populated with all non-hetero men who often repeated their yearly work contracts. They all cared for and lived on the ship with the structure of a small town. Arbor was nervous but found handling the details surrounding his skills the easiest. It was the personal queries that set him on edge.

And Danverse asked the first that could take a bad direction. "So why the *Santa Claus* of all places?"

Arbor swallowed and answered his best. "Well, I haven't had much luck finding new employment recently. The idea of being on a ship with a community of non-heteros sounds really appealing. Living off planet would be a nice change of scenery."

"You realize that living and working on board a cargo vessel is not a luxury appointment. Living in space for weeks at a time may not be the best fit for someone your size."

"Marc!" Mac paled in shock.

Arbor raised his hand in an attempt to calm Mac, who was nothing short of offended by the captain. "It's a fair comment, Mr. Smith. My ma is a naturalist. She pretty much hates technology in general and would rather do everything in her life without it. If the entire planetary cluster were reduced to third-world conditions, she'd be only too happy. She believes people are too spoiled in this generation. Before I was born, Ma found out I had achondroplasia, and she refused the procedure to correct the bone growth deficiency."

"She knew what would happen and allowed it? Why?"

"Because she believed I should be whatever nature intended. She'd only been medically scanned because my grandpa and grandma insisted."

"That kind of sucks. No offense."

"It's just my reality. She wanted me to be an artist when I grew up." He spun both hands back to front in the air as he chuckled. "Do these hands look like the hands of an artist to you? I can't even draw a crooked line. You can imagine her horror when I showed a talent for data coding. It was the ultimate lesson in irony. We fought about it, but she got over it, more or less.

"I was really good at it, but I still had trouble. One potential office refused to hire me because they thought I wasn't right for the company image. The job was coding in the back offices. I never would have seen the public during working hours. Captain, I learned a long time ago that this whole universe isn't made for any adult my size. I make do, but it's not always easy. It would be nice to finally find somewhere I can really fit in."

"With your skills, why do you think job hunting's been so hard?" Danverse's attention had never wavered throughout the interview, but at this moment, his question had a laser-like scrutiny.

Arbor squirmed in his chair. He'd hoped to avoid this line of his history but had known it was unlikely. Dwarfism was an easy scapegoat for his troubles, but if Mac and Danverse were as thorough as he suspected, they already knew the answer.

"My prison record is as much of a turnoff as being a dwarf to most employers. I'm assuming you've already read the charges."

"Yes, we have. Data hacking and falsifying government files. Mac's even read the magistrate's transcripts. I've never been the one to read novels. I'm all about the highlights. So, I prefer to hear your version."

"Where should I start?"

"How about why?"

"There was this guy—"

Mac snorted. "Isn't there always?"

Arbor couldn't help but snicker. "Yes, I think there always is. His name was Arthur. He was wealthy and attractive and I couldn't believe he wanted to date me. You can probably imagine, men don't line up for someone like me very often. So, I made him work for it. Three months, no sex."

"Did he do it?"

Arbor sighed in recollection. "Yes. Yes he did."

"So what happened?"

"Once I finally gave in, a vid of us having sex showed up on the Link. It was his proof to win a bet with his friends that he could bed a midget. Apparently, fucking me was worth ten thousand credits."

Danverse winced. "Ouch."

"You were in love with him, weren't you?" Mac was polite but supportive.

"Enough to hack his financial data records and delete, not steal, all of his money. Then I broke into Cluster Authority files and added him to the Most Wanted List as a violent pedophile. After that, I staged an arrest alert while he was at his nephew's birthday party. I'm told it was very humiliating."

"Damn! You don't fuck around when someone crosses you."

Arbor shook his head. "I'd never broken the law before. When the authorities came, I didn't fight and I told them everything. My history was clean and the magistrate wanted to go easy on me, but they were all major offenses that couldn't be ignored, so they gave me ten years."

Danverse chimed in, knowing more than Arbor had hoped. "But you only served five months and you're out with no parole conditions. Good behavior?"

A wave of sadness slumped his shoulders and forced him to avert his eyes. "Someone realized I shouldn't be in there."

An awkward lull came over the trio. Arbor's forehead creased while following the amber faux-marble line in the table surface. Coming up with another sentence was a study in random incoherence. Chest tightening, he drummed the table with anxious stubby fingertips as he tried to forget all of it. Was it suddenly hot in the restaurant?

"Those details aren't important." The subtle sympathy underlining Danverse's words surprised Arbor—it didn't seem like the captain from what he'd seen so far—and calmed his pulse.

Mac chimed in. "Did you bring a sample of your work?"

Relieved over the change in subject, Arbor nodded as he rummaged through his bag. "A lot of my effects were confiscated to pay my fines, but I managed to keep this. It's the pad I use for just about everything."

After pulling up the raw code on the screen, he handed the small pad to Mac, who scanned the object with reverence, his eyes flitting back and forth as he read the lines of data.

"This isn't the standard operating system on this device, is it?"

"No. The standard OS doesn't work well for me and I'm too impatient for updates. I hybridized the code to run smoother and clean out the bugs in the system. It's still fully compatible with all known tech languages, so I don't need other devices for most projects."

A delighted smile lit up Mac's face as he turned to Danverse. "I want him."

Please let there be a double meaning there. Mac was attractive and someone he could talk to about data streams and algorithms without watching their eyes glaze over. He was also seriously attractive. Had he said that to himself already? He hoped he wasn't blushing.

Danverse glanced between the two men, his scowl breaking Arbor's daydream. "I'm a little concerned about your ability to play well with others. The men can act like thoughtless adolescents from time to time. We have a nice little community built for ourselves, and I like it that way. I don't want a bunch of unnecessary drama breaking out in the ranks."

A growing fringe of despair welled inside Arbor as he watched another opportunity become splintered glass around his feet. The more he heard about the *Santa Claus*, the more he looked forward to being a part of it. Where would he turn next? He was nearing the end of his options.

Danverse continued. "Even so, I do believe in second chances. I think our whole crew was based on it, and it's a good thing. Remember that when you sign in for duty in three days."

Arbor's eyes went wide as he nodded like a smiling fool. "Thank you, Captain. I'll be there."

"And one thing... As you will be reporting to the head tech, you will be serving under Mac." Danverse leaned forward and his brow arched in command. "But you will not be *under* Mac. Are we clear?"

Well, shit. Given the way Mac rolled his eyes in embarrassment, Danverse and Mac were together. "Duly noted, sir."

Chapter Two

"I'M ALL IN."

The gruff man across from Priest pushed all of his chips into the center of the table. Cyber green numbers on the scorecard pad tallied the value, and Priest knew he could more than match it. This would be the last hand of the game.

The other four men watched with anticipation. After being eliminated earlier, all of them sat frozen, allowing cigar ash to build and ice to melt in their drinks. The bar's owner, Chuck, was probably sorry he'd allowed Priest to host the game in his back room. The game's stakes were reasonably substantial and he was the first to go down.

The five cards Priest held in his hand were basically garbage. In a normal game, the entire hand would have been folded long ago. He'd bluffed the guy into bidding everything he had, and it was time to make the payday happen.

Priest scrubbed the card edges against the perpetual two-day scruff on his chin, reached into his pocket, and felt the deck's remote control. The subtle button was smooth under his thumb as he caressed its edges.

"You got something in your pocket, Priest?" Chuck's eyes narrowed as he leaned forward.

"Yeah. My nuts. Wanna scratch 'em for me? Or, better yet, blow on 'em for good luck?"

A round of snickers erupted through the room, and Chuck backed off with a chastened grin. None of the men here would take him up on it. They were all hetero, and Priest wouldn't approach any of them under normal circumstances. All of them were coarse and brutish—not really his type. While he might not turn down a night of fun experimenting if any of them asked, Priest preferred men who didn't have the ability to physically hold him down and have their way with him.

Without changing his expression, he thumbed the remote and watched the holographic surface of his cards redraw themselves into three queens and two other off-suits. The deck would give him a winning hand based on what was available and unplayed. He only used the remote at key points to keep suspicion down, and made a point to reach into his pocket all through the game, whether he won the hand or not, to make the action look expected.

Priest pushed his pile of chips into the center to meet his opponent's. "Show 'em, baby."

The fine sheen of sweat on the man's brow gave away his confidence as he threw down three tens and an ace. When Priest showed his superior hand, his opponent's face fell. The rest of the men whooped and groaned in sympathy.

Clamping his jaw shut to control his grin, he raked in his winnings, not wanting to appear too eager. Priest was fit and no little guy, but these men were brawnier and he had no interest in fighting his way out of the room. Chuck gave him dirty looks even as the credits were transferred to his account, and sour looks came from most of the men even as they congratulated him.

The last opponent reached across the table and shook Priest's hand. "Good game, man."

"Thanks. I just got lucky." Priest made his polite thanks and gradually worked his way back into the main bar. The losing players were being good sports for the most part, but none of them had stellar reputations in the first place. Staying in the back room with the grumpy owner who he'd just fleeced a lot of money from might not be wise.

It was after 23:00 hours and the pub was filled to near capacity. The light panel's amber glow gave off a sultry mood, a reflection of the music weaving between the various conversations. Men and women, young and old, were in every semi-dark corner: eating, drinking, and making merry. Just the way he liked it.

Priest was elated and parched. He'd avoided drinks during the game to prevent any chance of making a mistake. The last thing he wanted, after all the work he went through to choreograph this outing, was for Chuck to start loading him up with booze or to be drugged by the opposition. With a new batch of currency in his accounts, there was no reason not to quench his thirst. With a little luck, the money could buy him a companion for the evening as well. Maybe two.

This was going to be a nice shore leave.

Sitting at the corner of the bar, he spied a young couple, dating or possibly married, enjoying each other's company. Priest watched from a nearby table for a few minutes. They seemed happy enough, but the guy was a bit pushy and overbearing. A clear sign of insecurity—perfect. The bartender served some florescent-green femme beverage in a stemmed glass to the woman and a clear drink on the rocks, in a short glass, to the man. As soon as the drinks were served, the man excused himself and headed toward the restroom.

As soon as he was out of sight, Priest made a slow count to ten, then sidled up to the woman and leaned on the bar. He gave her a sleazy smile and adopted the smarmiest accent he could muster.

"How you doin'?"

The florescent-green drink poised at her lips, she paused in disbelief with just a touch of horror. Before she could gather her wits, he continued.

"You're smoking, girl. Let's go find somewhere we can be private." His blatant gaze traveled up and down her body, stopping at the key zones from the neck down.

Her tone went from shocked to offended. "Excuse me, I'm here with someone."

"Not right now you're not, sugar." He lowered his voice so only she could hear as he leaned forward. "How could he leave such a *fine* piece alone—"

A solid hand clamped onto Priest's shoulder, spinning him until he faced the boyfriend. He looked a lot bigger up close.

Insecurity often equaled quick to anger, and this man fit the description. "This seat's taken. Get the fuck away from her."

All sleaziness disappeared, and Priest flipped into the pinnacle of penitent men. He raised both hands in apology. "Dude, I'm so sorry. I didn't realize you were together. I never would have..." Priest turned to the woman. "Why did you call me over here?"

The man's eyes went wide in disbelief as he turned on his date. "What the fuck, Shell? Again?"

As the couple argued, Priest shifted back, merging into the crowd of patrons. That went a lot easier than he expected. Slipping between people until he reached the other side of the establishment, he snickered as he took a sip of the man's clear drink on the rocks in the short glass. Collecting a free drink was rarely so entertaining. Luxorian vodka—the man had decent taste. Who knew? Too bad he was a total bruiser and liked women.

Now that he had a drink, Priest scanned the bar, looking for an appropriate playmate. A great number of men were attached to others. The kind that weren't looking for a third. It would be too much work to make any of those encounters happen. Bar-goers in a space station were usually travelers, so he was used to finding single men in abundance while on leave. From what he could see in this thick crowd, he was going to have to look a little harder.

The drink in his hand was already half empty when he spotted the man at the bar. He was lithe and pretty with rich, dark hair. It fell in a gentle wave, barely brushing past his shoulder line. The decorative tattoo running along his right cheek did nothing to stall his youthful appearance, but his confident gestures told the story of someone much older.

The bar was crowded, but he sat alone, biding his time and enjoying his drink. He paid no attention to the people around him. Aloof and uninterested, he presented an irresistible challenge.

With luck on his side this evening, Priest could be patient and wait for the blond sitting next to the beautiful man to vacate his position. Winning the poker game and collecting his drink without incident left him feeling invulnerable. The nameless blond paid his tab, and before anyone else could close the gap, Priest swooped in.

"Is anyone sitting here?"

The pretty man turned to Priest, giving off the slightest hint of a smile before shaking his head. As Priest mounted the stool, he noticed how the young-looking man's gaze roamed over him, and he turned back to his near-empty glass.

A bit of small talk would start off Priest's nighttime negotiations. "Are you traveling or arriving?"

"I suppose that in a space station this size it would have to be one or the other, wouldn't it?"

"Pretty much."

"A bit of both, really. Just arrived, but I'm heading out again soon."

Priest flagged the bartender, ordering another round for both of them. "Where ya hoping to land?"

"I'm booked to leave tomorrow morning to settle on Omoikane."

"Really? We end up in port there, but have a stop on Gamma Centauri first."

"Who's we?"

"I'm the head pilot for the cargo vessel, the *Santa Claus*. We have contracts with about half the planets in the cluster, but Omoikane is a new one. What's so special about it?"

"Oh, they have the most amazing technology. Light-years ahead of everybody else, they have the first prototypes for anything worthwhile. The data-coding techniques they use there are nothing short of revolutionary. They're building new memory caches that make the current ones look obsolete as soon as they're perfected. I even read about the first lifelike android, complete with synth-flesh and artificial intelligence capacity that rivals human beings." The pretty man paused, his posture suddenly awkward. "Sorry, the subject excites me, but I know that it can be painfully dull to others."

It was adorable how his cheeks colored as he averted his eyes. With a nervous hand, he tucked a lock of his hair behind his ear. Priest couldn't help but notice how he turned in his seat, opening his body a little more toward him.

"Not a worry in the least. I'm Priest, by the way."

"Priest? I'm willing to guess that's a nickname. Why would you be called Priest? You're hardly dressed like one."

He leaned in closer, taking in the smaller man's fresh scent. "It's like a big guy named Tiny. He's nothing of the sort."

A graceful snort turned his smile up a notch. "Well, that I can believe. My name is Costa. It's nice to meet you, Priest. I wanted to thank you for the drink."

Oh yes. All the signs were there and Priest was feeling good. This was a guaranteed bet. Why stand on ceremony when he could get the party started and make it last longer?

"Tell you what, Costa. We're both on borrowed time here, so let's just skip forward and find a place to smash your back doors in."

Costa's drink was in Priest's face almost as fast as his expression flashed its outrage. The alcohol stung his eyes much like the slap to his face, which nearly knocked him off his stool.

"What the fuck'd you do that for?" Priest wiped his face with his hands, pissed off at his soaking shirt.

"You pompous ass! I knew you were gearing up for some arsehole move."

"You were into it."

"With that cheap pickup? Are you congenitally deficient? What did you think you were going to do? Screw me like some cheap tart and drop twenty credits on the nightstand on your way out?"

"Well, not twenty—"

Costa's snarl was nearly out of control. "You bloody bastard!"

Priest had to grasp both of Costa's wrists to keep from being slapped again. The little guy was furious and starting to kick at him. It was all escalating way out of proportion. What the fuck? All he wanted was to get laid on vacation. If Costa didn't calm down quick, he was going to have to smack him one to get him under wraps. He was tempted to do it anyways, to pay him back for the first one.

Before he could make up his mind, a pair of meaty bouncers descended on the pair, snatching them out of their seats.

Priest resisted the hands crushing his arms. "Ow, shit! Wait a second, you fuckers! I didn't do nothing wrong, dammit!"

The owner, Chuck, pushed his way through the crowd and gave them a dirty stare. He nodded to the big men holding them as Costa snarled at being restrained.

"Get them both the fuck out of here. I don't want either one of them in here again. Make sure they understand."

The bouncer slammed Priest into a table and punched him in the stomach, side, and face, making Chuck's point. The world spun as he was hoisted off the ground and bent over a shoulder of solid muscle, then crashed on the sidewalk outside the bar with a painful grunt.

Face throbbing in time with his racing heartbeat, he looked up to find Costa sprawled on the ground beside him. The little shit was groaning, but they probably didn't have to rough him up as bad. He was so little. Priest's left eye was becoming harder to see through. It would probably be swollen shut before he knew it.

A shadow fell over them, and with his good eye, Priest found himself looking at a pair of Station Authority Officers in standard body armor, wielding riot batons. Neither one looked thrilled to see them.

"Fucking wonderful."

ARBOR'S BREATHING WAS a shade away from becoming labored. It was a small miracle his rapid footsteps weren't beating the *Santa Claus*'s walkways like a metal drum as he struggled to keep pace with Mac. His shorter legs were working hard to match the head tech's longer stride. If Mac noticed, he made no acknowledgement, and Arbor preferred it. The last thing he wanted was people making special concessions for him. He strived to be as normal as his condition allowed.

Mac was giving him the grand tour before the rest of the crew came back for the launch in two days. This was the typical routine apparently—for new members to get acquainted with the ship in advance before the whole crew descended. Mac told him that usually Captain Danverse or the Security Chief, Liam Jacks, performed the duty, but Danverse had business on the station and Jacks was taking a leave of absence. His partner apparently wanted to research his family history on Alpha Centauri. Arbor didn't understand why they had to leave the ship. Anything they needed could be found on the Link, but Mac said Hadrian Jamison wasn't tech savvy and wanted to do his visits personally. It made no sense to Arbor at all.

For an enclosed environment, the ship seemed enormous and out of scale for Arbor's size—like every other type of architecture he ever encountered. According to his historical research, special considerations used to be made to accommodate people with disabilities and conditions. However, with medical science nearly eradicating such occurrences, such provisions had all but vanished.

"After I show you around the rest of Beta deck, we'll tour the engineering areas. You can access the coding remotely through the system anywhere in the ship, but it's good to be familiar with the direct access ports in case anything ever goes wrong." Mac continued to speak as Arbor kept pace. "These are the restroom and locker areas. All the quarters on Beta deck run a circle around it. The gym is accessed that way and the shower room is in this direction."

At the end of the rows of lockers an open doorway led into the wide-open space with shower heads lining the perimeter of the wall. The tile surfaces shined, showing off the surprising cleanliness, but not a single partition in sight. Arbor's gaze rounded the room as he muttered aloud.

"Group shower room, gym, and lockers all connected. I think I've seen this porno-vid before."

Mac snorted. "On occasion, these rooms have been that porno-vid."

The idea of the entire crew using the facilities made Arbor a bit queasy. His breath quickened in a way that had nothing to do with his walking pace. "No private showers?"

"Sorry, Arbor. Only the captain's suite has a private shower." Mac caught Arbor's tense expression. "You'll find out modesty can be a little sparse sometimes on board. You'll get used to various levels of clothing and non-clothing during off hours. And don't worry. No matter what you may walk in on around here, no one will try to make you do anything you don't want to."

Arbor's brow nearly winged to his hairline. "Does that happen often?"

"Walk in on someone bumping body parts?" Mac shrugged. "It happens. Try not to be fazed by it. There're a few who're exclusive, but the crew plays around with each other a lot. What else is there to do on a ship for weeks at a time? The shower seems popular from what I hear. I'm not allowed to use the public shower. Cap'n likes to keep me to himself."

"He does seem a little dominant. If you don't mind me saying."

Mac grinned as his eyes glazed over as he drifted into some kind of daydream. "Yeah...he is."

Arbor stood looking up at the smitten tech. His mind wandering, Mac chewed his bottom lip with a dirty grin, reliving something of which Arbor probably didn't want the details. Even so, his orientation was far from finished and he needed Mac. On the tips of his toes, his hand barely reached up to Mac's chin as he snapped his stubby fingers out loud.

"I'm still right here, Mac."

Mac started as he came back to the present. "Oh, sorry. My mind drifted off to last night when... You don't need to hear about that."

Arbor chuckled. "Probably not."

"So what do you think?"

Arbor shrugged. "I'm still a little skeptical, but I'm getting over it." A shirtless man with a broad, hairy chest walked toward the shower room with a towel draped over his shoulder. Arbor turned around, his gaze following the rugged stranger. The man nodded to them both as he passed through the doorway. "Yeah...definitely getting over it."

With a chuckle and a pat on the shoulder, Mac ushered Arbor back onto the tour. "You know, I'm really geeked you came on. I have a number of guys who can help with the mechanical stuff, but no one I trust with keeping Mrs. Claus running smooth. I really needed help with the mainframe maintenance and upgrading."

"It'll be an adjustment, but meeting you guys showed me that this is my best option to get my life back in order. I'm looking forward to it."

"By the way, Arbor, I wanted to apologize for that 'under Mac but not *under* Mac' comment the cap'n made at your interview." It was cute the way Mac's face scrunched up in embarrassment.

"It's all right. I understood he was marking his territory. It was a little more possessive than I expected. That doesn't bother you?"

Mac shook his head with a smirk. "Nope. I'm just as bad. If I thought you were eyeing him up I'd have drop kicked your little ass out the door long before we got to your court history. Marc's a little domineering and harsh at times, but he's perfect for me."

"Sounds like you two were made for each other then."

"I think so. It wasn't easy. We both fucked up enough that it almost didn't happen. I don't even like to think about that. Sometimes I think we're both worried that the other will move on, so we both go overboard, but I think we both know that's not going to happen. Even on this ship, with all these healthy males, we don't have eyes for anyone else."

"That sounds strangely nice." Arbor tried not to sound wistful, but failed. It was a shame Mac was so attached to the captain. He was easy on the eyes, intelligent with a background in tech, and given the captain's clear dominant streak, had to be a bottom. It would have made him perfect for Arbor. Too bad he was so permanently attached. In spite of that, Mac would make a good friend on the ship— hopefully the first of many.

Hopefully.

Mac gave Arbor's shoulder a friendly nudge. "You have just as much chance as anyone. There's a guy out there somewhere for you. I know it. A hot stud who will want you so bad, he'd be willing to kill someone for you. In the meantime, you can test drive some of the crew. They like the new guys."

Arbor shook his head. He couldn't picture the crew wanting a man like him in that way even if he was fresh meat. And he certainly couldn't picture anyone needing him the way the captain and Mac found one another. Their intensity was a little scary and more than a little enticing.

"Do you think the captain would do that for you?"

"Do what?"

"Kill someone."

Mac reflected for a moment. "Let's hope we never have to find out."

IT HAD BEEN over six hours and Priest hated this holding cell. It wasn't his first experience. He'd been inside a few on various ports. Some were nicer than others. Drunken brawls in seedy bars had a tendency to magically spawn around him. He knew it couldn't always have been his fault.

This cell was relatively clean, if a tad confined. The neutral gray walls were cushioned to keep detainees from hurting themselves if they threw a tantrum. A vast open doorway facing the hallway was covered in fifteen-centimeter-thick, transparent plastic-hybrid glass. If it was exposed to the public, it would be like being in an aquarium. He lay on one of the four narrow beds mounted into the walls like shelving—two on each side, with the lavatory niched into the corner.

The swelling over his eye had gone down enough to know he wouldn't be blinded, and his side ached from the bouncer's handling. He didn't have to look to know he was sporting a number of spectacular bruises. Since there were no serious injuries, the station dumped them in the cell with marginal medical treatment.

He was still fuming from the night magistrate's decree right after being brought over from the bar. The court wouldn't even let him defend himself or listen to any explanation. It was made perfectly clear the station authorities didn't tolerate any disruption. The smug bastard wasted no time assessing fines for disorderly and drunken behavior. It completely wiped out all his winnings from the poker game and then some.

Priest could have made peace with the fact if the source of his poverty wasn't stuck in the cell with him.

Curled on his bunk across the room in silence, Costa had yet to speak a word since the plexiwall slid shut. Not that Priest was complaining. Right now, Costa's voice was the last thing he wanted to hear as he bided his time.

Harsh creases ran under Costa's eyes and split his brow. The beds weren't the most comfortable, and Costa couldn't lie still. Small movements had become more prominent over the last few hours. How much worse were they likely to get?

"You okay?"

Costa's disdainful glare drew a menacing arc in Priest's direction. "I'll be fine. My meds are back in my hotel."

"You sick?"

"I said I'll be fine. You should learn to mind your own business."

Priest rolled over to face the bunk above him. "You're looking a little rough, that's all. Just trying to be nice. Sorry I asked."

"I know what your idea of *nice* is."

"You don't know shit."

"I know it only takes a minute's chat with you to know you're an oversexed pig. Honestly, what kind of a desperate wanker uses a sad pickup line like that? How often has that really worked for you in the past?"

Priest shrugged as he rolled to the cot's edge and studied the floor. Looking back, he knew that kind of desperate effort was rewarded about one in every ten attempts. But Costa was so attractive, and he was giving him the signs telling him he was keen. One in ten. In his excitement, he spoke first, hoped for the best, and it all went to hell. It wasn't the first time his grand schemes had blown up in his face. As chaffed as he was by the situation and Costa's attitude, he wasn't about to give him the satisfaction of admitting it.

"I was in a good mood and wanted to have a good time. I thought you were a sure thing. Sorry you're such a frigid bitch."

"I'm a far cry from frigid. I just had no intention of being used by you as a cum bucket. Now, thanks to you, I've missed my departure to Omoikane."

Shifting off his bed, Priest stalked across the room, casting a shadow over the smaller man. "You can get all high and condescending if you want, but you could have just said no. I would have walked away. You weren't about to get ass-raped or anything. Instead, you had to go all psychotic and now we're in jail. I didn't slap you or start raging out." He pointed an angry finger scant centimeters from Costa's face. "That was all you. So stop blaming me because you picked a fight over being offended."

Costa's scathing gaze softened as Priest returned to his bed, sat on the edge, and rested his arms on his knees. Averting his eyes, Costa looked properly chastised.

"The authorities were a little quick to arrive to collect us both. What did you do?"

Priest shrugged. "I'm guessing the owner was pissed that I won a bunch of credits off him in a poker game. He was probably looking for an excuse to fuck with me and I know he has a few friends on the force. Thanks for giving him the opening. Now I'm broke because you can't take being asked out."

Costa sighed as he rocked himself into to a seated position. "Your proposal was vile and degrading. But you're right. I'm a touch sensitive these days. Perhaps I did overreact a little."

Now that his petulance was under control, Priest could admire Costa's beauty again. Legs crossed under, his slender frame's natural grace made the institutional mattress look luxurious. He was elegant and strangely fascinating. Too bad all he could count on was the uneasy truce Costa appeared to offer.

"I'm betting that's the closest thing to an apology I'm gonna get."

"Perhaps you're not a complete idiot after all."

"What was making you so touchy, anyways?"

After an extended pause, silence and a blank stare were Costa's only responses. Was he pissed off? Was he scared? Priest couldn't read him. If the pretty man wanted to keep secrets, it was fine. He was as entitled as anyone. But it rubbed like sandpaper to be snubbed when they were finally making a bit of polite conversation.

Priest huffed. "Okay then, what do we do now?"

"I'm not sure. I don't have much experience with this sort of thing."

Priest threw his hands upward in defeat. "Unless someone bails us out, we sit in here for another two days. Do you know anyone?"

"No. I just migrated from Earth alone. Surely you know people?"

"No one I want to know I'm in here." If he could keep the crew from finding out about this whole mess, it would be a miracle. Two days in holding wouldn't be his favorite way to spend his leave, but standard procedure would be to release a man in holding in time to catch his departing ship if he was part of the crew. It would get you off-planet with a minimum chance of creating more trouble. Paying passengers were screwed. It would be a close call, but the crew wouldn't have to find out about this.

Costa rubbed his temple as he hissed. "Then I suppose we sit here."

"I have an idea how we can pass the time." A leering grin with an arched brow accompanied his remark. Costa's eyes narrowed, a snarling frown marring his youthful features. There was no question reading his disgust.

"Don't be a twat, Priest."

Priest smirked. "Just thought I'd ask."

The pair sat in relative quiet for the next several hours, making small bits of conversation stretch out as best they could. Costa's headache grew progressively worse, and small tremors became visible in his hands.

"Are you sure you don't need a doctor?"

"I don't need bloody medical assistance."

Priest raised his hands in defense. "All right. Just checking."

Attempts at learning about Costa's past were also met with a barrier of refusal. Every question was answered with cold stares, silence, or brutal insults. If he continued being so resistant to Priest's curiosities, this would be a long couple of days.

"I wondered where my pilot ran off to this time."

Priest winced without even facing the voice from the corridor.

Costa swiveled around to the edge of the bed and stood, smoothing his clothes. "You must be Captain Danverse."

Priest was puzzled. Costa hadn't even heard of the *Santa Claus* or its itinerary before they wound up in this cell.

Danverse's arms crossed over his broad chest, his presence oozed authority, dwarfing the uniformed officer standing watch behind him. "I am. You must be Mr. McQuillen. I see you've met my wayward child."

"Hey, Captain." Priest couldn't hide the sheepish tone as he avoided the captain's eyes. Danverse might have been incensed at finding him in a cell—again—but it was hard to tell. He always held a minor annoyance with the world.

Costa sighed. "Yes, it appears that we've crossed paths."

"Is this something I need to be worried about during the trip? I don't like conflicts on board." Brow raised, Danverse held his head at a mild angle.

"No, Captain. The whole issue has been resolved."

"Conflicts on board? What are you both talking about?" Priest looked back and forth between them.

"Mr. McQuillen booked passage to Omoikane on the *Santa Claus* and let me know where to find you."

Now Priest was beyond confused. "How could he—"

Costa interrupted. "Is everything in order so we can leave?"

Danverse nodded. "Just about. I need to sign off on your releases. You'll be in my custody as long as you remain on planet. They said both of your fines are completed, so we can pick up your effects and head out. We'll be going back to the ship until we're ready to launch."

"Thank you, Captain. I appreciate your help and understanding."

"Your security check came up clean with your application. I figured it was just a misunderstanding with my pilot." Danverse's laser-like gaze burned over to Priest. "It wouldn't be the first time."

Priest cringed and lowered his head like the time his grandmother had caught him with porn. "Sorry, Captain."

"Get yourself sorted, Priest. We'll talk about this later when I decide what to do with you."

A wave of dread came over Priest as the guard escorted Danverse back down the hallway. Once upon a time, breaking the captain's rules involved restraints and physical discipline. Keeping his men in line usually ended with the offending crewman receiving a brutal fuck from the superior officer. Danverse got off on corporal punishment.

It wasn't a surprise to any of the crew. Their employment contracts stated all discipline was under the captain's discretion. At least until Mac arrived on board.

And thank the gods he did. Once Mac and Danverse became involved, all the aspects to law and order on the *Santa Claus* involving whips, chains, and deviant sex vanished. The two of them were an exclusive couple now, and perhaps he saved those impulses for the head tech, but it didn't mean Danverse had gone soft. He still knew how to maintain order.

Priest had trouble picturing Mac as a willing submissive. The idea of him bound and whipped during sex wasn't the image that came to his mind. But Priest shouldn't be shocked. Mac wouldn't be the first man in his life to surprise him with his appetites.

Once he made sure the captain was out of earshot, Priest grabbed Costa by the arm. "What's going on? How did you book flight when you've been stuck in here with me since we got bounced?"

Even with the visible strain around his eyes, Costa's smile was almost arrogant. "I'm very resourceful."

Chapter Three

"THIS WILL BE your quarters as long as you're on board," Danverse said.

Costa scanned the spartan room. The metal walls were plain and unadorned, but he could hardly expect more from what was basically a motel room. Once upon a time, he wouldn't be caught dead in a place like this, but so much had changed over the years. The *Santa Claus* was functional and safe, which was a far cry from some of the questionable shelters he'd found himself in prior to the chance to migrate.

This would have to do. He had little choice.

"Thank you for your help, Captain. Allowing us to stop for a decent meal after calling in at my hotel was particularly appreciated. The Station Authority's menu was inedible." Costa rolled one piece of luggage into the room and dropped a shoulder bag next to it in the middle of the floor. It would be nicer if there was so much as a rug in this place.

"You'll be staying on the ship until we launch. Then you're free to do what you want. I don't want any more trouble."

"Nor do I." Costa let out an exhausted sigh as he examined the minimal amenities. "It's not the most luxurious I've ever been in, but the *Santa Claus* appears to be a reliable ship."

Danverse's spine straightened. "Maybe not the prettiest, but he's a sturdy vessel and where we make our home."

"He? It was always my understanding that, out of tradition, all ships were referred to as 'she.'"

"This is a non-hetero crew. The ship's AI, Mrs. Claus, is the only female I have on board."

A small grin curled Costa's mouth. "I see."

The bed was a good size for his petite frame, with a few shelves over the generic desk and chair. Storage compartments were visible in multiple locations, and the walls were split by the light panel illuminating the room. It was a functional, if not glamorous, method of travel.

"It'll be a while before we hit Omoikane. It takes about seven weeks to get to Centauri Gamma with a two-day stopover and another six weeks after that. Long way to get where you're going."

Costa shrugged as he critiqued the nightstand fixed to the wall. "It wasn't my original plan, but it's taken me this long to be able to migrate away from Earth. A few more weeks won't make a great deal of difference."

"You only have a few bags. Traveling awfully light for someone relocating across the universe. Do you have any family back on Earth?"

He paused for a moment and turned to the captain, maintaining his veneer. "They've been gone for some time now."

Was that a hint of compassion he noticed in the captain's eye? It was difficult to place for sure. Danverse watched his every move since they were released from the Station Authority, scrutinizing and evaluating. Costa would have been offended, but was more impressed the captain was being so thorough. The man demanded respect and given Priest's reaction to Danverse arriving at the cell, Costa imagined he was used to receiving it.

"So, do you want to tell me what happened with you and Priest?"

"There's very little to tell." Costa cringed and ran his fingertips across his forehead. "I really feel quite stupid. Priest rubbed me the wrong way and I overreacted. I didn't mind him chatting me up. I wasn't planning on shagging him. After an attempt at being pulled by an adolescent child earlier, the conversation was refreshing. I just hadn't anticipated his rude proposition. It set me off."

Danverse grinned, paired with a mild snort. "Priest has a gift for that. A lot of the men on this crew are like that when we have newbies on board. One look at you and you're going to get a lot of attention. They don't mean any harm, but the libidos on this ship can run a bit racy at times. I need to know if there's a chance there'll be a repeat of this."

"He simply said the wrong thing at the wrong time. It won't happen again."

"That's fair. Make no mistake, though. Once we take off, I'm in charge. We have a nice little extended family on the *Santa Claus*. We appreciate visitors. They make some of our trips real interesting, but I don't tolerate dissension in the ranks. Living in space has its challenges, but we love it. This voyage will be as pleasant as you make it."

"I'm just looking for a little peace and quiet during my travels."

The captain gave a satisfied nod. "Glad to hear it."

"Don't tell him I said so, but try not to be too hard on him. He was only defending himself."

"I'll consider it. Priest is a good guy, but needs direction. His mischievous streak turns him into a scam artist if he's not reined in. Priest loves being on the *Santa Claus*, but like everyone else, he has to play by our rules for the safety of everyone on board. He needs the reminder from time to time."

"I see." A fresh surge of pain crushed Costa's eyes closed as he pressed the heel of his palm into the crease of his brow.

Danverse's gruff voice became as kind as his nature likely allowed. "Are you all right? I didn't want to say anything until we were in private. You look like you've been running a little harsh since before I saw you in the station. Dr. Bosch takes good care of all of us. He's more than happy to see passengers in sick bay. Recruiting him was one of the best things I've ever done."

"Thank you, Captain, but I will be fine." The pain had been rumbling for days, but Costa pushed it aside and put on a smile. "It's late and it's been a very tiring day. I just need a proper lie down to rid myself of this migraine. The beds in the cell belonged in a condemned hostel."

Danverse didn't seem convinced, but conceded. "All right, if you're sure. Contact us if you need anything. Breakfast service will be at 08:00 hours. A lot of the men stayed on the ship on this port. You'll get a chance to meet a few come morning."

Costa gave a gesture of thanks. "I'll be sure to set myself a wakeup com for the morning. Cheers."

The doors slid shut with the captain on the other side and only then did Costa begin to slump, showing the wear of the last few days. As if waking from hyper-sleep wasn't stressful enough, finding himself in holding for a pub brawl wasn't improving his first days in the planetary cluster.

Holding a brave face for the captain had been a trial. The pain daggering through his skull was growing worse with each passing hour. There was too much inside to contain without help. He couldn't have waited much longer for Danverse's exit.

Staggering, he fell to his knees in front of the larger piece of luggage. He cursed as he struggled to unfasten the catch and tear the bag open. Personal effects spilled onto the floor as he rummaged through the contents with shaking hands. Where was it? He knew it was in this case. It had to be here. He was nearly in a panic when he felt the object and wrenched it into the open air.

The small black cylinder fit easily into his slender palm and he sighed in relief. Wasting no time, he tipped his head back and pressed the button, dispensing two drops on his tongue. A rush of ecstasy pushed the thorns out from behind his eyes and the world around him became unimportant and tolerable. The noise diminished into a subtle din.

"Oh yes...yes, yes, yes," were the only words slurring from his lips as he lay down on the floor in the middle of his quarters, tiny giggles bubbling forth as he let the drug take effect.

ONE BY ONE, all sets of eyes turned in Arbor's direction as he entered the Mess Hall. It was intense enough he wished he'd taken Mac up on his offer to eat with him and the captain a little later. He refused, wanting to get an early start and make a good impression. With the curiosity buffeting him in every direction, being a third wheel now felt like the better option.

Too late to turn back, Arbor gripped the strap on his shoulder bag, held his head high, and strode into the room. He tried not to cringe at being on display as he surveyed the room to get his bearings.

Rows of tables in a tight grid formation were randomly occupied by eating crewmen. From what he'd been told, the population was lighter than normal. About half the men stayed on board during this docking. A lot of the crew had served in the Centauri Civil War and had little interest in this particular planet or its space stations.

A serving rack with trays and silverware sat to one side of the food service line. Getting a tray was simple enough—the stack was within reach—but the utensils were at a bit of a distance. Determined not to look a fool, Arbor stretched to his limit and retrieved his cutlery. He knew others were watching, but he stamped down the impending swell of humiliation even as it heated his cheeks.

Trying to maintain a sense of dignity, Arbor walked up to the service line as the sound of another crewman caught his attention, making him turn around. Collecting his eating effects was a handsome male with light brown hair and brown eyes. Handsome but not too pretty, he wore a shirt that showed off his muscled, but not too muscled, torso. Average in height, he bore a pleasant smile as he stepped up behind Arbor.

The man called out across the buffet line. "Hey, Erron! Got anything good today?"

The door behind the service zone swung open and a young man shuffled through, carrying a tray of food. Arbor wasn't thrilled to see the jade green locks held back by the cook's cap. Didn't they have any standards of decency?

Erron struggled to settle the tray in its resting place. "You haven't started complaining yet, have you, Priest?"

"Oh, hell no. Not if you keep feeding us the way you do." A broad grin erupted on Priest's face as he shifted closer to Arbor.

Realizing he was holding up traffic, Arbor tore his sight away from the new arrival, a new warmth quickening his breath. The giddiness starting to form dissolved as he caught sight of the height of the food line. With a sigh, he set his tray on the shelf—nearly level with his chin—and reached into his bag for his expandable steps. He hated using it, but there was little choice.

The flat panel hadn't cleared his satchel before a pair of arms reached around his chest from behind and hefted him off the ground.

"Here you go, little buddy," Priest said.

Shock and rage boiled over as Arbor swung the collapsed stool behind him. He struck Priest with a bang, causing him to yelp, and the pair crashed to the floor in a heap. Scrambling to stand, Arbor took another shot at the stunned crew member, slamming him in the shoulder with a snarling grunt.

"Ow! What the fuck?" Priest ducked, holding his arms up as he curled in a ball to protect himself.

Arbor was livid. "Don't ever fucking do that again!"

His chest heaved as he struggled to contain the shame and anger warring inside him. The idea of being seen as helpless was something he couldn't accept. Years of peoples' repeated doubts crashed into his memories. Not even on board one day and he couldn't go without being reminded of his limitations. Would that ever change?

Priest stayed down in defense, as Arbor brandished his weapon, faltering only when he noticed the absolute silence in the room. If everyone was curious about him before, now they were staring with a look of unerring disbelief. Scanning the crowd, his spun his vision to each man, all mirroring a twisted expression of shock, with a hint of revulsion. Arbor understood the look all too well. Being different was one thing, being a freak was something else altogether.

With a deep breath, Arbor turned away from Priest as he expanded the panel into its step-stool configuration. Trying to center himself, he did his best to smooth his clothing.

"Sorry." Unable to meet Priest's eyes, Arbor's voice was meek as he tried to restore the meager threads of his dignity. "I didn't need any help."

Climbing the stool allowed Arbor a normal vantage point of all the breakfast offerings while Priest picked himself up off the ground. He didn't look over at him, he felt angry and humiliated enough for one day and it was only starting.

"You're Arbor, the new data tech, right? I'm Erron." The green-haired cook's smile was warm and unassuming.

Arbor barely nodded.

"What can I get for you?" Erron pointed with a ladle at the tray of scrambled eggs. The handle was abnormally thick and Arbor couldn't miss the unsteady tremor of the cook's hand holding the spoon. When Arbor didn't respond, he shuffled to the left, his foot dragging as he moved sideways, and pointed at the tray of hotcakes.

Afraid to speak and do something else wrong, Arbor only nodded again. He couldn't stop watching as Erron switched utensils to another wide-handled spatula and added a proper serving of hotcakes to a plate with much difficulty. The cook chewed his lower lip as he focused intently on his awkward movements, but ultimately was successful.

With another stressed effort, Erron added a few sausages to his plate as well. "Take these too."

Arbor accepted the plate as Erron handed it across the buffet to him, a relieved smile gracing his face. Placing his breakfast on the tray, he couldn't help but feel uneasy at the idea of eating the food, given the cook's peculiar condition.

"Don't let Priest get to you. He doesn't mean anything by it, but forgets that not everyone wants help. He should know better." Erron's brow flattened, shooting a pointed look behind Arbor, but Arbor didn't follow its direction.

"Thank you." Arbor climbed down his step stool with a quiet nod. He folded it down, stashed it away, and moved his breakfast down the line. After grabbing a fruit juice, he walked along the outer edge of the room and selected a table with a wide berth from the rest of the diners. He kept his head down so he wouldn't have to look at their incredulous stares.

Excellent work. In one day on board you've alienated yourself and the ship hasn't launched yet. What shall I do for an encore? Carefully climbing into his chair, he tried to tamp down the anxious burn in his chest. He held his head high, even though he didn't feel the confidence he tried to portray.

Sipping at his bottle of juice, he studied his breakfast. While a little untidy due to Erron's shaking, everything looked cooked to perfection, and the scent strived to override the destruction of his appetite. Even so, he couldn't make himself do more than nudge things around as he stared at his plate with distaste.

"You can't catch what he's got."

Arbor was startled to find Priest standing next to his table, carrying his own breakfast. "What?"

"He doesn't have a disease." Pulling out a chair, Priest sat down across from Arbor, who was having a hard time muffling his surprise. "I saw you watching how his hands shook. You were a little put off by it."

"I was not."

Priest's brow rose as his head bounced. "Yeah, well, you might want to *not* not stare so hard next time. People around here are pretty protective of him, his partner especially."

"He's partnered?"

"Um...yeah. You're surprised by that?" The words were almost lost as he shoveled a large forkful of scrambled eggs into his mouth.

"No...no, of course not. What happened to him?"

"Erron had a stroke last year. It was pretty bad, happened right here in the Mess Hall. Doc Bosch fixed him up, but I guess his motor skills are a little toasted."

Watching Priest's enthusiasm over his food made Arbor think twice about his own. Taking off a small wedge of hotcake with his fork, he regarded the pleasing color and texture. The bite was tentative, but even his reluctance couldn't deny the quality.

"This is really good." The second bite went down even faster.

Priest smiled. "Yeah it is. Erron's one of the best food slingers this place ever had."

"What did he mean by the comment that you should know better?"

"I picked up a box out of his hands he was having trouble with a while back. He chewed me out so bad I wished Doc hadn't fixed his speech. Sometimes I don't think first. I was just trying to help. Same back then as now. Erron said I better come over and apologize."

Arbor shook his head. "It's all right. I'm a little touchy about being independent. Comes with being looked at like an infant your whole life just because you're small."

"I can see that. Tell you what, it won't happen again. Promise."

Priest reached out his hand to shake Arbor's. It was a gesture of respect and kindness Arbor hadn't seen often and it helped quell the morning's complications.

"Thanks." Arbor couldn't help noticing a fading bruise ringing Priest's eye. "Did I do that to you?"

"What? The shiner?" The man's laugh was hearty and charming. "No, a bouncer roughed me up the other night. Captain made sure I'd be safe to fly the ship, but had Doc Bosch stop short to teach me a lesson."

A new kind of blush surfaced on Arbor's face. Had he really been so enraptured by Priest's arrival he glossed over such an obvious mark? It wasn't subtle in the least. What was next? Hiding a giggle behind his hand like a tittering schoolgirl? What an awful thought.

"That's good. I'd hate to think I was responsible for that."

"I'll get razzed enough that the little dude beat my ass on the chow line."

"You picked me up like a toddler to see over the counter." Arbor couldn't control the dark scowl as he enunciated each syllable.

Priest winced. "Okay, when you say it like that, it makes a lot more sense. Tell you what, let me make it up to you."

"Go on."

"You play poker?"

"I've played some. Why?"

"I'm planning a game the night after we launch and get under way. I'm just getting the table filled. Fifty credits gets you in."

Arbor's head tilted as he contemplated the offer. "That sounds like fun."

"Just a heads-up. This game is strictly for adults."

It was impossible to ignore the way Priest peered up at him through his lashes, chewing his lower lip as it curled in a lecherous smirk. The heat in his voice underscored every gesture. It didn't take Arbor more than a millisecond to calculate what the man was really saying.

"Strip poker? Seriously?"

"It gets to be a little bit more than that." Priest's grin stretched from ear to ear. "What else is there to do on a boat full of non-heteros? Come on and play with us, Arbor. It'll give you a chance to get to know some of the guys. Maybe even better than you expected."

A predatory gleam in Priest's eye and the way he unconsciously licked his lips as he waited for an answer gave Arbor pause. The plotting grin told Arbor he should run—not walk—away. It sounded like this game had all the hallmarks of a night you wished to forget. An "adult" round of poker with a group of strangers—what could possibly go wrong?

Nude vids of yourself showing up on the Link kind of wrong. That's what.

It did sound like fun though. And Arbor had resolved himself to finding a way to fit in on the *Santa Claus*. He couldn't stay living like an outcast for the rest of his life. The small community on board had a better chance of assimilating him than the rest of the planetary cluster. Word would likely spread over the scene with Priest earlier and it was doubtful it would be favor him. Getting to know a few others might not be a bad idea.

It had been a long time since he'd found himself in any kind of social setting. Since before he ended up in prison, in fact. Is that what was making this so hard?

A new kind of anxious heat flushed his chest. He knew he was probably being hustled for fifty credits and should ignore the seductive grin Priest threw his way. But he was so many things Arbor liked in a man. There was nothing about him that was extreme or overdone. Priest's eyes were such a rich shade of brown. Would he still notice them if the cocky man was undressed? There was only one good way to be sure.

"All right, Priest. Count me in."

EVEN THOUGH HE wasn't allowed off the ship for the rest of the leave, Priest couldn't be happier to be on board. The

Santa Claus was a safe place for him and he doubted if he'd ever leave it for more than a few days in port at a time. It was where he belonged.

The metal hull was solid, and Mrs. Claus was always available to answer questions. His meals were covered, he had a place to bunk, and a group of men to play with when the voyages got lonely. What more did he really need?

Content and pleased with himself, the tap of his footsteps down the hall was a welcome sound. His new poker game was nearly arranged. Only one last person was needed to fill the table and he knew right where he'd go next.

"Mrs. Claus, is passenger Costa McQuillen in his room?"

The matronly voice was pleasant as always. "Yes, Corporal Jones. Mr. McQuillen has been assigned to Beta Deck, Room 236."

"Excellent." Costa should be feeling guilty enough over the whole bar-to-jail debacle that maneuvering him into playing shouldn't be too difficult.

Priest could use the extra credits to make up for his losses on the station, but a chance to get to know the elusive beauty more intimately was worth the effort. Even if it was simply due to winning the game, bedding Costa would be quite a prize.

The real trick would be getting him to play along.

The electronic chime for Room 236 rang out as Priest thumbed the access pad on the wall. Hands locked behind his back, he rocked back and forth on his heels as he waited for a response. Coming through the speaker, Costa's rich, accented voice bolstered his resolve.

"Who is it?"

"It's me, Priest."

"Come in."

The door slid open and Priest stepped inside, only to be stopped short as Costa worked to pull a long-sleeved tunic over his lean, bare torso. There was something oddly exotic about the slender gentleman. Priest's mouth went dry at the sight of his tender, smooth flesh, making him wet his lips to fight the effect.

Costa was a stark contrast to the majority of the men on board. Most came from military or working-class backgrounds. Rough hands and lusty appetites were not uncommon. Being poised and borderline aristocratic were not typical traits among the crew.

Nimble, tight muscles disappeared under the snug, dark fabric as Costa straightened the hem, facing away. His dark hair was damp, and the thought of him in the shower brought an inappropriately soapy image to Priest's mind. Costa reached up with his elegant hands and released his hair from the tight collar, exposing a circular-shaped scar below the base of his skull, only to be hidden a moment later.

The unusual size and location of the mark drew Priest's curiosity. It was only a brief glimpse, but unmistakable. He wanted to ask about it, but decided to hold back. Given Costa's lack of interest in talking about his past, Priest worried he might only piss him off and then who would he get to finish his poker game? He was running out of viable options.

"Just get back from the shower?" Priest knew the question was obvious, but it kept him from making a comment that would likely get him thrown out.

"Yes, and you can keep those horrid little thoughts running through your head to yourself."

Priest snorted. "So now you're a mind reader?"

"I wouldn't need that skill. It's not that difficult a read." Now that his clothing was intact, Costa busied himself with collecting his shower effects and carefully returning them all to the wall storage.

Priest deadpanned at the insult. "Thanks. Missed you at breakfast. You okay?"

"Everything is fine. I simply needed some extra sleep after that whole incident in the bar. I'll make up for it at lunch."

"Well, you can't stay in your room for the whole trip. That would be a waste. I was wondering if you wanted to join me and a few of the guys for a poker game after launch."

Costa turned with a cocked brow. "Why do I feel that any game you're organizing has some insidious fine print attached to it?"

"Well, it is an adult version of the game."

Costa huffed in annoyance. "Why am I not surprised? I turned down your first offer to—how did you so kindly put it—'smash in my back doors.' Why would you think I would subject myself to an opportunity for you to try again?"

"Aw, come on. Come play with us. You're the one who said you're not frigid. Now's the time to prove it."

"You must be joking." Arms crossing his chest, Costa held his ground.

Priest shrugged with a cheeky grin. "What else are you gonna do for the next seven weeks?"

"I could enjoy the rapture of eating shards of glass or driving metal spikes under my fingernails. If that fails, there are plenty of entertainment vids to watch. The monitors here are actually far better than I would have expected—"

Both men were shocked into quiet as the monitor mounted to the wall roared to life, pages of data scrolling and shifting around the screen. Crew member images and personnel files vanished in a pile as one window layered over another. Deafening noise from all the information being accessed spilled through the room.

The panel illuminating the room flickered and a kaleidoscope of flashes reflected across the walls as Mrs. Claus began speaking. "Mr. McQuillen Danverse personnel files thank you very much travel to Omoikane Access Denied without valid authorization..." Her matronly voice rambled on without pause or an end in sight. Something was very wrong.

Priest was motionless in the cacophony of light and noise. Costa's brow furrowed as his cheeks flushed. His stance grew rigid and his mouth drew tight. The crease above the bridge of his nose deepened as the monitor went dead and Mrs. Claus went silent. Everything was back exactly as it was before.

"What the fuck was that?" Stunned and wide-eyed, Priest twisted his finger in his ear to restore his hearing. "Mrs. Claus, are you okay?"

Her reply was as sweet as usual. "Diagnostic protocols show my systems are functioning within normal parameters, Corporal Jones."

Creases formed around Costa's eyes as they narrowed in discomfort. "It's clearly some sort of error. It's not the first time since I came on board."

"Really? We should get ahold of Mac and let him know. He doesn't like it when things go screwy. Especially if it's Mrs. Claus."

"Feel free."

"Now about the poker game..." Priest's enthusiasm deflated when he recognized the pain in Costa's face. It matched his experience in the jail cell. "Are you okay?"

Costa snarled in condescension. "I'll be perfectly fine, Priest. It's simply a sudden migraine. Could you please sod off now? I'd like to take my medication and have a lie down."

Something about his sharp tone made Priest feel small and stupid. "Okay. I'll check up on you later."

Shifting his weight between his feet, Costa said nothing as he fixated on Priest edging his way to the door, his piercing stare harsh and unwelcoming. With a quiet nod, Priest left the room. The door closed with the usual soft hiss, but it might as well have been slammed in his face.

Priest had been rejected before—who knows how many times he'd said the wrong thing and been told to go to hell—but there was something off this time. He knew Costa was capable of being snotty and rude, but this was more like embarrassment. What brought this on—his instant headache? Something didn't add up, but he knew direct questions would get him nowhere. What else was he supposed to do?

There was something more going on, but Priest was at a loss as to how to figure this out.

Unable to help, Priest drifted around the halls for a bit. He didn't have a work shift until it was time to launch, and he wasn't allowed off-ship due to the details of his release. After going up and down in the lift a few times, there didn't seem to be anyone free to spend time with him.

The sound of Mrs. Claus's voice nearly startled him. "Corporal Jones, you have a private text message."

"From who?"

"Passenger Costa McQuillen."

Priest's brow twisted in confusion. "I'll take it in my quarters."

The short trip back to his room was muddied with confusion. Why didn't Costa just summon him back? Why the private message? Was there going to be a giant fuck off waiting for him back at his quarters? The idea brought forward a wave of dread.

Inside his room, he queued up his monitor, the display showing the incoming message. His chest tightened a bit as he debated over the possible contents. Why was he so concerned about a com from a pretty man he barely knew? Shaking off his ridiculous apprehension, he opened the mail, its cyber-green letters in full view.

To: Priest
From: Costa

My meds have kicked in and I wanted to message you to say that I think the poker game is a brilliant idea. This will be a good chance to meet some of the crew and keep me from growing stagnant on the trip. And it's an adult poker game at that? It appears as if I'll be getting to know some crew members more intimately than I'd originally planned. Ha Ha.

It sounds as if I need to know more details to be sure I'm prepared for all the fun. Com me back when you have the opportunity.

Ta.

Dumbfounded, Priest read the copy over more than once. What the hell happened? While he was glad that he had his sixth player, Costa's change of mind sparked a whole new set of questions. Where did the happy person who wrote this com come from? After what he'd said earlier, Priest had no doubt that Costa was hands-off for the voyage.

Now he wasn't sure what to think of him.

Chapter Four

"FIVE-CARD DRAW, ladies. We're all here to have a little fun."

"Anything wild?"

Priest scoffed. "Wild cards are for pussies."

"So you're making a lot of wild cards?"

"Fuck off."

A series of snickers and chuckles erupted from the six men surrounding the recreation room table. The rest of the ship might have had hard metal walls, but Priest loved the deep rustic red surfaces surrounding them here. The lush furniture was a joy to sit in, and from the corner where they sat, the rest of the amenities were accessible. Outside of his personal quarters, this was the most comforting space on the ship.

On Priest's left was the burly, shaved-headed security guard, Barrus, and Teddy, one of the ship's navigators. Arbor sat across from Priest, nervous and excited, stealing glances at Priest as he introduced himself to the others. The men were being polite, but word was spreading about the crazed incident in the Mess Hall, and he noticed the crew being extra cautious in their dealings with him. Priest hoped this game would undo some of that. He still felt guilty for picking up the guy and causing the whole mess.

On the right was James, Barrus's handsome husband and chief supply officer, and Costa, looking incredibly stunning as usual. Casual conversation filled the room.

Every man was chatting Costa up in one way or another, and Costa was charming them all, joking along as he tucked his hair behind his ear with a graceful hand. Costa's smile was delicate and provocative, the iridescent tattoo highlighting his right cheekbone. He knew the effect he was having on the men and was loving every second.

It was a nice, if not curious, change.

After James collected the funds and the chips were divided, Priest set up his deck of cards. Selecting Poker on the holographic menu, the images drew up a classic set on the surfaces of every card.

James broke in before the shuffle could begin. "Go over the house rules, Priest, for everyone's sake."

"All right, ladies. Once the game starts, no quitters. Shirt and pants are worth three hundred and your skivvies are worth five. First man broke and naked agrees to be the willing playmate of the winner. Everyone else can do what they want once the clothes are gone. No requirements there."

Costa interrupted, his voice containing a silky, playful quality. "I don't see anybody here that wouldn't be worth the effort of playing until the end."

The sultry mirth in Costa's eyes only made Priest want to win more. The chance for a night of Costa under him would be a prize better than the credits. And the way others around the table were eyeing him, Priest would have to use every skill in his arsenal to win.

Priest shook his head to clear his thoughts and get back to the task at hand. "If you cheat, you're at the mercy of the rest of the players, no rights of refusal."

"Ha! You know how that turns out, don't you, Priest?"

Narrowing his eyes, Priest didn't even give James the benefit of looking at him. "No one needs to air out the dirty laundry at the table."

Teddy started laughing, passing a dirty leer his way. No one needed to be reminded what happened when Priest got caught trying to fix the game to get Erron into his bed when he first arrived on board. Teddy and Carson, the head nurse, took their turns on Priest that night. At one point, they didn't bother taking turns. It had been fun, but his ass still hurt if he thought about it too much. Priest couldn't have said no, really. He got caught, and they were his rules in the first place. Priest might have been a scoundrel, but he owned up when it mattered.

"Speaking of cheating, where's the remote to this deck?" Barrus's accusing brow framed his pointed stare.

Priest pulled the metallic cylinder from his pocket. "Right here, Barrus. The one and only. You can watch me put it on the shelf so everyone knows I'm not scamming."

Getting up from his seat, he made a big theatrical show of placing the remote on a shelf on the far wall. It was visible, yet well out of reach of all players. Not having access to it galled him—especially with Costa in the game—but he didn't want anyone accusing him of not playing fair. Not this time at least.

"This deck has a remote?" Costa's quirked brow was a gorgeous accompaniment to his beautiful grin. "Did you happen to have this rather suspicious deck of cards with you at the poker game you won just before we met?"

Priest tried to look innocent as he shrugged, but he couldn't control his smirk. "I might have."

"Now I'm not so sure I'm feeling sorry about your loss of currency to the magistrates."

"Don't worry. I'm planning on winning some of it back tonight." Priest ran a heated stare over Costa's body as he wiggled his eyebrows. "And then some."

Costa laughed along with the challenge. "You're certainly welcome to try."

"Are you sure you really want to play this in the rec room? Out in the open?" Arbor hedged in his seat a bit, but had yet to refuse the game.

"There's not too many people out and about right now." Teddy patted Arbor's arm to reassure him, but Priest caught the subtle tension as Arbor's vision flashed over to Teddy's pony tail and the heavy tattoos spilling out from under his sleeves, reaching over his wrists and hands. There was barely any skin showing through the bright graphics. Arbor's expression flattened slightly. He nodded to Teddy with a hesitant smile, but shifted a tiny bit closer to Costa.

Priest shrugged. "It's nothing they haven't seen before."

"Okay." Arbor straightened his back and squared his shoulders. "I'm good."

The men gave a series of approving grunts and nods. There might be a chance for Arbor on board yet. Priest pulled out his chair, giving it a wide straddle as he sat down. With a broad grin, he rubbed his hands together in excitement.

"All right, ladies. It's time to play some poker."

"I'LL RAISE YOU seven fifty. If you want to stay in, Priest, it'll cost you your underwear."

Priest was not happy. He sat in his chair with only the thin fabric of his briefs separating him from the cushion, while everyone else was only shirtless.

Except Arbor.

Somehow the sneak sat with a majority of the chips, fully clothed, and looking quite proud of himself. And now he was forcing Priest to offer up his last piece of clothing to stay in the game. He had no choice, really. The amount of chips he would have, if he folded now, would make it hard, if not impossible, to work back up to the top.

The rest of the table had folded, so no one else was involved in this showdown.

Costa's teasing was infuriating. "You seem stressed, Priest. You're not concerned over the outcome of this hand?"

"Nope. I'm just making sure what I want to do here."

Priest could feel the atmosphere thicken as all players waited with bated breath for his decision. He chewed his lip gently for effect, already knowing he was staying in. The five cards in his hand were two sevens and three jacks—a full house. It wasn't an absolute winner, but being his first decent hand, he wanted to make this one look good.

Following Costa's lead, Barrus chided right along. "You're certainly taking your time making a decision."

"I just wasn't planning on fucking a midget tonight."

Arbor gave off a loud snort. "I'm not a midget. I'm a dwarf. Besides, who said you were going to be the top?"

Loud howls of laughter burst out around the table as Arbor matched Priest's stare. A heat colored his cheeks as he took in the fact Arbor had got one over on him. He'd fix that.

"All right, you little fucker. I'm in."

A chorus of catcalls and whistles erupted as the first chance of elimination came alive. Priest shook it off. He wasn't planning on being the first one out. It would disrupt his plans for the flirtatious Mr. McQuillen tonight.

"Good luck, Priest." Costa leaned over the table on his forearms, pushing his smooth chest forward, and winked.

When Priest tore his gaze away from Costa, the cards in his hand shimmered and re-drew themselves into five plaques of random suits and rank.

What the fuck just happened? It took everything he had not to start screaming as he stared at his now useless hand.

Even then, Priest couldn't help but look up at the remote sitting untouched on the shelf above.

"Is something wrong, Priest?" Costa blew him a kiss.

"No... No. I'm fine." Confusion slowed his reaction as the reality sunk in.

He was about to lose.

The worst part was, if he told them the cards malfunctioned and he had a full house before he bet, not a single person would believe him. It would be seen as some sad attempt to keep from being the party favor of the night. Fuck. He was screwed. In more ways than one.

He knew he should have spent the currency and ordered a second remote.

"C'mon, Priest. You can't bid anymore, let's see those cards."

He couldn't tear his eyes away as Arbor laid down his hand—two pair. It was almost a joke to show his own, but he was stuck. When everyone saw the mismatched, impotent cards he held, the uproar was much louder than he expected.

"What the hell, Priest? Did you really think you'd bluff your way into that pot?" James could barely breathe, he was laughing so hard.

Priest found Costa staring at him, not even watching the scene unfolding. "I guess I didn't think this one through." The crease between his eyebrows felt particularly deep at the moment. Was it possible to be annoyed and confused at the same time? The glee in Costa's eyes was unmistakable. He knew what happened and had to be responsible. But how?

"I'd like to rake in my winnings, but there seems to be a piece of clothing missing from the pile." Arbor beckoned with his finger toward the chip pile.

"It's a little chilly in here tonight. How about I keep 'em on and give a special show to the winner at the end?" A chorus of snickers and refusals answered his suggestion.

Arbor snapped his fingers and pointed to the pot. "Drop 'em, flyboy."

Stunned, Priest couldn't help but see the dwarf sitting up tall and proud in his seat, a near arrogant grin of his face. Where this show of confidence came from, Priest had no idea. He was trying to decide if he liked it or not when the rising group of whistles and chants of "drop 'em, flyboy" derailed his train of thought.

Pushing back his chair, Priest stood tall as the raucous noise grew in volume. Arbor's gaze was trained on him, daring to burn his skin. When he hooked his thumbs into the waistband of his snug grey briefs, he swore Arbor gasped. The arrogant expression had shifted into longing, as if he hadn't seen a naked man in years. Perhaps he needed a little thrill?

Carefully, he grazed his thumbs down his hips, exposing the flesh running from his hip down to his groin, making a point not to reveal anything too fast. Sliding his hands around to his backside, he uncovered his ass, keeping his cock hidden from hopeful eyes.

The chanting continued as he leaned forward far enough to touch the floor, peeling the tight fabric down the muscles in his thighs and calves until he stepped out of them. He pulled his chair under him and sat, using the table to keep himself decent from Arbor's vision as he tossed the pair of underwear onto the table.

"I believe those are yours for now."

Standing up in his seat, Arbor took the briefs, keeping a tight hold on them as he happily scooped up his winnings. "I didn't get to see much there, you big coward."

Priest shrugged and smirked. "You gotta win to get a proper look at the good stuff."

PRIEST STOLE ANOTHER glance at the slender male sitting next to Arbor. Costa was down to a pair of silky, shimmering boxer briefs and Arbor was still fully clothed. Everyone else was sitting in the nude waiting patiently. All of Costa's chips were in the middle and his briefs had just been wagered. This would be the last hand unless his luck held out.

The temperature at the table had increased. As the number of losing players increased, so did the bawdy comments and hands—not of the card variety—disappearing under the table. The arousal level in the room was at a near peak, except for Priest. Although, the anticipation was having an effect on him. As the prize for the evening, he was being saved for the winner as the others sized up each other's equipment and made lewd suggestions of how the night would end between them.

Costa played right along, his frigid streak from the other day completely nonexistent. Sultry innuendo kept issuing from his lips in contrast to the others' crude comments. He was completely at ease in this crowd of roughnecks. Costa was guaranteed a partner, or partners, this evening. If he lost, it would be any number of the remaining players. If he won, that person would be Priest. And that's what the pilot wanted from the beginning, right? Costa could still come back and win this thing.

Please let Costa win.

Barrus cheered, eager to move things along. "C'mon, people. Let's see if this is the end!"

Arbor leaned forward and splayed his cards out in a fan. Three sevens and an ace of hearts graced the table. Whistles of approval filtered around the room as the tension built. A small sheen glossed Arbor's forehead, belying the centered calm he displayed.

"What do you have, Mr. McQuillen?"

Costa studied his cards before collapsing them into a stack. He dropped them face down into the pile of chips as he turned to Priest with a cheeky smile.

"Your hand is much better than mine, I'm afraid. Although I have to admit it's worth the fifty credits and a pair of my favorite knickers to see Mr. Kittering have a good time. Congratulations on your win. I hope you enjoy your spoils."

Arbor's beaming grin widened as each player shook his hand in turn, congratulating him. He was genuinely happy. Accepting each handshake respectfully, Arbor never took his eyes off Priest for more than a second.

Costa shimmied out of his underwear as James transferred Arbor's winnings to his account. Arbor climbed out of his seat and hurried around the table to his prize.

"Do I finally get a good look now?"

Priest couldn't help but admire the earnest request. He gently slid his chair back, hoping not to disappoint the grateful winner. While Arbor's gaze took in every inch of his winnings, his hand stood poised to reach out, but held still. It was as if he didn't know what to do next. The near-innocence of it made Priest smile.

"I'm all yours for the evening. Would you like to take me to your quarters?" Priest motioned to the game surface. "Or would you prefer me on the table?"

A sudden light went on behind Arbor's eyes, brightening his face. He started nodding so fast it was almost comical. "My quarters. Definitely."

Priest gathered the cards and remote while Arbor unearthed his clothing from the stacks of chips. Everyone else was starting to get real friendly and invading each other's personal space. If he couldn't be a part of it, Priest didn't want to see what Costa would be up to this evening. It was time to go.

Besides, given Arbor's excitement, the evening could still be fun.

"Okay, let's go," Arbor said.

"Give me my clothes and we'll head out."

Arbor tucked Priest's attire deeper under his arm. "You're fine as is."

Priest gasped as Arbor's stubby hand circled around his bare cock and balls and started walking for the door. A loud refusal sat on his lips, but perched frozen with the bold move. Since he loved his happy parts, Priest was forced to follow along, trying to ignore the laughter of the other players as they watched the spectacle.

"Be careful." Priest gritted his teeth as Arbor led him to the lift like his dick was a leash. The doors slid shut with a familiar hiss.

"Relax. I have no intention of injuring the goods. I need you fully functional. Mrs. Claus, take us to Beta Deck please."

Given Arbor's hesitation earlier, Priest had no idea where the cool bravado was coming from. What was it about these new guys going cold to hot in a flash? Head high and chest forward, Arbor had yet to let go of his junk, and being trailed around like a dog was diminishing the potential fun of the evening. He wondered what was next as he thanked every deity he could think of that no one else had seen him.

The lift came to a stop and the doors opened to no less than three crewmen waiting for the elevator.

All three men couldn't help but take turns looking at Arbor, then Priest, and then Arbor's grip on Priest.

"Excuse us, gentlemen." Arbor gave Priest's dick a tug, and the miniature crowd parted. Priest followed along, his face and chest burning with embarrassment. Whispers and snickering disappeared behind the closing lift doors.

Reaching his room, Arbor hesitated. With a glance back at Priest, he stretched to the tip of his toes to reach the access panel. Once they stepped into the room, Arbor finally released his grip.

Priest inspected himself immediately. Nothing hurt, so he was good. Even so, standing naked in Arbor's quarters felt weird, so Priest found himself snooping around the small space.

Arbor's quarters were the same as everyone's, except for how small he looked inside of it. The proportions were all skewed in comparison. The bed had to be too high to get in and out of easily, and climbing into the chair at the desk couldn't be any fun on a regular basis. The higher shelves were empty and were likely to stay that way. Arbor could never reach them. It was odd enough watching him reach out to place Priest's clothing on top of the side table.

An unusual scent caught his attention. He noticed it when they first walked in, but being used as a pull toy had distracted him. Rich and sweet, it took little to follow it to the source.

Sitting on the edge of Arbor's desk was a stuffed animal: a handmade monkey constructed of dense woolen fabric, like old socks. With a faded brown body and white face, hands, and feet, it was in good condition despite its obvious age. The colors were faded and it sported a few visible stains if you looked hard enough. Bringing the sock monkey to his nose, he could smell the cloves and cinnamon emanating from deep inside. It was wonderfully real and not synthetic in the least. Someone had gone to a lot of trouble making this little item.

"Where did this come from?"

Arbor blanched when he saw the doll in Priest's hand. Striding over, he took the monkey from Priest and returned him to his place on the desk.

"Please leave Mr. Wiggles alone. My mother made him for me. He's very old."

Priest's eyebrow couldn't arch any higher. "Mr. Wiggles? Your mommy made you Mr. Wiggles?"

"I was just a kid at the time." The flush to Arbor's face and neck had nothing to do with arousal. "He was a security blanket of sorts. Can we not talk about this? I finally have a naked man in my room and I don't want to think about my mother right now."

Priest chuckled. "All right, all right. Well, you won. What are going to do with me?"

Whatever bravado Arbor walked into the room with had evaporated. With his arms pulled close to his side, he fingered the hem of his shirt. A glint of fear appeared in his eyes now the decision stood in front of him.

"I'm not sure."

"What would you like to do?" Priest hadn't expected Arbor's hesitation, so he saw no harm in moving things along. He hadn't organized the poker game to sit around and share stories.

Arbor's voice became tiny, even for his size. "I'd like to touch you...and make sure this is really happening."

"I think that's a good start."

Arbor edged forward, his nervous fingers brushing Priest's hips even as his gaze roamed around the man before him. Standing so close, he tipped his head back with an anxious smile to look at Priest's face.

"Can you lie down on the bed? I can reach you better that way."

Priest nodded with a smile as he climbed onto the bed. It must have been gigantic for the dwarf. Sprawling out on his back, Priest watched Arbor scramble around, climbing up using a small crate planted at the foot of the bed.

Half kneeling, half lying down, Arbor stopped alongside Priest's relaxed torso. Arbor reached out with tentative fingers, grazing the hairs on Priest's chest, sending a shiver through him. He was still annoyed at how he'd been brought through the hallway, but all the titillation during the game left him with a craving that overrode his moment of humiliation. He could deal with that later. Right now, after having been denied more than once, he needed this.

Arbor's small hands splayed out across his chest, the pads warm and smooth against his skin. It was so polar opposite to the rough hands of the other crew members. Arbor had likely never worked hard labor in his life, assuming anyone would have let him.

"Can I kiss you?" Arbor's timid question surprised Priest so much he repeated it in his head twice before he could respond.

"Of course you can. This is all about fun. Why would you ask that?"

Arbor averted his eyes. "Because I know you don't really want me. You said yourself you weren't planning on fucking the midget. I just want it to be good in case I don't get another chance like this again."

As soon as the words were uttered, Priest wished he could take back his stupid comment. Once again, he'd spoken first without thinking and someone got hurt. Now he felt like a total fuckup. How many more times would it happen before he learned? It was no wonder Arbor was hesitating once the reality started setting in.

Priest rolled forward, cupped Arbor's head in his hands, and covered his mouth with his own.

A pleading whimper escaped Arbor as his lips parted. Following the invitation, Priest dipped his tongue inside. Arbor's hand fluttered to meet Priest's, and the kiss went from nervous and timid to starved for attention. Every touch, every sound drew them both to a near frenzy. Priest struggled to find the urge to separate them enough to breathe. The kiss alone left him hard.

"You need to be naked." Now, Priest was into the evening's fun.

Eyes lidded, Arbor he tore away his clothing. Priest would have laughed at how eager he was, but instead found himself entranced.

Arbor's skin was unblemished and his body held a nice musculature. His limbs were shortened, so the proportions were diminished, but it looked good on him. Balanced with his untamed hair, the smattering of fur in the center of his chest drew an enticing line down his flat stomach. It ended at a tight snarl above an ample dick, well out of proportion to the rest of him.

"So much for the idea that a small guy comes with a small cock."

Arbor blushed. "Too bad it's neglected so much."

"Not tonight it's not."

If it was possible to make Arbor any hotter, that did the trick. Without a word, he urged Priest over onto his stomach and straddled his hips. The touch of Arbor's buttocks atop his own was delicious. He knew exactly where Arbor's cock rested by the heat along his spine.

Arbor might have had small hands, but there was a proper strength in them as he began kneading Priest's lower back, working his way north. Each movement ratcheted Priest into a new level of want, teetering on going straight to the main event.

But Arbor took his time, touching the flesh with his hands and signing each work with a wet kiss. Priest was so hard he was afraid he'd spend himself into the bed.

Priest's voice was raspy and muffled in the bedcovers. "Holy shit...Arbor, can I fuck you?" Arbor's hands stilled. An unwelcome tension radiated from the contact and Priest never expected the stern reply.

"No."

One quiet tiny syllable contained a volume of anger and hurt. Priest immediately backpedaled.

"It's all good, dude. This is your night. Do whatever you want with me."

A few seconds later, Arbor exhaled and the massage resumed, causing Priest to quickly return to the state of euphoria. Arbor only paused long enough to climb over to the nightstand and open the drawer. Straddling Priest's thighs, he took a firm grip of the pilot's buttocks. When Arbor pried them apart and dove in face first, Priest buried his face in the pillow to muffle the wanton howl.

Arbor's coarse chin burned the valley between Priest's haunches as his tongue began licking and burrowing into the tender opening. This time it was Priest's turn to whimper with need. He couldn't stop himself from arching into the contact. When Arbor pulled back, Priest wanted to cry.

At least until a slippery fingers traced the ring for a frustrating moment and slid inside.

For long minutes, one hand squeezed his ass while the other strummed the knot inside his channel, causing Priest to spit out harsh moans with each stroke. Another finger was added before long, prepping him in the best way possible. Arbor might not have had long fingers, but damn it, they were getting the job done.

"Shit...Arbor...Fuck me...please..." Trapped in a haze of mindless lust, Priest couldn't keep himself from begging.

For a moment the fingers disappeared, leaving Priest empty. Arbor's weight shifted, and his impressive organ began pushing its way inside. Needing to be plundered so desperately, Priest ignored the knowledge of Arbor's girth and encouraged it. The perfect thickness, Arbor's cock couldn't avoid Priest's prostate.

"Oh shit!"

Arbor stopped, a tinge of worry in his voice. "Are you okay?"

"Do that again."

With a chuckle, Arbor pushed his whole body forward, impaling Priest to the base. He pushed back with a grunt, a wordless demand for a driving pace. Arbor did not disappoint, slamming into him as hard as he asked. Priest didn't care what happened next, as long as Arbor didn't stop. The pounding inside was building everything into a gradual detonation he eagerly awaited.

Then Arbor pulled out.

Priest panted as he complained. "What the fuck?"

"Roll over already." Arbor's chest heaved with exertion, his eyes narrowed and commanding.

Without another protest, Priest flipped onto his back, following Arbor's silent request to pull his knees to his chest. Even in this vulnerable position, Priest admired Arbor's hefty cock, a piece of wet stone jutting forward between his shortened thighs. Crawling forward, Arbor lined himself up and planted his pole back inside. Priest cried out in relief at the welcome intrusion.

Priest flexed, trying to convince Arbor to start moving. Arbor reached over to a small bottle on the bed, poured a thin drizzle of oil into his palm, and began rubbing his hands together. Priest hissed when the slick grip enveloped his waiting cock, spreading the oil over every square centimeter of Priest's genitals. Only once it was a purple, glistening column did Arbor rock his body, burying himself completely into Priest.

Keeping control was proving to be a lost cause. Arbor was proving his talent for using his hands, and his big dick was smashing all sense out of Priest. His voice was raspy, pitching with each thrust.

"Can't last much longer."

Arbor snapped his hips harder. "Then don't."

An uncontrollable howl broke loose as Priest erupted, each arc of release spattering his stomach and chest. He couldn't stop himself from clenching down on Arbor's cock with each pulse, and Arbor's self-control went up in flames. He buried himself as far as he could go as he came hard, every muscle in his body a new study in sculptural relief.

Unable to hold on any longer, Priest dropped his legs, even as Arbor slipped out and fell backward on the bed. Both men panted for long minutes as they cursed and giggled through the aftermath.

"Damn, Arbor. For someone who doesn't get out much, you do good work." Priest's cheek ached from his grin. It might have been permanently etched on to his face.

"Well, if this was going to be a one-off, I wanted it to be worth it."

Priest nodded, even though Arbor couldn't see. "Oh yeah, I'd say you succeeded."

"When you tell people about me, be sure to tell them the good stuff."

"Have no fear. Your review shall be stellar."

Arbor rolled over and climbed up against Priest's chest. Priest draped an arm around him, floating in postcoital bliss, enjoying the intimacy. How long they stayed wrapped around each other was hard to determine. Priest refused to check the clock, even as Arbor's fingertips drew lazy circles around his nipple.

"Are you all worn out?" Arbor's question held a subtle taunt.

Priest peeked down at Arbor even as his cock filled. "You good for another round?"

"I get all night, right? Isn't that the rules?"

Priest gave out a lusty growl as he rolled over onto his hands and knees. "I am your willing playmate, sir."

Chapter Five

"WHAT THE FUCK is this, Priest?"

Mac watched as Arbor scrambled out of his Mess Hall chair and stalked toward the *Santa Claus*'s head pilot. When they sat down to dinner, Mac noticed an edge of discomfort running through Arbor, but Mac had put it off to being the new guy. Now he knew there was something specific bothering him. The sudden vitriol pouring off Arbor made Mac get up and follow him, if only to avoid another public incident with Priest.

Arbor thrust his personal datapad into Priest's line of sight. "You want to tell me what this looks like?"

The raised eyebrows and thin smirk on Priest's face spoke volumes. "It looks like Mr. Wiggles."

"Mr. Wiggles?" Craning his head over Arbor, Mac reached over and turned the screen by turning Arbor's wrist. "Oh cute! You have a sock monkey! Is this picture in Engineering? Why...?" Mac's expression deadpanned as he realized what was happening. "Oh, wait...there's a ransom note attached. Shit." Frowning, Mac turned on Priest. "You didn't."

Arbor didn't wait for a response. "The message said, 'Come to Engineering or you'll never see Mr. Wiggles alive again.' Then I went to where the holo showed, but he wasn't there. Then I got another com that sent me somewhere else." Arbor jammed a finger into Priest's chest. "Where is he?"

Priest's mouth went tight to contain his laughter. "I have no idea."

Arbor's jaw tightened and his whole body quaked in rage. "Bullshit! You're the only one who's been in my room, so it has to be you!" A few snickers could be heard from other dining crew members. It was clear multiple people were already involved and watching this new scene.

"Arbor, it's a prank." Mac placed his hand on Arbor's shoulder in a vain hope to calm him down. "Every so often the crew snatches a personal effect and they pass it around from one person to the next. They send an encrypted ransom note to make the owner run around. It's kind of an initiation of sorts."

"Has it ever happened to you?"

Priest snorted. "He's the captain's boy. We like our nuts where they are, thank you very much."

"Why would you do that to me?"

Priest shrugged with an exaggerated disbelief. "It was just a little payback."

"Payback for what?"

Eyes narrowing, Priest leaned forward until his nose nearly brushed Arbor's. "You led me down the hall, in front of people, by my dick. Just evening the score a bit." Crossing his arms over his chest, he straightened slow and deliberately, and gave Arbor a taunting grin.

"I can't believe you did that to me."

"Why are you making such a big deal about this? We're just having a little fun."

Arbor spun to Mac, his eyes nearly crazed. "They stole my personal property! Make the captain force them to give it back!"

He stepped so close, Mac had no choice but to put up his hands to create some distance. "First off, no one makes the captain do anything. Even me. Second, you're best off playing along. Eventually, they get tired and one day it'll show back up at your quarters unharmed. The more upset you get, the longer it plays out."

Arbor snarled. "I'll just talk to the captain myself."

"Arbor, you know he had reservations on you being able to fit in. Even if he sides with you, he'll just see it as if you can't get along with the crew."

Arbor's eyes glistened and his voice quivered. "Who has him, Priest?"

The smug grin bled away into sad regret as Priest shook his head. "I don't know. Each person picks the next handler. He could be with anyone right now."

"I'll hack the encrypted coms. That'll show me who has him." Arbor's torso was racked with tremors as he ground his teeth.

Mac hated to do it but had to throw a warning at Arbor. "Don't. You don't have security clearance and you'll wind up in the brig and off the ship at the next port. Arbor, calm down. Nothing's going to happen to Mr. Wiggles. Why don't we sit back down and finish our dinner."

"No thanks. My appetite's gone."

Arbor turned and stormed out of the Mess Hall, knocking over a chair that made the mistake of being in his path. Mac gripped Priest's arm when he made to follow. Crew members who had been watching began whispering among themselves.

"Don't, Priest. Let him calm down."

Priest's whole body slumped as his voice grew repentant. "I want to say I'm sorry. I never thought he'd get this mad over it. It was supposed to be funny."

Balling up his fist, Mac laid one solid punch to Priest's shoulder.

"Ow! What was that for?"

"For being a stupid asshole. Arbor's had people making fun of him his whole life. How did you expect him to react?" Mac couldn't help but sigh in defeat. He really liked Arbor and wanted nothing more than for him to find his place on the *Santa Claus*. But if he didn't learn to control these kind of reactions and stop being so hypersensitive, it would only egg the guys on and make him the very outcast he was afraid of becoming.

HOURS LATER, ARBOR could still picture Priest's expression before he marched out of the Mess Hall. A man couldn't fake the way his face sagged, the remorse he saw in Priest's eyes. Worse, Arbor was the victim and, for some strange reason, he felt horrible for making Priest feel that way. The other night with Priest had been so much fun, but becoming attached to the first man you fuck after a period of nothing was something he'd like to avoid.

Arbor sat in his quarters, staring at the space where Mr. Wiggles should have rested. He knew Mac was right. It was an adolescent stunt performed by adults who should know better and he should just roll with it. Why couldn't he?

What a stupid question. He knew perfectly well why.

His mother had made Mr. Wiggles after the first time he'd been called a freak and actually believed it. The artist commune in which he grew up was supposed to be a tolerant community, a safe place for one and all. A shame no one informed the other children.

Working for several nights, she crafted the doll out of a series of fresh socks she had knitted. She hadn't even bothered using the threadbare ones that were too worn to wear. This monkey was special. Stuffing him with natural fibers, she put a center of cloves and cinnamon in the body. It was supposed to be a naturalist method of repelling insects. Arbor didn't care. He loved it and even had new sticks put in over the years when the scent faded.

Mr. Wiggles was a sign of her unending love and acceptance and made life easier when being different was hard. And life for Arbor had never been easy. Normally, when the days were difficult, he would hold onto Mr. Wiggles, breathe in the spicy scent, and remember his mother's support.

With him gone, he only had one other option.

"Mrs. Claus, I'd like a private connection to Alpha Centauri."

"Communication link will be established in one minute, thirty-eight seconds."

Such a short time to wait, given the distance, but each second held on like forever when your life was crumbling.

"Link established, Mr. Kittering."

Arbor climbed into the chair facing the screen. "Com link me to Mariah Kittering, Nine Muses Art Collective, District Gamma-Seven."

An anxious flutter rose in Arbor's chest as the monitor over his desk came to life. Lines of code scrolled down, giving a hurried status report as the connection was established. With a sharp flicker, the screen changed to the image of an older woman sporting a series of long, graying dreadlocks, swirled into a pile atop her head. Creases marked the corners of her eyes and mouth, giving away her age, but it was the harsh line between her eyebrows that caused Arbor concern.

"Ma? Are you okay?"

She looked agitated and flustered. "Arbor? Can you hear me?" With a clumsy hand, she kept touching random controls on the screen. "Am I using this thing correctly?"

"Ma, stop touching things. Everything's working fine." Her image kept turning colors as she huffed and continued trying to adjust settings. "Ma! Stop already!"

With an angry huff, Mariah dropped her hands to her sides in defeat. Arbor tapped a few icons in the corner of the screen and her image stabilized.

"It's a travesty that there's some technology we can't do without. If I didn't need this contraption to communicate, I'd have burned it on the last Sabbat."

"Please. No more images of you dancing naked in the firelight with the clan. I'm still permanently scarred and haven't found a reliable method to give me amnesia to cope with the trauma."

"I'll have you know you were conceived during one of those firelight dances."

Arbor shuddered. "Stop telling me things like that."

Mariah chuckled, her laugh sultry and alive. "Of course, my darling boy. How are you doing? You look tired. Have you been sleeping?"

"It's been a rough night."

"Is the time stamp on this thing right? It's awfully late. What's happened that's so bad you'd call on me at this hour?"

Arbor's whole body deflated as he exhaled. "Do you ever think you're ruining your last chance to make something of yourself?"

"You know I don't believe in last chances. Nature always reclaims itself at some point. Tell me what's happened."

"The crew played a practical joke on me. I got really angry, and made an ass of myself. In the process, I upset some people. I guess I just needed to hear a friendly voice that isn't on board."

Mariah's smile was warm and succoring. "I would have thought you'd curl up with Mr. Wiggles and ignore it all."

"That's the problem. They stole Mr. Wiggles and are holding him for ransom."

"Oh, Arbor." Mariah snickered before drawing a motherly sympathy across her face. "That's so awful."

Arbor dropped his head into his hands. "Crap. Even you think I'm being ridiculous."

"Ridiculous? No. But I do think you're making too much of it. You'll survive this, just like everything else. I named you Arbor to impart a spirit of the tree's renewing strength and endurance."

"Too bad you got more of a stump."

The unhappy look on Mariah's face found no humor in Arbor's self-recrimination. "Shame on you, Arbor. You've always been too hard on yourself."

"The world is always hard on me."

"It doesn't have to be. You could come back and be an artist here in the commune, instead of dealing in all that unnatural technology. It could be easier here for you."

A sudden flash of annoyance spilled into Arbor's voice. "Ma, the commune is where I got my first taste of how shitty the world can be. Remember?"

"Those little boys were awful, but what can you expect from the offspring of experimental performance artists?"

"At least I have something I do here that I enjoy. Even if I'm a strange minority."

"You are not strange. You are as nature intended."

Arbor hated it whenever she said that. It was a stock answer from the naturalist community. It supposedly nullified every argument surrounding his condition. It always put his spine on edge and brought out the worst in him.

"I didn't have to be. You could have fixed it. You knew about the achondroplasia before I was born."

Mariah's brow quirked in distaste. "I was only scanned because my parents insisted on it after I was drawn into the hospital due to an accident. When the doctors told me they could correct the condition, they kept referring to you as 'the fetus' in this cold way that made you sound like a science experiment. Those sterile people kept saying how they could *fix* you. They wanted to change my baby who could live perfectly healthy without their intervention. All in the name of vanity." She shook her head in undeniable refusal. "Why in Great Mother's graces would I consent to such a travesty? I refused then and still hold my position, even now with everything that's happened."

"I'm so glad you could find your moral center at my expense." Arbor knew how nasty it sounded, but he couldn't restrain his need to lash out.

Mariah frowned. "You're hardly sick, Arbor, and your life isn't in jeopardy. It's merely inconvenient."

"Inconvenient?" Arbor growled in outrage. "Do you have any idea how hard my life has been? To be regarded as some kind of medical throwback or carnival sideshow attraction?"

"You struggle too hard to be normal, Arbor. Normal is highly overrated."

"I'd love to agree with you, but I've never known what that's like."

Mariah straightened in her chair, reinforcing her position as head of the household. "Oh, stop whining, Arbor. I've never treated you as anything but perfect in my eyes and I've always done everything in my power to make you believe that."

"Except for the one thing you could have done before I was born."

This wasn't a new argument, but it held new fuel since all the events before and after prison. The whole struggle for acceptance on the ship had worn his already thin skin. If he wanted to get a rise out of his mother, he succeeded. Her volume rose, scolding him through the hidden speakers.

"I have watched you make more than one mistake in your life and blame me for it. I am growing tired of being your scapegoat. Nature is blessed in the variety it generates. Stop hating yourself for being different. You are responsible for only yourself and your own choices. You didn't end up in prison for being a dwarf." She struck her hand down on the table as an exclamation point. "You ended up in prison because you were angry over what happened with that sad excuse of a lover you fawned over."

Arbor slapped the screen, spinning it out of position, and ended the connection. He couldn't listen to any more of it. Sharp gasps hissed through his teeth as tears perched at the edges of his eyes.

What the hell was he doing? His mother was absolutely correct, and he knew it. He was healthy and sane and understood her values. Being a dwarf was the result of nature's random number generator—the lottery no one would want to win—and accepting the fact had never been easy. Some days were easier than others, but today was not easy. Considering how many times they'd had this argument in one form or another, it was amazing the woman still took his com. Arbor wasn't sure that he had the same level of compassion inside himself.

With his nerves so frayed, Arbor knew better than to com her back. It would just drag the two of them into the same circular conversation. She would start trying to make amends, and he would target her naturalist ethics. This was why they couldn't talk too often. He wouldn't forgive himself if he ever saw her cry because of him.

Arbor squared the monitor and settled in his chair. Touching a pad on the edge of the panel, a holographic keyboard appeared on the desk, scaling itself to the size of his hands.

Dear Ma

I'm so sorry if I upset you. There are things I haven't told you about Arthur and being in prison that have made me touchier than normal. You're right. I've spent a lot of time wanting others to like me. I just haven't convinced myself they can like me in spite of being a dwarf.

Being on the Santa Claus could be good for me, if I could only figure out how to fit in. I just wish I was better at that and less of a social reject.

Even so, none of this is your fault. It never has been. You're the one person in all the universe who knew how to make me feel loved. So don't listen to me when I'm being a brat.

I'll check in again soon when I'm having a calmer day. You deserve better than this.

Love, Arbor

Arbor sniffed as he rubbed the wetness along his eye. With a deep breath, he drew strength from the knowledge he loved his mother and pressed the send-message command.

Being upset always weathered him, so Arbor decided a shower might make him feel better.

PRIEST'S BOOTS STRUMMED a rapid beat on the floor as he rushed back to his quarters. Off-ship personal coms weren't very common for him, so he wasn't going to miss out on the rare occurrence. His hand was still touching the access panel as he pushed between the doors of his room.

He jumped into the chair like an excited child and activated the screen.

"Hi, Dad!"

"Morning, Eugene!"

Priest winced. "Not so loud. No one calls me that around here. I don't want that to change."

"It's your given name, boy. You should wear it proudly." Larry Jones was a tall, forthright man, and the knowledge his son rejected being named after his elderly grandfather was no small source of friction between them. Priest kicked himself under the table for starting up a problem so soon. Why couldn't his mother have called instead?

"It never really fit me and kids made fun of me all the time because of it. But I don't want to talk about that. How are you guys doing?"

"I'm doing all right." His father's voice dropped a notch. "Your mama's been better."

A sharp pinch in Priest's chest extinguished his excitement. "What's going on?"

"She had an accident driving one of the seeders. Wasn't taking her meds and she passed out in the field and crashed into a silo. She was hurt pretty bad." Priest opened his mouth, but Larry held up his hand to interrupt. "Doctors are fixing her up, but there's some leftover nerve damage that isn't healing correctly. Motor skills in her right hand and leg don't quite work like they're supposed to. She won't be able to drive any of the machines anymore, so that's one less hand to get the crop out on time."

"Are you gonna make it?" The idea of the family farm in distress worried him. Growing up on the farm, Priest knew the long hours and endless work involved in being successful. Their livelihood was entwined in each season's crop.

"We're putting in a lot of extra hours, but we think so. It'll be close. It's next harvest we're a little worried about."

Priest let out a relieved breath. "Sounds like you have time to hire someone on to cover."

His father looked away from the screen as his mouth grew tight. An extended silence filled the room as he hesitated to speak. Priest waited patiently to hear what could be so difficult to say.

"We want you to come home to the family business."

Priest shook his head. "Get David to help. He likes farming."

"Your brother David's been working here for the last nine months. You'd know that if you kept in touch better."

Priest cringed at the statement. It was only a matter of time before his father started wielding guilt as his weapon of choice, at which he was viciously adept. Steeling himself to weather the blows would take a miracle.

"I can't, Dad. I have my life here."

Larry sat up tall, the tilt of his head and body the one he used when lording over his children. "It's time you grew up and stopped hopping around the cluster and helped out with what matters. The farms are growing fast as the governments transition off synthesized rations. Almost too fast. You can run all the equipment and make a fine life for yourself here."

"But I don't want to be a farmer. I never did."

Larry's eyes grew cold. "You think you're too good for us?"

"No! I never said that. I never thought that. But I wanted more than that."

"Like what?" Larry scoffed. "How many crazy schemes have blown up in your face as you work to make yourself rich? Are you any closer yet? Still hoping to become a celebrity?"

Every word Larry said made Priest feel like little Eugene all over again. "I was never happy there, Dad. You know that. After the Civil War, you couldn't expect me to go back to a regular life."

"There comes a time when a man has to cast aside his wild ways and settle down and do what's right."

A surge of anger filled Priest. He hadn't spoken with his father in months and now he was proselytizing the virtues of a life of farming without once asking if Priest wanted such a life. Even this com was more of a request—or command—of what *he* wanted, not Priest.

"But it's only right if it's what you want, right, Dad?" Priest shook his head as he held his temper in check. "I need something else in my life. I was never good being grounded on Alpha Centauri. I like being head pilot on the *Santa Claus*."

Larry's face twisted in displeasure. "Head pilot? It's a cargo freighter, boy. You need to stop making it sound bigger than it really is. That was always your problem. Tall tales and reckless dreams. You've spent a lot of time carousing around on that ship, visiting worlds and partying it up. Any partners yet? At least for more than a night, Eugene?"

The cheap tactic nearly made Priest laugh out loud. Larry Jones never asked a question during an argument if he didn't already know the answer. It wasn't as if Priest didn't want a permanent partner. He had yet to find one unique enough to keep him interested.

Priest tried to maintain a respectful tone even as he wished to do otherwise. "You don't understand. I don't know exactly what I want, but it's not something ordinary. Not something standard. I know deep down I'll never be happy on the farm. So, I'm sorry, but I'm not coming back to it."

"I can't say I'm not disappointed in you, Eugene."

Priest shrugged, not even wanting to look his father in the eye. "Wouldn't be the first time you've said that to me."

"Probably won't be the last either if you keep on like this."

Priest closed his eyes to take the sting out of the last comment. "So glad you commed, Dad. You started up the 'Eugene the Worthless Son' song and dance faster than usual. Tell Mom I love her."

He disconnected.

Rolling forward, he held his head in his hands as the air escaped his lungs through his clenched jaw. He knew his father was being harsher than normal. His mother was hurt and the old man was probably blaming himself for everything.

But taking out his anger on him wasn't fair. He might have been traveling the cluster, but Priest never forgot his family. Priest would give anything to make his father proud of him, but nothing short of doing whatever the man said would ever be enough. The quintessential patriarch, he was used to being followed and crushed out opposition.

It wasn't to say he was an evil man. Priest loved his father, and the lack of approval ate at him. If only he could go back to how their relationship functioned before. There were so many good memories growing up, living back on the farm almost sounded like a good idea. Almost.

From the first time Larry Jones taught his son to drive while sitting in his lap and manning the controls his feet couldn't reach, little Eugene learned to like thrills and excitement. It didn't take long to flourish into a need to escape the routine, common life on the family farm. A taste for the good life was only a step away.

He wanted more than waking up each morning to work the land, doing the same tasks each day, all day, until you went to sleep at night. Life on his family's farm rarely meant a day off except during the winter months, and what could you do when you were snowed in? There had to be something else out there for little Eugene.

Too bad he hadn't quite found the exotic, perfect life yet. There was a way to make himself happy. He knew it. Priest was still working hard to find it, but at least he would earn every gram of his success. He'd never asked his family for money once he moved away. He never leeched off his mother and father and made their lives hell like other reckless people around whom he'd grown up.

No, he would make his way under his own power. If only his father could ever understand that.

Frustrated and uncomfortable in his own room, Priest grabbed his shower kit and headed out the door.

COSTA SIPPED A mug of tea as he sifted through restricted personnel files. The room's beverage dispenser was a grateful comfort. In his haste to send away the captain when he first arrived, the simple amenity had been missed. If he hadn't overheard one of the crew in the hallway the other night, he might never have enjoyed his steaming drink.

Pages of information sorted themselves on the monitor, but Costa wasn't watching. He didn't need to see to know what it said. As long as he stayed relaxed and gentle, the headache floated on the fringes, barely out of reach. Last night he'd been hit with another blinding attack. It took two doses to get it under control and make him normal again. Today, however, was a good day.

But would it stay that way?

The trip was proving to be longer than he anticipated. His supply was rationed for a seven-week trip. The stopover and extended voyage could be a problem. When they arrived on Gamma Centauri, he would have to seek out a chemist.

Perhaps Priest would have some ideas. He had to have a number of unsavory contacts of which Costa could avail himself.

Priest's file came up on the screen. Costa snickered at his given name of Eugene. It was no small wonder why he insisted on his nickname. A former farmer turned pilot with lofty ambitions. Priest had a long list of minor incursions with law enforcement—all nonviolent. His help would be required to complete his plans.

It wouldn't be hard to persuade Priest. The interest he showed was impossible to miss. It was almost a shame to send him off with the dwarf at the poker game, but a little denial was good for the soul. Priest was an attractive man, although Costa was unlikely to admit it aloud, and his immaturity boasted a good time should it be necessary. A night with Priest would not be a hardship.

No, not a hardship at all.

He sighed at the perpetual quiet in his quarters. How he missed talking late into the night with his brother all those many years ago. It kept him sane and centered knowing his efforts had saved the two of them from a horrible future.

But it didn't last and now look where he was. Running away from the home he knew, hoping to find a new settlement with the most precious cargo he'd ever possessed.

An ache built behind his eyes again. Without looking or touching, he deleted all his search evidence and shut down the monitor. It was happening faster than before, but there was so much in his head these days.

While he was confident he could entice Priest to his side, would he stay there once he knew everything? Costa couldn't be sure. When the moment came, he would have to tread carefully.

It wasn't as if Costa didn't know how. Precise planning had taken him this far, and it would take him to Omoikane as well.

A twitch in his hand gave Costa pause. How long had it been since his last dose? There was only so much. It had to last. The twitch gave way to a small itch—he couldn't focus on its source.

Crossing his arms over his chest, he tried to still the impending shiver. It was not time. He needed to wait.

Sitting on his bed, he found his sight trailing to the nightstand. He fought the urge for several minutes. Reaching for the drawer, he pulled out the black cylinder. The simple device held a fascination for Costa he was not happy with.

Dropping it on the bed, he turned away in some vain attempt to ignore it.

The pressure in his head gave a soft blur to his thoughts. If he was addled, he couldn't keep his control. And a lack of control on this ship could be disastrous.

Perhaps one dose to get through the night would be enough. Then he could leave it be for at least another day.

Retrieving the cylinder, he dispensed a single drop onto his tongue then shoved it in the drawer to remove the temptation for more. The buzz in his head receded and he felt more like himself. Before long, his mood elevated and the idea of getting out of his room sounded like a wonderful idea. What chance was there another crew member would be up and about? He could use some company for the night, but he felt dirty.

Perhaps he'd go take a shower.

ARBOR WISHED THE shower room didn't make him so apprehensive. He wasn't in prison anymore and there wasn't any reason to be scared. If only he could make himself believe the words he told himself.

Entering the locker room, he could hear showers in use. Someone was already inside. Since he boarded, Arbor had made a point to bathe when he was alone. He knew it was absurd to be nervous, but he kept telling himself he'd get past it all. He almost turned back, but he really wanted the hot water to wash off the memory of his fight with his mother.

He could do this.

He sat on the bench and started undressing, noticing the clothing next to him. The navy shirt hanging off the end was the one Priest was wearing the night of the poker game. The idea of Priest naked, and the option to clear the air after his anger over Mr. Wiggles, sounded like a good reason to get over his shyness.

Removing the rest of his garments in quick order, he headed for the sound of running water with a towel in hand. His newfound confidence was only marginally complete. Arbor stopped short at the doorway and surveyed the room first.

Streaks of soap ran down Priest's back in sudsy lines, tracing the mounds of his backside as he lathered his head and neck. Heated memories of being inside that ass filled Arbor's cock. Another venture inside would be such a good thing. The only thing stopping him from walking in and helping Priest scrub his nethers was that he wasn't alone.

Two showers away, Costa rolled his head as the water washed over him. Priest kept stealing glances in his direction and the smile on Costa's face proved he knew it. Neither man had noticed Arbor.

"Why are you standing so far away, Priest?" The playful tone Arbor remembered from the game was on Costa's lips.

"Getting too close to you has gotten me in trouble. Trying to decide if it's worth it, I guess." A fresh run of soap coated Priest's chest and stomach as he turned, half facing Costa. The move was a veiled invitation, giving Costa a better look without being vulgar.

"Surely I'm not that terrifying. Come closer so I don't have to shout."

Priest flashed a defiant smile. "I can hear you fine."

Costa met his smirk and locked eyes with Priest. When Priest didn't move, he nodded and the water over Priest's shower turned off.

"Shower on," Priest said. When nothing happened, he gave Costa a look. "Turn that back on."

"It seems to be malfunctioning. I'm afraid you'll have to use the one next to me now." The shower between them came to life.

Reluctantly, Priest reached out and tested the water before stepping into the spray and resuming his shower. He'd barely rinsed off when he yelped and jumped out.

"*Ah!* Fuck! That's cold!"

Costa giggled. "Oh my, another malfunction. It appears only my shower will be safe for you." Dipping his head into the spray, he slicked back his hair and ran his hand over his graceful body.

Priest stood unmoving, fixated on the display. "You sure you want to share with me?"

"I would even be happy to wash your back, if you need it. Or you can return the favor to mine."

Priest licked his lips as he stepped forward, stopping short with a cautious hesitation as if expecting something to go wrong.

"Come to me." Costa reached out, his gentle hand tracing a line down Priest's chest, all the way down until he had a handful of Priest's growing erection.

As Priest shifted closer, both men took new handfuls of soap and began a new round of caresses. Slippery foam swirled around and between them as they slid their bodies against one another. As Priest dipped his head down to Costa's eager mouth, every shower turned on simultaneously, filling the room with eager rolls of steam.

With a quiet gasp, Arbor slid back from the doorway, hoping he hadn't been seen. Heart pounding, he found himself gripping the towel so hard it bit white lines into his palm. He sat back down, gathered his clothes, and redressed quickly. The last thing he was going to do was walk into the middle of what was going to happen next—or sit back and listen to it either. Could this day go any further down the toilet?

He shouldn't be mad at Priest. The other night was supposed to be about having fun and he didn't have any claim on the man. Arbor shouldn't be surprised, really. Costa was beautiful. Who wouldn't want him more? But would that still be the case if they knew how much more there was to Mr. McQuillen?

As he forced his legs into his trousers, Arbor wasn't sure what upset him more: the sight of Costa in Priest's arms, or the reality that Costa was a freak—a para-human.

Chapter Six

PRIEST WAS FORTUNATE Costa allowed him to get dressed before dragging him out of the shower and to his quarters. He was convinced his underwear was inside out, but the way the Costa urged him through the door, he wouldn't be wearing them long enough for it to be an issue.

Costa slammed his mouth on Priest's as the door slid closed, frantically attacking the clasp of his pants. They barely pulled away long enough to pull the shirt over Priest's head and resumed the needy, desperate kiss.

This was heaven. The exotic man wanted him—something Priest had nearly convinced himself was a blind man's fantasy. But Costa came for him, wanting him, and he couldn't say no. There might not be a next time.

"Off, off. Get them off." Costa yanked at Priest's pants and briefs together, scratching his hips with his urgency. It was a little more crazed than Priest was used to.

Priest grabbed Costa's wrists. "Easy, there. We got time."

"No. Need you. Need you now." Costa's pupils were black pools with little color surrounding them, and when he pulled back his hands, his fingers twitched on the fringe of self-control. His lust appeared barely lashed down and Priest couldn't tell if he should be flattered or concerned.

Stripping away the remainder of his own clothing, Costa positioned himself on his bed. Priest wanted him, but should he? When Costa lifted his legs in invitation, Priest's erection won out. He kicked off his shoes and couldn't get naked fast enough. He nearly pounced.

Their cocks slid against one another as Priest ground their hips together. Costa's lithe but strong legs wrapped around his waist and crushed them tighter as their kiss became sloppy and reckless.

Costa chanted against Priest's mouth. "Inside me. Inside me."

"We need some lube." Priest raised himself on his arms as he looked around the room.

Costa spit into his hand and reached between them and slicked Priest's cock, causing a moaning hiss to spill out of him. There wasn't time to think. Costa shifted his hips and forced himself on the newly greased organ. The cry he let out made Priest go still.

"Wait, wait. I don't want to hurt you."

With a surprising flex of those fit legs, Costa dragged Priest forward, burying him all the way in one thrust. "Hurt me."

"Oh shit." The heat and friction were mind-bending. Spasms of pleasure streaking through every extremity, Priest found himself frozen in place. Clearly, Costa wasn't feeling patient. He rocked his hips, forcing Priest's cock almost out before driving it back in to the hilt. Both men shouted out at the motion.

Costa focused his piercing eyes into Priest's. "Fuck me, please. Make it hurt. Need you, Priest."

Losing himself in the fervor, he could only nod and give the man under him exactly what he asked. Digging his feet into the bedding for leverage, Priest pumped as hard as he could. Whenever he tried to be gentle, Costa demanded a more punishing rhythm.

This was not going to be a drawn-out affair. Living out the fantasy he imagined from the moment he first caught sight of Costa, coupled with plunging in and out of that sucking wet heat, was bringing Priest close to the end.

"I'm not gonna last much longer."

Costa arched, grinding his leaking hardness against Priest's belly. "Please fuck, don't stop!"

Understanding what Costa was doing, Priest tightened his core, giving a firmer surface for his frottage. The wetness soaking his stomach was more than the sweat forming between them.

Costa rolled forward, sealed his lips over Priest's, and screamed into his mouth as a flood of semen sprayed between them. Each surge was paired with Costa's channel clenching along Priest's length, and he gave in. Buried as deep as he could go, he came long and hard, letting Costa's spasms milk him dry.

Still engaged, Priest wrapped his arms around Costa and rolled them over so he was on his back. Costa's slight weight over him was damn nice.

Eventually, Priest softened and slipped out, the rush of fluid coating his deflating member. Yes, he had come hard. Priest was pretty sure he'd emptied his balls, and this contentment made all the earlier cat fighting between them a fleeting bad dream.

Costa placed a small kiss on his lips and dismantled himself from Priest's arms. He stood graceful and soiled, skin flushed and hair disheveled, the contrast making Priest want him more. A few steps to the wardrobe storage and Costa slipped a thin robe over his body. Without even looking back at Priest, Costa ran a hand through his hair, taming the still-damp locks.

"That was very enjoyable, Priest, but I need some rest. I'm sure you have duties early in the morning as well." Costa was quick and harsh, the rigid countenance Priest hated reappearing. "Make sure you don't leave anything behind."

The bright sunshine warming Priest's soul dulled. "Oh. Sure." One moment he was basking in the aftermath of an unplanned liaison and now he was being dismissed like an anonymous bar trick. It wasn't as if Priest never knew the pain of rejection, but this one was unexpected. Given the way Costa had pursued him, a small glimmer of hope had sparked, but it was quashed now.

Rolling off the bed, Priest began gathering his clothes, not caring to clean up before dressing. He needed to move faster and get out, but he couldn't find the urgency. Everything was leaden, mired in a sudden fog.

Costa's gentle hand directed Priest's gaze from the floor to his own. "Come now, Priest. Let's not make more of this than it really is. It was just a shag. A very good shag, mind you, but just a shag. We both needed to vent a little frustration and I have no doubt we will do so again. But for now, you need to go."

Silent, Priest nodded and finished dressing. The idea of more opportunities to play around with Costa eased the sting of being kicked out, but far from extinguished it. Something about Costa made him want more. When the door opened, he looked back at Costa, whose impassive veneer was showing a minor fracture.

Costa sighed softly and his shoulder dropped a fraction of a centimeter. "I'm not the kind of man you want to fall for, Priest."

MAC COULDN'T HELP but talk with his mouth full. Lunch was mouthwatering and he'd missed breakfast working. Arbor had taken up his invitation to eat with the captain and himself for a change. Mac thought it would do them good to have a nice civilized meal, showing the captain Arbor's ability to be part of the crew wasn't a piece of fiction. Other crew members were keeping their distance from their newest acquisition, possibly not wanting to be pulled into a new piece of drama.

Arbor had been a little preoccupied for most of the meal, and Danverse was being polite, but his usual gruff self. Not much conversation flowed between them.

"We had another one of those glitches last night. This time in the shower room."

Arbor didn't look at Mac as he swallowed another spoonful of soup. "You don't say."

"Is this something we should be worried about?" Danverse cocked his head at Mac. If it involved the ship functions, he made it his business.

Mac shook his head. "I don't think so. It's probably just a bad piece of code that's crept up. Mrs. Claus is a sophisticated piece of tech. Arbor will help me sort it."

A small smile appeared on Arbor's face "That's what I'm here for."

"Sounds good. You let me know if it becomes something more serious." Danverse reached out and stroked the back of Mac's neck. The loving gesture was a mix of dominance and approval, causing a warmth in Mac's chest and sometimes other areas. When the captain began stroking his thumb along the base of his skull, Mac's eyes fluttered and his breeches became tighter than a moment ago.

Arbor shifted his sight, shying away from the display. Mac shrugged, dislodging the captain's hand before he became too aroused. When the captain gave him an unhappy glance, he nodded in Arbor's direction. Danverse dipped his head in understanding, but Mac knew he'd have to make up for it later in the evening. It would be worth it.

Mac cleared his throat. "Sorry about that, Arbor."

"Nothing to apologize for. You guys are good together. If you have someone in your life that can bring out that kind out of reaction, you should take advantage whenever possible…"

Arbor's voice trailed away as Priest walked in with Costa McQuillen by his side. His face wasn't giving away much, but his rapt attention said it all.

"Priest or the passenger?" Danverse hadn't missed it either.

Arbor turned back, stirring his soup in lazy arcs. "Priest is a grown man. He can do who he wants."

"Sounds like you don't care much for Mr. McQuillen." Danverse's question was filled with scrutiny. He was testing Arbor's compatibility with passengers as much as his interaction with the crew.

Arbor shrugged. "I don't know him well enough to say much."

"I wasn't aware they'd started bumping uglies." Mac watched the pair gather their meal and sit together, having a pleasant chat. McQuillen was a bit regal, making it hard to get a proper read on what might be going on between the two men.

Arbor's nose crunched as he grimaced. "I think I walked in on their first time in the showers last night."

Danverse shrugged as he took a drink. "It happens."

"You don't have a problem with stuff like that going on?"

His lips flattened as he shook his head. "It keeps the ship running smooth. It always has. The men spend long weeks at a time with only each other, bottled up on the ship. It can get a little lonely sometimes. As long as the work gets done, and everyone's consenting, I don't mind that they let off some steam together." The captain paused for effect. "And they have to keep their dicks off my boy too. That's the most important rule."

Arbor snorted and Mac rolled his eyes. Marc Danverse would never change. He was possessive and gave Mac no reason to believe he wasn't completely devoted to him. It went both ways. The two of them were hopelessly besotted with one another. Mac could live with that.

"A word of advice, Arbor." Danverse spoke up, the authority never leaving his voice. "Priest is a good man, but he's got great expectations of what he wants. Passengers are often like a new rocket to play with on the *Santa Claus*, especially the pretty ones. New toys always lose their shine."

"I guess."

Mac chimed in. "Most passengers just come and go. No pun intended."

Danverse chewed his lip while he controlled the grin threatening to break his composure. He reached out and bopped Mac's forehead with the heel of his hand. "Hush, boy, the captain's being serious here." Danverse turned back to Arbor. "As I was saying... Eventually, Priest'll find someone who will let him be himself and leave him with something good. Until then, think of this voyage as a chance to meet new people and make yourself part of the family."

Arbor's head tilted as he absorbed the captain's speech. "I hope I can figure out how to be around long enough to see that happen."

"If you relax and learn to take everything as not being a new way to fuck with you, you'll manage. I pick all my crew very carefully, Mr. Kittering. They may be thoughtless at times, but they're not cruel. And with a few exceptions, they all enjoy each other's company at any given time. It's nothing to be ashamed of, and nothing to worry about. Sometimes a fuck is just a fuck. Learn to enjoy it and things get a lot easier for everyone involved."

"Are you saying I should start sleeping with everyone in the crew?"

"Only if you want to, and not to be worried if other men want do the same thing. It doesn't necessarily mean they don't like you."

ARBOR HAD BARELY slept for the last two days. Reports of occasional malfunctions had sprung up in various places on the ship, so Mac had him tracing down anomalies in Mrs. Claus's subroutines. With no evidence of hardware degradation, it pointed to coding flaws, which was why he'd been hired.

He scoured the lines of data for hours at a time, but not finding a conflict in the code wasn't what was keeping him up at night. He was already convinced of the cause, and it all pointed to Costa McQuillen.

It was a giant accusation and Arbor knew better than to blurt it out loud. Due to his outbursts since stepping on board, his reputation was frayed enough, so he had to be sure before saying anything. The biggest question still loomed over him: should he say anything?

Stories of pariahs were used to frighten children when he was little and, since so few were known to exist outside of Earth's territory, hard knowledge in the cluster was limited. Many people believed them to be dangerous. Was it true?

Was the crew of the *Santa Claus* at risk with Costa McQuillen on board? He watched Costa turn the showers on and off before he seduced Priest into... It was best not to dwell on details outside of the code. What else had Costa done? Were the malfunctions a remnant of his presence?

His personal distaste for the man aside, Arbor couldn't prove enough to make an issue of it. He couldn't bring anything to the captain's attention without proper evidence. More reliable data was required.

"Mrs. Claus, I need a secure, encrypted Link back to Earth databases. Upload my personal sniffer program from my secure server and use it for all data transfer."

"As you wish, Mr. Kittering. Secure Subspace Link connection to Earth will be established in two minutes, forty-six seconds."

Arbor could feel perspiration dotting his brow. Using his personal hacking software was against the magistrate's decree and all copies were supposed to have been deleted. All except one he hid on his personal datapad, buried deep inside other software as a series of fragments waiting to be assembled. He hadn't planned on breaking the rules, but a lot of time went into making it, he couldn't destroy it outright. Following these orders, he hadn't touched any of the applications he'd written that landed him in prison, but this was important.

The sniffer would be able to bypass dynamic firewalls and go unnoticed on the Link once it had copied itself into the proper information centers. When all was complete, it would self-delete, leaving no evidence. He knew he shouldn't be using this, but until he verified his suspicions, he needed to keep any knowledge of his task away from prying eyes.

"Connection established, Mr. Kittering."

"Activate sniffer, scramble all incoming transmissions and decipher on my personal datapad."

Arbor lay back on his bed as the thin plaque came alive in his stubby fingers. Convinced the data was private, he started his search.

"Define para-human." Several sites gave similar results. He tapped the page with the most reliable stats, watching the text spill over his screen.

While it is argued para-humans have existed in small numbers throughout history, after the Great Migration, where nearly half of the population of Earth traveled to settle in the Alpha Centauri cluster, para-human appearances grew exponentially. The most commonly accepted theory is the numbers were the result of environmental damage and the genetic engineering efforts to combat it. Extra-normal abilities resulted, ranged from a wide gamut of physical and psionic effects that typically manifested during the onset of puberty. Testing of children became a political platform as sympathy fluctuated.

Arbor tapped the words "political platform."

With the world population diminished, Human Fundamentalists argued the need to defend the human race, and Evolutionists argued para-humans were the next step in humanity's path. Public opinion for both sides wavered but never took hold enough to force government intervention.

The name Haphic Delmedge appeared at the top in the list of relevant links, so Arbor followed it.

Haphic Delmedge was a para-human with the ability to walk through walls. He was convicted of raping and murdering twenty-three children in their own beds before authorities constructed a method to capture him. The outcry to protect the children pushed the Human Fundamentalists into the majority.

In the interests of global security, all para-humans were marked as second-class citizens, relieved of most basic civil rights, and required to perform duties in the service of their communities. Various restraints and safeguards were applied to protect the populace.

Tracing the feed into a government site, Arbor unearthed the safeguard schematics.

Non-technological controls were the use of a manufactured drug called Calm. A sodium pentathol derivative, Calm inhibits higher brain functions, creating euphoria and inducing complicity in activity and honesty. The effect also suppresses the activity in the brain governing most para-human abilities. Controlled substance. Black market varieties can induce sessions of heightened arousal and compulsive sexuality, depending on the dosage and formulation.

An image of a small, circular metal disk appeared on the page.

A pacifier was implanted at the base of every para-human skull, connecting directly to their nervous system. When activated by their sponsor's remote, the device sends micro-surges of painless electricity into the spinal column and brain stem of the individual, rendering them harmless. Tampering with the device would set off its function.

Shocks to the spine and brain, painless? Who the fuck came up with that load of nonsense?

All para-humans were marked with a series of identification numbers tattooed across their right cheek. The numbers were tagged to their DNA, marking them down to the bone, preventing removal.

All para-humans not safe to be within the general population were placed in Quarantine, a facility equipped for the containment of extra-normal powers.

Touching the feed to Quarantine, Arbor looked over the blueprints for the building. Adaptable tech was placed in each room, or cell, to counteract a tenant's abilities. It seemed appropriate. It was a prison, right?

A wave of cold nausea ripped through him as he found the crematorium on the building's south side. Why would they need such a thing? The answer floated before him but he refused to latch onto it. Better to stick with hard facts relevant to his search, but questions kept erupting in his head. Who created this thing?

The search for Quarantine's architect brought up the name Anthony Swaden. It took nothing to pull up his personal files the military had marked classified. The first one was about fifteen years old.

Anthony Swaden: promoted to Head of Global Security after being awarded the contract to combat the para-human problem. Unmarried, 45 years of age. Designer of the pacifier, ID number technology, and Quarantine. System updates and designed upgrades are performed through Swaden's master connection to the Link, referred to as the Hub.

Swaden is actively meeting with heads of other districts to implement expansions of his systems. He can be found at most times with his longtime companion, servant/attaché; para-human number 006251.

Arbor touched Swaden's name and a holo of the architect appeared with a young, slender man by his side. The mannerisms didn't match, but he was a replica of Costa McQuillen with a short, bleach-blond schoolboy haircut. The attaché was respectful but content, despite his social status. Swaden was tall, broad, and handsome. His shirt's top buttons were open, exposing a hint of his chest, in lieu of a tie. Unusual for a businessman of his rank and status. A bit of a maverick? The pair looked close, their body language lacking the proximal distance of a purely professional relationship. Minimizing the image to one side, Arbor touched Swaden's companion's ID number 006251.

A new file appeared with a government ID image of the same young man. The data came from a classified database of cataloged para-humans. The resemblance to Costa was uncanny.

> *Designate number 006251. Poll Gilliard, tech-empath. Born in the British Collective, EU District. One of five on the planet. Possesses the psionic ability to read and write code to any machines with a digital brain. Allows for control of all technology that uses data for implementation. It is theorized that few data sources can be permanently blocked from his influence.*
>
> *This ability marks him as highly dangerous to global security. Abuse of his abilities could be devastating unless sponsored to an appropriate service. If not, he is marked for retirement.*
>
> *Subject is potentially powerful, but remarkably fragile. Projectile or other low-tech weapons are a proper defense against his abilities. Physical force recommended.*
>
> *Responsible for the death of Anthony Swaden and dismantling of the Para-human Containment Program. Deceased.*

What? Swaden was dead at the hands of his servant? That was a thread Arbor's curiosity couldn't ignore. He put in a search for the details of Swaden's death. It didn't take long to pull up the classified Global Security death certificate.

Anthony Swaden was found dead in his home, gunshot to the head by his own weapon. His DNA ID had been overridden to activate the pistol, which confirmed the criminal investigation reports that his attaché 006251 was responsible.

006251 was found dead in the Hub, Swaden's gun beside him. Time stamp links 006251's time of death to match the time frame of deactivation of all para-human restraints and facilities. Coroner scans show radical damage to tissues in all brain quadrants. Having reached across the Link globally at one time, it is theorized that 006251 reached beyond his limitations, resulting in multiple massive strokes and hemorrhaging that froze his autonomic functions and ultimately caused his death.

The deactivation of all passive countermeasures resulted in a massive revolution of the para-human community. Global enactment of the Pariah Revolution Control Directive was initiated.

The revolution between humans and para-humans was a common Earth-history lesson, but this directive was new. Wasting no time, he sifted through the military communiqués, finding the orders disseminated right before the final siege. When Arbor pulled up the details of the directive, he paled. Every para-human cataloged was listed providing explicit extermination instructions. There were so many. Special weapons had been designed, capable of adjusting to combat specific power sets. The para-humans didn't have a prayer. The directive's final report was equally bleak.

Tens of thousands of lives were lost on both sides, but the para-humans failed in their battle for freedom. The humans had long-term planning on their side, and the release of all pariahs was a surprise to everyone, including themselves. While no known survivors exist, para-human activity is illegal in all districts.

Arbor's stomach churned at the reality. It sounded like the para-humans were disorganized and unprepared, and lost in spite of their abilities. What could have possessed 006251—Poll—to kill his sponsor and start this mindless anarchy? Was he insane? Why would Poll do such a thing?

Arbor needed to understand. He pulled up Poll's activities using his DNA ID but found nothing of interest. Subtle dead zones in various timelines suggested he was adept at erasing his trail. Unsanctioned uses of his powers, perhaps? Outside of the blank spots, there was nothing notable in Poll's history prior to the shooting. All records of Poll's personality profile said he was dedicated to Swaden. There were implications of a romantic liaison between the two as well, even if it was considered illegal. It wasn't surprising. Timelines showed they'd been together for at least fifteen years. It wouldn't be the first time an owner bedded down a slave.

Had Swaden done something to turn his lover against him?

After double-checking his connections were still private, Arbor dug through Anthony Swaden's DNA ID stamps. Being a high-ranking official, there was a constant feed on his location and activities, even if they were restricted. What caught his attention were a few black holes in the feed several days before the shooting.

Arbor's hacking had shown him how Earth's Global Security kept DNA ID traces on all citizens and archived a running log for the purposes of "maintaining freedom." All relevant events were tagged for future investigation and forwarded to various security departments. Nothing was ever deleted.

But sections of Swaden's time code appeared to be missing. When Arbor pressed harder, he had to admit he was impressed with the man's ingenuity. The sections weren't deleted, they had been marked to be ignored by standard Link algorithms. If Arbor hadn't been looking so closely, he might have missed them.

The first altered file was a security vid. The audio data was damaged, but the visuals were intact, except for a certain amount of visual artifacting. Arbor suspected Swaden tried to delete the file but had to settle for hiding it instead.

Swaden was in the vid waiting in what looked like a lower level of a parking garage. He paced in circles, kicking at debris, edgy and snarling. Another person entered the scene. It looked like his attaché, Poll, but with long dark hair. Did he have a twin? It looked like a younger version of Costa McQuillen. Was Swaden having an affair? Kinky, but seemed unlikely. A quick DNA ID cross check showed no mutual locations for Swaden and the lookalike in the history.

An argument broke out over something impossible to hear until Swaden pulled out a small device and the other man fell to the ground, thrashing and spasming as he clawed at the back of his neck until he exhausted himself on the ground. No doubt the pacifier in action. It was horrific to witness, even through the poor quality of this vid. *Painless, my ass.*

A chill raced down Arbor's spine as he watched Swaden reach into his jacket and draw out a gun. He couldn't bring himself to turn away as Swaden put two bullets in the young man as he lay on the ground, standing over him until all movement stopped.

Arbor swallowed down the nausea. There was more to know. He couldn't stop now.

The second suppressed file was a communication from Swaden for a pickup to be sent directly to Quarantine. The vid continued, showing a team of men collecting the corpse and sanitizing the area.

Arbor's hand shook as he rewound the vid and selected the dead man, marked as Designate 006252. Following the DNA ID trail, he found two more hidden files on the man's timeline. One was an acquisition order for 006252's arrival at Quarantine. Immediate incarceration for unlicensed power usage. The next was an incineration order—marked complete.

Arbor set down the pad and rubbed his face in disbelief. Was there anything about this story that wasn't a horror? He wanted to stop, but he still had questions.

Reaching into the para-human registry, he pulled up Designate 006252.

> *Designate number 006252. Costa Gilliard, tech-empath. Born in the British Collective, EU District. One of five on the planet. Possesses the psionic ability to read and write code to any machines with a digital brain. Allows for control of all technology that uses data for implementation. It is believed that few data sources can be permanently blocked from his influence.*

His powers are identical to his twin. Insufficient testing has been available to determine which one's skills are stronger. This ability marks him as highly dangerous to global security. Abuse of his abilities could be devastating. Must be sponsored to an appropriate service. If not, he is marked for retirement.

Subject is highly intelligent, having solicited appropriate sponsorship for his and his twin brother, Poll, 006251, to prevent being sequestered in Quarantine for security purposes. Powerful, but remarkably fragile. Projectile or other low-tech weapons are a proper defense against his abilities. Physical force recommended.

Deceased. Exterminated and incinerated via Quarantine order A1-sw7762.

006252's name was Costa? The image accompanying his file was a younger version for Costa McQuillen, except the tattoos across his cheek were iridescent numbers instead of abstract designs.

Arbor gathered the details and assembled the best theory he could, incomplete as they were.

Did Poll, a para-human, upon finding out that Swaden, the architect of para-human enslavement, murdered his brother, kill him in protest and then release all the other para-humans in defiance? The release was handled poorly and without direction. An act of passionate revenge? So many were killed because of it. The implications of the act were mind staggering.

If Costa was a rare survivor, being a para-human would leave him a target. It would make sense to change his name and traffic himself to the cluster. But all records confirmed the brothers were dead. Costa Gilliard was dead. Arbor had watched Swaden pull the trigger and read the incineration order. The DNA ID confirmed it.

He didn't understand. What the fuck was going on?

Even if he somehow survived, Arbor wasn't convinced Costa was harmless. In spite of all the hardships he must have endured, there could still be a real danger to everyone on board. There were still the strange instances on the ship he hadn't defined. And what did Costa want with Priest? Beyond the obvious?

It was frustrating only being able to confirm so much. The answers he had were pieced together without a solid reference, and he was damned if he was going to walk up to an unlisted para-human and ask.

Until he knew more, Arbor resolved himself to keeping quiet. There was no need to cause a panic if there wasn't a reason for it.

He would, however, plan to be better prepared in case a crisis surfaced.

Chapter Seven

YESTERDAY, MR. WIGGLES was sighted in sick bay. Naturally, he was nowhere to be found when Arbor chased after him. How much longer could this go on before they became bored?

Arbor was doing what he could to insinuate himself into the crew in general, but conversations coming to a halt as he entered a room would grate on a saint's nerves. The men were being polite, but they weren't exactly welcoming him either.

Trying to find some truth in Captain Danverse's wisdom the other day, Arbor spent his time attempting to not find achondroplasiaphobia in every crew member. He repeated to himself being a dwarf did not make him a freak, hoping it would sink in. He said hello to people as they walked by, which often made them look twice before returning the sentiment. Even the chef, Gamin, was kind when Arbor accidentally walked in on him and his green-haired cook, Erron, engaged in a fierce sixty-nine session on the kitchen floor.

Arbor apologized for the interruption and said he'd come back later. Gamin just waved. His mouth was full.

It wasn't the first time Arbor had walked in on crew members in various sex acts. Did they not understand the idea of using their quarters? Or were they blasé about the whole activity? He couldn't be sure.

Maybe Danverse was right about setting aside his uptightness and aligning himself with the crew's idea of fun. Well, now wasn't the time to decide, he had work to do.

Following a path of corrupted data, Arbor found himself in the hallways near the cargo bays. Scanning along the wall, he tracked the source of this disruption behind one of the bulkhead's maintenance access panels.

As many times as he tried, his equipment couldn't get an accurate connection with the tech behind the wall. The panel was shielding the memory caches enough to make this harder than it needed to be. He needed to reinitialize the minor system to purge the foreign data out of the operating software, but it he couldn't access it remotely, he'd have to do it direct.

Stowing his pad in his bag, he examined the panel. With his short arm span, the handles were spaced too far apart to make this simple.

"Mrs. Claus, unlock maintenance panel AJ-62, please."

The magnetic locks disengaged with a pair of soft *thunks* behind the wall.

"Panel AJ-62 is now unlocked, Mr. Kittering."

He scratched his head as he planned his next move. He couldn't grip both handles at once, so he'd need to do them one at a time. The first handle shifted with a twist easily enough. The panel moved slightly but didn't open.

"Okay, I can do this."

Placing one hand on the panel to steady it, he turned the second handle. It released easily, causing the door to come out of the wall. It was heavier than Arbor anticipated, and without the leverage of using two handles, he couldn't control it. The dense metal section fell against his chest and face and teetered backward as its weight began to topple him.

His feet buckled as a pair of large hands snatched the panel from his hands.

"Whoa, careful there!"

Arbor fell back on his butt as the newcomer pushed the panel to one side, setting it on the floor with a weighted thud. He should have been complaining about his sore ass, but he couldn't stop ogling his savior. Up, up, up, his gaze went over the handsome stranger. Swollen with muscle under his mocha skin, the seams of his tight black shirt were in danger of bursting at any moment. Sculpted quads stretched his breeches in indecent ways as he knelt down next to Arbor. A mix of embarrassment and interest flushed Arbor's cheeks.

"You okay there?" The pistol strapped to the man's hip marked him as security.

"Yeah, thanks. The panel was heavier than I expected."

"You should have asked for help."

"I didn't know anyone else was around. Sorry about that."

"It's all good. You're Arbor, right? I'm Angus. Nice to meet you."

Angus reached out, offering his hand. Arbor was so caught up in Angus's chocolate eyes, he almost forgot to take it. His stubby hand all but disappeared in Angus's grip.

"Nice to meet you too."

With a minimal effort, Angus pulled Arbor to a standing position. "What are you doing here?"

"Cleaning up some data corruption. Needed to patch a hard line in here behind the panel. Felt like popping it open and seeing if I could squish myself."

Angus's chuckle was deep and rich. "Sounds good. Anything else you need help with here?"

"Well..." Arbor had a sudden inspiration. Other crew members took advantage of a situation. Why couldn't he? He ran his hand up the security officer's leg, feeling the dense power coiling through it. "I have an idea of something I could help you with."

Angus raised an eyebrow. "Really? You think so?" Angus didn't stop his hand or say no as Arbor tracked his way across his fly. The mound inside was thick and solid like the rest of him. Arbor pressed his palm against the mass, and when Angus stood perfectly still and made no refusal, he took it as permission.

The zipper gave way easily, and Arbor needed both hands to heft Angus's ample genitals into the air. The weighty orbs didn't fit in one hand and he couldn't get the other around the spongy shaft. Angus was so tall, Arbor barely had to lean forward to stretch his mouth over the head. He dug his tongue into the open slit as he sucked and stroked the shaft, coaxing it to harden. Angus's cock filled his mouth now. What did he plan to do with the complete beast?

Angus placed a gentle hand on Arbor's head and wrist and extracted himself. His voice was deep and sympathetic.

"I...I'm sorry. I'm just not really into this."

The scorching heat in Arbor's face had nothing to do with arousal. "Oh. Sure."

Angus stammered as he made himself decent once again. "I-I should go. It's not you, really. Leave the panel there. I'll get it once I come back around."

"Yeah. No problem." Arbor couldn't even watch as Angus turned and resumed his rounds, vanishing around the corner.

Well, that was a great way to bolster one's ego. Most men he knew wouldn't turn down a blow job from a toothless whore, so Arbor's self-esteem was floating somewhere near the bottom of the recycler filter, placing him underneath the residual scum the machine always managed to miss.

With a shaky inhale, he swallowed down the humiliation.

Plugging into the exposed circuit access, Arbor performed his job. He purged the system and reset its parameters for proper functionality, making a log of relevant variations to look at later. At least he thought that's what he'd done. The shame in his head was deafening. Was it possible to feel so unappealing and sexually frustrated in the same stroke?

Angus was nice enough about the whole thing, but he probably wasn't interested in the first place. Arbor knew he must have come on too strong—the big guy's reaction was probably automatic at first but didn't know how to stop the whole fiasco before it got so far. Then again, maybe Arbor's skills were so deficient Angus gave up before he could make more of an ass of himself.

It had been a while since Arbor remembered what pure rejection felt like. He hadn't made an attempt to seduce a man in so long, he'd forgotten. The last time anyone made him feel so downright unappealing was somewhere around the sex vid incident he wound up in prison over. Somehow he didn't have many hopes for the rest of the crew's interest in him.

Only one person on board made him feel attractive and wanted.

The trip to Beta Deck was a vague memory as he extended himself to reach the door chime. The door slid open to Priest in a pair of red briefs dragging a towel over his still-damp hair. It was hard not to notice him in this state. The clean scent of shower soap was fresh on his skin.

"Hey, Arbor. What's going on?" Priest's natural smile chased away some of the doubts in Arbor's mind. He looked pleased to see him.

"Are you free? Can I come in?"

"Sure." Priest stepped aside to give Arbor a path. As he passed, Arbor resisted the urge to run his hand over the barely covered bulge before him. He didn't know if he could recover from being turned away twice in one day.

Climbing up on the bed, Arbor took in the near-naked man before him. The red briefs hugged Priest in all the right ways, and his lightly furred chest and legs held starring roles in Arbor's dreams for the last several nights. As attractive as he found Angus earlier, Priest was kilometers ahead on the scale. But even as perfect as Priest was to Arbor's eyes, he still didn't feel worthy somehow—especially not today.

"What's up?"

"Priest. I have to ask you a question and I want you to be honest." Arbor took a deep breath and marshaled his nerve. "If I hadn't won the poker game, would you have still slept with me?"

"That's stupid. Why would you even ask that? What happened?"

It took three tries to get the words out of his mouth, and they were barely audible once he succeeded. "I threw myself at Angus earlier and he turned me down. He couldn't run away fast enough."

"Arbor, Angus doesn't sleep with anyone." Priest's face twisted in a mocking shade of ridicule. "He's celibate. Waiting for his *one true love*. Yeah, I'm sure there's a long fucking story of virtue and dumbass promises to go with it, but what a waste with a dick like that."

"So, he didn't—"

Priest knelt down in front of Arbor. "He would have done that to anyone. Not just you."

"Oh."

"You're a good guy, Arbor, when you're not getting pissed and kicking my ass with that step stool of yours. You're not bad looking either. I'd like to think that I'd have worked my way over to you. The poker game just sped up the flight plan. Especially after the guys caught sight of you in the shower and saw what you were packing. I'd need to see for myself."

Arbor scrunched his face in disbelief. "You think I'm good looking?"

"You've got an expressive face and have a hot bod on you, dude. I hope I get another round soon."

Scooting to the edge of the bed, Arbor placed his hands on either side of Priest's face. "Is now too soon?"

With a wicked grin, Priest stood, peeled down those red briefs, and kicked them into the corner of the room. Shoving Arbor deeper onto the mattress on his back, Priest crawled over him. Dismantling Arbor's clothing with a practiced hand, his breath ghosted over the newly exposed skin.

"I'd say now is perfect."

SO SATED HE refused to rise, Priest barely lifted his head, observing the mass of pearlescent white streaks drying over his torso, all the way up to his neck. If this was a study in red, he could lie perfectly still and everyone would think he'd been a murder victim.

Rolling his head to one side, he found Arbor lying on his back. Chest still heaving, his thick, lazy tube of shiny flesh rested across his thigh. Damn, the things Arbor's cock made him crave. He'd never let anyone fuck him with so much force before, but it was so damn good.

It was an awful thing to disturb this languid moment, but the drying fluids pulling at the hairs from his chest to his groin were starting to hurt. Minor quakes still rushing through his body, Priest pushed himself upward to a seated position.

"I'm going to need a new shower." Priest slapped Arbor's leg to rouse him. He checked the time stamp glowing on his monitor. "C'mon, we can finally show you off to a bunch of the guys."

Arbor snapped forward. "What do you mean a bunch of the guys?"

"This is when a bunch of the maintenance guys finish working out and shower together. Grab your pants, you can borrow a towel."

"I can wait." Shoulders dropping, Arbor turned slightly away from Priest, his arms crossing in his lap.

Priest searched his hamper for a pair of shorts. "You're the one who wanted to hook up with Angus. This is the best way to drum up some business."

"Go without me."

"You're almost as nasty as I am. Come on." The blue pair of shorts he found was dirty, but so was he. It couldn't make anything worse.

"I said I don't want to go."

Priest stopped short of stepping into the garment. "Why are you being so pissy about this?"

"I don't want to be in a shower with a bunch of horny guys."

Now Priest was a little annoyed and confused. "It's not like anyone's gonna rape y—"

"*I said no!*" Arbor's rage and fear were all too palpable.

Staring at the wall, Arbor clutched his arms tight. Tiny, panicked gasps of air matched up with an uncontrollable shake affecting his whole body. Priest knew what this looked like. It was the same reaction as he witnessed on surviving soldiers in the Civil War. It was the fringes of terror.

Being a pilot, Priest was removed from face-to-face skirmishes that left their invisible scars on the men and women left behind. But he had seen enough of them to know what they were.

"Arbor?" Priest stepped around the bed, forcing Arbor to look at him. "When did it happen?"

Arbor's eyes were moist and vacant. "When did what happen?"

Priest stooped down in front of him, keeping his voice soft. "When were you raped?"

"I wasn't." Arbor's hands gripped tighter and his gaze dropped into his lap.

"No offense, but I'm having a hard time believing that. Was it prison?" Arbor's eyes flashed wide as he sucked in a mouthful of air. "You can tell me if you want. I won't say anything."

Arbor rocked back and forth. His mouth shifted like he wanted to speak, then clamped shut more than once. Priest was patient, waiting for him to decide what to do.

A tear brimmed along the edge of Arbor's eye. "I wasn't...but I was...sort of... I don't know..."

Priest brushed a knuckle down Arbor's arm, wanting to show comfort, but worried about startling him. "You're not making sense. Tell me what happened."

Without looking up, Arbor gave a shuddering exhale. "Prison was so scary. I was in for hacking government data files, but they put me in maximum security with all the murderers and rapists. I saw inmates get stabbed in the common area on two separate occasions. I was just trying to keep my head down and get through my sentence.

"I got caught in the shower by five or six guys. They surrounded me when I was rinsing the soap out of my eyes. One guy picked me up off the ground and when I fought back, they beat the shit out of me." A tear rolled down to his chin as his voice broke. "They were all laughing as they held me face down on the floor. I couldn't stop them. The first guy used his finger on me and said he liked how tight I was. He got on top of me and was just about to shove it in when the guards burst in."

Priest wiped away the stray tear. "Oh shit, Arbor."

Fists clenched, Arbor snarled as more tears threatened to fall. "They went after me because I was little, because I was different. They saw me as an easy target. They held me down because I wasn't strong enough to take care of myself."

"Arbor, most of us would have gotten our ass kicked against six guys. That's nothing to be ashamed of."

Arbor sniffed. "The sad part was that I wasn't supposed to be in maximum security with all the violent offenders in the first place. My ex's family pulled some strings as payback for having him arrested at his nephew's birthday party. Even the warden said he didn't understand why I was there. They didn't look into it until I got attacked. The court was so afraid there'd be an investigation, they released me only five months in without any major parole conditions."

Priest placed his hand along the back of Arbor's neck, unsure if he would accept any comfort more substantial. He was shaking so hard, and had yet to even meet his eyes.

His voice lowered to a whisper. "I never told anyone about this. Not even my mother."

"Why not?"

Arbor gave a feeble shrug. "Because I feel so stupid about it. I didn't even get raped, but I keep reacting like I did."

Priest dipped his head down so Arbor could see into his eyes. "They used your size against you and made you feel powerless, right?"

"Yeah." A ragged exhale and another tear fell.

"That sounds a lot like rape to me."

An enormous pause followed as Arbor processed those words, and the severity of his tremors abated—not completely, but they quieted into something less frightening.

"Yeah. It suppose it does."

Long minutes passed as Arbor sobered, Priest refusing to move. Arbor reached up and squeezed Priest's arm. When his breathing slowed, he wiped his face and stiffened his back, looking a little ragged, but more like himself.

"We're landing on Gamma Centauri tomorrow night. What do you do when you're there?"

Priest shifted back, accepting Arbor's evasion. The subject was hardly resolved, but this was enough for one day. He could respect that.

"There's a tavern I like to stay at off the main drag called Avers Inn. It's a little rough, but they've got good food, cheap drinks. You know, the staples of life."

"We're only staying forty-eight hours before we shove off again."

"Yeah, but my leave got cut short last time. I want to have some fun before we ship off to Omoikane."

"You got arrested with Costa McQuillen from what I heard."

Priest picked his shorts back up off the floor. "Not one of my stellar moments. He was a snotty little bitch, but he's turned around lately."

"So I hear." Arbor crossed his arms over his chest and turned his head. It sounded a little bit bitter. Was that a sneer?

"What's that supposed to mean?" Priest slid his shorts over his hips and for the first time ever, Arbor wasn't paying attention.

"I saw what happened in the showers. At least the beginning of it. I can pretty much imagine what happened next."

"Spying on me?"

Arbor scoffed, but his tone lost none of its sharpness. "Hardly. I just walked in on seeing that pariah controlling the showers and climbing all over you."

"A little jealous?" Priest mocked Arbor, but he was finding himself less sympathetic as he trash-talked about Costa.

"Not even for a second. I don't know what you see in him."

Priest shrugged. "He's gorgeous and lets me fuck him. What other reason do I need?"

A disgusted glare accompanied Arbor's words. "If you want that dirty freak touching you, that's your fetish, not mine."

"Could you stop calling him that?" Priest couldn't help being defensive. Arbor had no right to be so foul.

"What? A freak? Pariah? It's what he is."

Priest couldn't believe what he was hearing from Arbor. The bigotry he was spouting was seriously pissing him off. "What's your problem with Costa? He hasn't done anything to you."

Arbor bounced off the bed to the floor, his narrowed eyes never leaving Priest's. "You don't even know what he's capable of, do you? He could be affecting your thoughts and forcing you to do what he wants."

"Pretty sure I'd fuck him anyways." The smug remark did its job and angered Arbor further, making his voice rise.

"I'm already pretty sure he's responsible for random problems that are going on in the ship's systems."

Priest bent down so his face was in Arbor's. "So what?"

"It's only a matter of time before something bad happens."

"Now you're just imagining shit." Standing tall, he turned his back on Arbor to try and control his rising temper.

"I should tell the captain about him and have him locked away."

Priest spun and stalked in close to Arbor. "If you really wanted to do that, you'd have done it already. Why don't you tell what's really going on here, Arbor."

"What do you mean?"

Priest shoved a stiff finger into Arbor's chest as he spat. "You just have a problem with Costa because he's para-human. Period. Nothing else. Fucking bigot."

"That's ridiculous." Arbor slapped Priest's hand away.

The rant came pouring out of Priest's mouth. "You think I don't see how you react to other people?—"

"Now you're being as stupid as people say you are."

"—how nervous you get around Erron's green hair and stiff movements, or Teddy and Costa's tattoos? You hate anything that doesn't fit your fucked-up narrow standard of what's normal."

"And what's wrong with wanting things to be normal?"

Priest's volume went through the roof. "Guess what, Arbor? You need to stop hating everything that's abnormal, because look in the fucking mirror! By your standards, you're a walking advertisement for abnormal!"

The anger and shock splashing across Arbor's scarlet face couldn't be disguised. Snorting angry breaths, if he clenched his jaw any tighter, his teeth might crack. Pushing past Priest, Arbor snatched up his clothing. He shoved his feet into his pants, too much in a hurry to bother with his underwear.

"At least now I understand why you'd bother with me in the first place. You only want a man who can pass for a carnival sideshow attraction so you won't feel so ordinary."

Not even buttoning his pants, the rest of his clothing under his arm, Arbor jumped up and punched the door access, stomping out of Priest's quarters.

Priest couldn't punch the panel to close and lock the door fast enough.

THE BLACK CYLINDER was too light in Costa's hand. It was the last dispenser he had, and the saving grace it contained—Calm—was low. If he didn't find another source when they landed, he wasn't sure what was going to happen. The dosages weren't lasting as long as before and he needed more than usual to stave off the headaches. What had he done to himself?

He could fix this. He simply needed to make it to Omoikane. From there he could undo everything.

The door chime rang and he dropped the tiny lifeline to the floor. He gasped as it fell in slow motion, bouncing along the floor until it came to rest under the nightstand jutting from the wall, thankfully unbroken.

The chime rang again, interrupting his compulsion to retrieve the device. He was strong. It could sit there and he'd retrieve it later. It was not time for another dose.

"Just ignore it, Costa, and go and see who's at the bloody door."

The itch along the back of his hand made it tremble as he opened the door.

Priest stood in the doorway, wearing a red T-shirt and blue shorts, hair freshly damp from a shower. "Hey, Costa. Having a shitty day. Thought I'd see what you were up to. Can I come in?"

"If you must, but only for a short while."

Costa's gaze slid over to the Calm dispenser as he made room for Priest to enter. He appeared unaware of the towel still in his hand as he turned in the center of the room, weight shifting back and forth. When the door slid closed, Priest settled, but chewed his lip as silence filled the room. It ate at Costa and fed his impatience, making even semi-polite conversation an effort.

"By the way you're fidgeting, I can only assume you have something you're simply dying to say. Perhaps you could make it quick? I have several things that I need to be doing shortly."

Priest cleared his throat. "It's no secret between you and me that you're para-human. I was just wondering...can you control people's minds?"

"If you're going to be absurd, you can sod off."

Priest's shoulders sank and he turned his head away and toward the floor. "Sorry. It was a stupid question. I got into an argument with Arbor earlier."

"Regarding what?"

"Over you. He saw what you did with the shower room the other night."

Costa paused. Playing with Priest that way had been reckless no matter how much fun. It would only be a matter of time before his secret was spilled among the crew if he didn't restrain himself in the future. How much damage had been done so far?

"Would he inform the captain?"

"I think he'd already have done it if he really cared. I think he's more pissed at me than anything."

Priest clasped his hands behind his back and rocked his weight on his heels. His face was nothing if not penitent. From what little Costa knew of the man, only one thing made him feel anything close to guilt.

"Is it your goal in life to have a row with everybody you sleep with?"

Priest scrunched his brow as he stared off at nothing in particular. "Sure looks that way, don't it?"

A growl barely stayed silent as Costa's ediginess bordered on impatience. He needed Priest's help ultimately, but if he was torn between romantic engagements, it would certainly make things more difficult. Having the man show up at his quarters to deal with the debris of a disagreement with another man was not at the top of his list. In fact, hearing about it was grating his already frazzled nerves.

"Are you all right? You look like you're having another headache." Priest's concern was oddly welcome to hear.

Costa reached up and rubbed the aching point between his brows. "I wouldn't go as far as saying *another* headache. It's more like the same one that never seems to end. It's simply a question of how strong it is from one day to the next."

"How strong is it today?"

"Tolerable—"

Costa shrieked as a dagger of white-hot agony seared through his skull. All at once, he could sense everything. All the voices, all the data, every scrap of information down to its essential binary code crashed through his thoughts at once.

His head was too full. How far could he go before it exploded?

"Costa! What's wrong?"

Knees slamming into the floor, Costa curled into a ball, trying to hide away from the shocking invisible noise. It was too much to absorb, and instinctively he pushed it away, vainly trying to save himself.

"Holy shit!"

Costa heard Priest's scream, but he had other worries. He felt the monitors burst with energy and the lights strobed out of control. Mrs. Claus began screaming out incoherent commands, her deafening consciousness clashing with his own and splintering. The room filled with audible debris, choking his ears. He could feel Priest's hands on his body, trying to settle him down, but he was being lost in ones and zeroes.

The door lock engaged. Every attempt to center himself and stop the chaos was only causing more. Priest was trapped in here with him and he could feel the environmental systems collapsing. If something didn't happen soon, cold and lack of oxygen would take over and this would be their tomb. The thought of others dying filled him with despair.

No. He'd come too far. He couldn't fail now.

Forcing his eyes open, he managed to focus on the black dispenser under the nightstand. Every centimeter of his body screamed at him as he scratched at the floor, struggling to crawl to the tiny object of salvation.

He snatched up the little device, desperately trying to shut out the cacophony around him. Ignoring the spike of binary overflow driving through his skull, he tilted his head back and opened his mouth. Nothing happened. He fumbled with the cylinder, his fingers too numb to dispense it.

The terrified sob wrenched out of him. He couldn't save them.

"I got you." Priest pulled Costa back against him. He took the dispenser and aimed it over Costa's waiting tongue. One drop hit, and Costa urged him for one more. The metallic taste ran down his throat, the drug instantly absorbing through the skin.

The noise and pain retreated, and he was able to put the tech back in place once again. The room calmed as he settled into the arms surrounding him.

"Are you okay, Costa?"

Costa nodded, too numb to speak out loud while he waited for everything to settle. This was one thing he'd never wanted anyone to witness. The humiliation only lasted until the heat from the Calm suffused through his flesh, bringing a rush of joy and contentment.

"What is this shit?"

Normally, he would stay silent, but the warmth of the Calm made Costa want to be compliant. "It's called Calm."

"I thought that stuff was supposed to turn off your powers."

Costa shook his head, a light giggle escaping him. "Not anymore. My skills are much stronger these days. It does, however, rein them in and make them more manageable."

"How long does it last?"

"Not anywhere nearly as long as it used to." The fact didn't bother Costa so much at this point and time. The Calm was doing a fabulous job of adding sunshine to his world.

"How much more do you have?"

A sad, dramatic sigh issued out of Costa. "What's in that dispenser is the last of my store."

"This feels almost empty."

Costa ran a finger along the cylinder's shell. "I've rationed it out to the best of my ability, but I wasn't supposed to be in space this long. Being arrested and missing my flight to Omoikane wasn't in my original plan. I only came to the *Santa Claus* because you were heading there in spite of the extended time line."

"Is there anything I can do?"

"I need to find a chemist on Gamma Centauri who can make a new supply for me."

"I might know a guy."

Sitting upright, Costa smiled at Priest's willingness. He'd never needed him more.

"I had hoped that you could help me, Priest, but you must be aware that this is completely illicit. If either one of us gets caught, I can't even begin to explain the consequences."

"Don't worry. I'll com him once we get closer and set up a meeting for you."

"Thank you, Priest. You treat me better than I deserve at times." A new heat rose in Costa's chest. His pulse quickened and every square centimeter of his flesh felt so wonderfully sensitive. The urge to touch and be touched grew with every second.

Looking closer at Priest, Costa could see by the way his loose clothing draped over his chest and hips there was nothing underneath. The thought was simply too compelling. He crawled into Priest's lap, facing him, and began stroking his nipples through the red material.

"What are you doing?"

"Thanking you." He cupped the firm flesh of Priest's chest. The pressure in his palms sent rushes along his arms and into his spine.

Priest grabbed Costa by both wrists and pulled his hands away. "No. This isn't right."

"Are you saying that you don't find me attractive?" With his wrists confined, Costa leaned forward and ghosted a husky exhale along Priest's neck. When Costa's tongue snaked out, he tasted the salt and hint of soap still present on his skin.

"I never said that." A shudder came over Priest as his hold on Costa's wrists drifted away.

"Then you should allow me to continue." Costa stood just long enough to divest himself of his lounging pants before settling back into Priest's lap.

"Maybe we shouldn't—" A soft, wet kiss silenced Priest, who returned the kiss with restraint, but didn't stop.

Costa moaned as he ground his bare erection against Priest and was greeted by a fresh hardness Priest's shorts couldn't restrain. "Shh, Priest. I know you want me. I can feel it."

"But..." Priest's eyelids were beginning to gain weight and his voice was more breath than words.

"I need your skin against me." Costa planted hungry kisses on Priest's lips, jaw, and throat. "I need you inside me. Don't be gentle. Just take me. Please."

"But..."

Costa could feel Priest's resistance crumbling under each swipe of his tongue and each grind of their cocks. "Now."

Nodding in silent need, Priest shimmied out of his shorts and rolled Costa onto his back, where he braced himself against the bed and nightstand.

Chapter Eight

GAMMA CENTAURI LOOKED like every other planet from orbit. Blue water, green continents, and white swirls of clouds interrupted the surface like an antique glass marble. Suspended in the vast blackness, holographic images of the globe were available in every tourist shop Priest ever found in port. The image drew the fascination of voyagers who couldn't capture it for themselves but were willing to pay for the unique opportunity.

Priest understood. He used to be one of those people. It's why he'd become a pilot on the *Santa Claus*. Every time they approached a planet, his chest fluttered knowing he was experiencing something so many others did only through a media proxy. It made him feel special. It made him feel unique.

But today he didn't care.

Sitting in the pilot's chair with Teddy at the navigator seat beside him, Priest waited for clearance from the station on the main continent. Once they received it and the flight path telemetry were sent, Teddy would feed it to the goggles sitting on top of his head. From there, it was his job to land this giant craft.

Usually, he couldn't wait to get into the pilot's seat. But today, he couldn't muster up the enthusiasm.

Teddy swatted him on the shoulder. "Priest. You're up."

"What?" Priest looked around, confused, following Teddy's finger until it led to the flashing data on his dashboard. Flight information was uploaded and the ship was cleared for landing. "Oh. Sorry."

"You all there, Priest?" As usual, Danverse was supervising from his podium.

"I'm good, Captain."

He slipped the goggles over his eyes and the flight path and relevant data scrolled over the lenses. Turning on the inertial dampeners, he took the controls and steered the ship for the planet.

The ship hit the atmosphere without so much as a shudder. It was an effort to stay focused, but Priest had no real difficulty in bringing the ship safely to the ground. It was so uneventful, he hardly remembered the landing sequence after the fact.

Taking off his goggles, Priest went through the routine of shutting down the engines and other non-essential systems with the rest of the bridge crew.

"That was quite an easy landing, Priest. It's never been that smooth." Danverse's arched brow framed an accusing stare. Priest took a look at the inertial dampeners. They were up on full. He'd been so dazed he forgot to bring them up gradually to stage a rougher landing like he always did in the past to guarantee his position. Shit.

"Yeah. I guess we hit it just right this time. Probably won't happen again."

"Mmhmm," was all the captain said in return.

Once the ship was secure and powered down, Priest avoided the bridge crew's questioning stares and headed for his quarters.

The hallways were eerily quiet. Most of the crew must have already disembarked. One of the downsides of being the head pilot: you were always one of the last people off once you came into port. The lift was loud without the white noise of the engines he took for granted. The absence of crew on Beta Deck was no better.

"Mrs. Claus, are Costa McQuillen and Arbor Kittering still on board?"

"Costa McQuillen and Arbor Kittering are no longer on board the *Santa Claus*."

Huffing at the response, he stalked down to his own quarters. Priest wasn't sure why having Arbor gone bothered him so much. Maybe he would have liked to say goodbye, even if it was only for the next forty-eight hours.

Inside his room, he pulled his overnight bag out of storage and checked to make sure it had all the required gear for an off-ship excursion. There were a few changes of clothes, his deck of cards and remote, his personal datapad, toiletries, lubricant, and a few prophylactics in case he came across someone so dubious he needed coverage against any infections he and the crew weren't already inoculated against. Although, it wasn't likely. You had to love Dr. Bosch's thoroughness.

Snapping the bag closed, Priest found himself wondering if Costa would be all right.

The man was an addict, but given what the drug was for and what happened without it, Priest couldn't say no. He was no innocent, but setting up a meet with his chemist buddy brought a wave of disquiet he was having trouble shaking. Litmus made as many unsanctioned meds for people who couldn't afford it as illicit concoctions with no medical purpose. If currency was involved, he held no prejudice over the reasons.

Priest had told Costa to wait for him, but Costa must not have felt he needed Priest to complete his deal. The site of the meet was private. Priest hadn't been involved. He only got them connected. Now he wished he hadn't.

Mr. McQuillen was all grown up and could make his own decisions. Costa was using him. He had some agenda he wasn't sharing on this trip. It was no secret to Priest that the sex with Costa was fueled by the Calm side effects. He knew that, but he couldn't deny he wanted it either. His attraction to Costa was a mystery. Maybe he was hoping Costa might see him as a proper suitor instead of the convenient oaf.

Hopefully, everything would be fine. Although, he wasn't exactly sure why he was feeling so protective.

Checking his com one last time, he found the mail from Arbor at the top of the list. Why did Arbor have to send over all that data he snatched from the Earth Global Security files? Priest hadn't even had the chance to read the files, but he knew it was all about Costa. It didn't matter. The files would all have to wait until they were on their way to Omoikane.

Priest rubbed his face in frustration. What was he supposed to do about Arbor?

He liked the guy—a lot. But why did they have to argue? The sex between them was *fucking amazing*. The things Arbor's cock made him beg for, he'd never admit to another living soul. Priest wished he could get Arbor to switch roles and let him fuck for a change, but considering his prison experience, it wasn't likely. Under the circumstances, he could forgive the imbalance in their nights together. Maybe someday he could help Arbor work through that. It would be worth it.

Assuming Arbor would ever speak to him again, let alone get naked.

Arbor's volatile temper was a challenge, and his attitude toward Costa was outrageous. Priest wasn't sorry he threw his bigotry in his face. He had no right to say those things. If only Arbor saw what Priest did. No doubt a self-esteem boost would make Arbor's outlook on the less conservative a little more realistic.

The trick would be getting there, because otherwise the unrealistic fantasy of getting them both in bed at once was completely off the table. Priest snorted. As if that was possible.

Priest growled as he slung his pack over his shoulder and locked his door behind him. It shouldn't be this hard to manage his relationships with friends and crew members. He should have been strutting like a peacock for having both men in his stable, so to speak. They were all in this for a good time. Weren't they? They wanted close friends that screwed each other stupid until they couldn't see straight, right?

All the air left his lungs in a defeated gust. Maybe he should just get a hooker to make himself feel better tonight.

THE TRANSPORT DROVE away, leaving Costa at a residential tenement near the edge of the market district. Each set of buildings was a high stack of units fit tightly together for maximum volume of tenants. The structure was relatively solid, but flaws in the details screamed low-income housing. On closer inspection, the area was dirty, and the sad attempt at landscaping was amateur at best.

Costa frowned and began muttering to himself. "What a charming area. I don't know how people aren't falling over themselves to live here."

Checking his information, he made careful steps along the cracked walkways until he found the apartment section he was looking for. The fractured Plexiglas in the outer doors was dodgy, but Costa had to remind himself of some of the hostels he'd been forced to hide in before he could migrate off Earth. Being an illegal on a planet filled with spying, paranoid bigots didn't afford him many opportunities for luxury.

"I suppose that finding a dealer in any self-respecting posh resort would be a little much to ask for."

The sound of metal grinding against metal assaulted his ears as the double doors wrenched open. He cringed so hard it made his shoulders ache. Unless the walls were thick, which he highly doubted, there was no way he hadn't announced his arrival.

He took the stairs to the third level, because he had no intention of setting foot inside the lift. The stench of urine was too strong. No one was visible, but faint voices could be heard through the walls of various apartments. The strips of light panels on the ceiling were dull and out in sections, throwing off a cascade of faded shadows along the filthy walls.

If his need weren't so urgent, he wouldn't endure the anxious needles pricking his spine. Costa would only be too happy to conduct his business and leave as quickly as possible.

After checking his details one more time, he found the correct door. The chime controls were equipped with mechanical buttons rather than a touch panel, and the wall beneath it bore a grimy streak. Many unwashed hands had been at this location.

This had to be the right place.

Costa didn't wait long after pressing the call button before a tinny voice crackled into the hallway. "Who is it?"

"I'm a friend of Priest's. Litmus is expecting me."

"You're late."

Uneasy in the hall, Costa grew impatient. "I'm afraid that transports are hardly racing to get to this ruddy little corner of the world. Let me in already."

"All right, all right. Turn off your rockets, champ. I'm comin'."

The door ground open to a younger man with pale skin and short, spiky black hair, tipped in vermillion. A pair of scratched safety goggles hung around his neck and he wore a tattered, sleeveless undershirt and striped pajama bottoms.

"You must be Litmus."

The young man zeroed in on Costa's facial tattoos. "And you're obviously Priest's buddy. Get in here already."

As Costa stepped inside, Litmus leaned out, scanned the hallway in both directions, and closed the door. The apartment was claustrophobic and horribly cluttered. It appeared to be basically one space for the kitchen and living area, with adjacent doors he hoped led to a lavatory and bedroom.

"Well, Priest did say you were pretty."

"While it's wonderful to be appreciated, that's not what I'm here for."

"No worries, princess. I like my men bigger than you. My boyfriend's a bouncer at Zippo's in the Market District. Give me a second. I'll get your stuff."

Litmus vanished through one of the extra doors, leaving Costa standing alone in the squalor. Gently, he reached out his thoughts. Very gently. He'd only rationed himself a single dose to hold the migraine at bay and stave off arousal flashes. A little self-control was warranted today. Finding no incoming or outgoing transmissions, he was satisfied there weren't any surprises waiting for him. Thankfully, the dull ache behind his eyes decided to stay still for a change.

Smiling, Litmus returned to the main room. "I do like that you transferred the currency to my account in advance."

A small object was placed in Costa's hand. "For some of us, it's like making money appear out of nothing." He examined the cylinder to refill his dispenser. "This is less than half of what I ordered. Where is the rest?"

"That's all I can make right now. I'll have the rest in five days."

The panic in Costa's chest was instant. "Five days? We'll be shipping out in two! What do you suppose I do then?"

Litmus hissed, motioning with his hands to lower the volume. "There's nothing I can do. I can't get my hands on enough raw mats to make more until then."

This couldn't be worse. The voyage to Omoikane was six weeks long, plus whatever time it would take to complete his task. How would he manage to stretch out this supply the way he was consuming it? This new batch was supposed to be more potent, and hopefully he wouldn't need as much, but it wasn't what he asked for when this transaction began.

"If I find out you're swindling me—"

"Calm isn't something I deal in. There's no street value in it. No one uses that shit. There are cheaper ways to get the same high."

"What about more expensive methods?"

Litmus arched a brow. "Does it look like I live on the wealthy side of town? Plus, I don't have the kind of equipment to synthesize stuff that complex. The authorities keep a tight watch on that stuff. You have to have an approved medical license just to look at them."

Costa huffed, the anxiety making him unsteady. "The high is not what I'm after. How can I get more?"

"Fucked if I know. I had to hack the chemistry database to fabricate it. That's some serious designer shit there. I don't know anyone else who could get you more before you planet hop and keep things quiet." Litmus sat down on the weathered sofa and pulled a metal box from beneath it. Shoving a stack of random items to the floor, he opened it on the cluttered table before him. "I can set you up with something else if that'll help. I have some kick-ass hallucinogenics."

"Nothing else will be even remotely sufficient. Do you not understand what Calm is made for?"

"Yeah I do, but those problems didn't really migrate to this end of the galaxy."

"I should take my funds back."

Litmus sighed as he closed his little metal box. "Look, you're a friend of Priest's. Otherwise, I wouldn't do this in the first place. Making that shit could get me a lifetime's worth of hard time. Anyone else around here heard about this and they'd snitch about an unlicensed pariah running around, hoping for some kind of reward. It may not be illegal in these parts, but you can bet the authorities would crawl up your ass wanting all your life details if they found out. Now, I'm doing the best I can, but you didn't give me enough time."

"You could have let me know."

"I didn't know until a few hours ago. It was too late, and it's not like you have any other options."

The dealer was correct. Costa didn't have a plan if this one didn't succeed. He was lucky to have gotten this far. His own research had come up empty and Priest only knew of one person he could trust for the task.

Costa squeezed the cylinder in his hand like it was a lifeline. "I'm still planning on refunding myself for the product you didn't provide me."

"Whatever makes you happy."

Turning around, Costa took the two steps to the outer door, cringing at the loud scraping as it opened. Standing in the doorway, he turned back to face Litmus, pointing the cylinder at him.

"You can count on the fact that I'll know if this is real before we're off planet."

The dealer simply grinned. "Fabulous! Then you won't be knocking on my door bitching about it."

SAMPLING A GLASS of good bootleg bourbon usually made Priest happy. Tonight, it lacked the same effect. Costa had commed him earlier and told him he'd see him back on the ship before launch but didn't give him any details on how things went with Litmus. He'd known Litmus for a number of years, and in most cases, he was a good guy, but like most dealers and other disreputable types, he'd likely sell out his sources rather than risk going to prison.

He hated sending Costa to the seedy side of the miniature city making up this space station, but there was no choice. Someone with Costa's refinement should never set foot in such a place. But, he couldn't go without the Calm, and Priest didn't know of any other way to provide it.

He knew Costa was hardly a fragile flower. From what he knew of para-human history, Costa had to have been exposed to many disturbing things in his lifetime. It didn't keep Priest from feeling somehow responsible for him. If their first meeting at the bar hadn't gone so off-kilter, Costa would have made his trip and not run out of supplies before he arrived.

Helping Costa take the dose in his quarters yesterday was awful. Every piece of tech went insane at once, and he felt the airflow stop during the chaos. It was going to be dangerous to get him to Omoikane without an incident, but it was the least he could do.

Costa needed him, and he'd take what he could get in return.

It wasn't as if he expected the two of them to walk off into the sunshine together. He knew once Costa's business on Omoikane was complete, so was his need of Priest. Costa was not about to become a permanent member of the crew and be his partner, nor did he want him to be. So why did he find him so compelling?

Was it that he found Costa so exotic? His accent, his beauty, the roguish tattoos across his cheek, all coalesced into something Priest found overly enticing. It added up to something one would never find in a farming community on Alpha Centauri. Was the reason so simple? What an awfully shallow motivation. If Priest were a deeper man, he might be concerned.

He took a deep swig of his drink to clear his head. This was a forty-eight-hour leave to enjoy himself, and he intended to make good on the promise.

Avers Inn was a little quiet, but it was off-peak hours. The waitress set a plate of prime rib with all the fixin's in front of him. He wasn't positive if it was real beef or from a similar native animal, but it looked and smelled right, so he was going with it.

The knife went through the meat the way it was supposed to and there was the correct kind of juices pooling on his plate. The piece he cut had just the right amount of pink and the taste made him give off a decadent groan. This was not synthetic. Only Gamin and Erron could cook synthetic rations properly when forced. Off ship, Priest was not about to be subjected to anything less.

This tavern might have been a little rough and the patrons not all members of the pinnacle of society, but he liked the place. It wasn't central to the station, so it thrived on word of mouth. If you hadn't heard about it, you'd probably never set foot in the place.

Priest knew the owner, Rushman Avers, was a shrewd businessman and hard worker with a reputation for rule-bending. The inn was everything to Rushman and he wanted it to flourish no matter what. If he had to replace top-shelf liquor occasionally with cheap knockoffs to keep from running out, so be it. His other main flaw was his inflexibility. The inn could benefit from better marketing, but the man was too bull-headed to change his long-running strategy. Rather than work behind the scenes promoting the business, he spent far too much time with the customers, micromanaging the whole affair.

On top of it all, Rushman's personality switched moods like binary code: from one to zero in an instant. He could be joking it up with patrons one moment and have them barred the next. His temper was explosive. Priest had no difficulty believing the man had three divorces and two annulments in his history. Why any woman would stay with the fat, balding ass for any length of time was beyond him.

Rushman's famous temper was why the nice waitress catered to Priest—wasn't Jenna her name?—who sat at a table instead of the bar where Rushman was bartending this evening. After all the stress with Arbor, he didn't want to test his luck with the owner's combustible persona.

What was he going to do about Arbor?

It would be so much easier if he could wash his hands of the guy and keep it casual, but he liked him way more than he should. If only it was easier. Arbor was too caught up in trying to create some kind of fiction called normal. He had a lot of self-loathing built up and had to admit it if he was going to ever find a little joy in his life. It was too easy to make it all crash around him.

Priest still felt awful about the whole sock monkey thing. There was no telling whose hand the toy was in now, and if the prank didn't run its course, it would tarnish Arbor's standing with the crew in an unrecoverable way. Right now, it continued because Arbor couldn't find any humor in it. Yes, it was childish, but that's how the guys entertained themselves at times.

Arbor hadn't spoken with him and ignored his messages. Having had the time to settle in on leave, Priest was regretting the whole mess. He would have given anything to take back the argument between them. It was a rotten thing to make Arbor face his faults so harshly, even if it was the truth. Arbor needed the mirror to see himself, but the delivery could have used more work. Sleeping with Costa afterward hadn't made him feel any better. If anything, it only complicated every aspect of the incident.

They weren't attached to each other, and Arbor knew Priest had played with Costa. There was nothing new there. He was allowed to fuck whomever he wanted. He was a free man. It was all about having fun, right?

Then why did he feel so shitty about it?

He enjoyed both of them. Costa was beautiful and unattainable, yet his passion was addictive. Banging him was a bedpost notch other men had in their dreams. The man was a prize. However, the beauty was a mask. There were untold secrets Mr. McQuillen was keeping, Priest was sure of it, and everything happening between them was of Costa's making. At least Priest was enjoying the ride.

Arbor was something completely different. The man had issues—lots of them—but when he could set them aside, he was charming. He was handsome, unique, and his size kept Priest from feeling dominated even when he was being pile-driven by Arbor's award-winning tool. He never would have imagined Arbor's skills could draw out the types of noises he filled the room with when they were together. It was a kind of mutual satisfaction hard to find among casual friends. Something about Arbor made Priest want to put a smile on his face. Why, he wasn't sure.

Both men suffered from harsh pasts, bringing out Priest's protective side in different ways. When they got back on board, he would have to check on both men and make sure they were all right. He wanted Costa to be safe, to protect him from his secrets. Arbor was wounded, and he wanted to bandage him back to health.

Was that even possible for either man?

Thinking about his problems blunted the flavor of his meal. The majority of his steak was a vague memory and the last few bites were dull, but the food wasn't the cause. The waitress replaced his drink as the cutlery clinked on the empty plate. With nothing better to do, he swiped his hand across the DNA ID reader to pay his bill, its sleek black panel mounted into the table. When this drink was finished, he was heading back to his hotel room to decide what to do next.

The front door opened and a flush of excitement warmed his chest as Arbor wandered in.

Arbor looked weathered. Shadows darkened his eyes and little unstoppable movements were visible in his hands and feet. He looked so alone standing in the tavern's entryway. Priest was about to hop off his stool when Arbor caught his eyes, a tiny gasp filling his chest.

The excitement collapsed when Arbor turned away and headed for the bar.

A dark hole opened underneath him. Arbor didn't want to see him? If that were true, what was he doing here? Questions began flitting through his head as he sat frozen in his seat, unable to approach, until Rushman's graveled voice bulled through the room.

"You turn your little ass right around the way you came."

Arbor's response was tight and confused. "What?"

"I don't want you around my customers. They'll start thinking I cater to carnies and gypsies."

"I just wanted a drink."

"I don't serve your kind here. Push off."

Arbor snarled in offense. "What did you say to me, you fat bastard?"

Rushman slammed down the rag in his hand and rounded the bar. Stomping forward, he bent over until his face was breathing in Arbor's. If Rushman was trying to use his size for intimidation, he'd picked the wrong target. Arbor was rigid and unyielding. Fists tight and body thrumming with restraint, he was furious, not frightened.

"I don't serve freaks. Get the fuck out."

Arbor slammed his forehead into Rushman's nose. The break was a ghastly noise as the insufferable ass screamed and fell to his knees. Rushman's hand flew to his face and blood ran freely between his fingers. Arbor stood unmoving, fixed on the spectacle.

"Oh shit!" Priest kicked over his stool as he raced forward, grabbing Arbor by the arm. "We need to go. Now!"

Arbor stood in place, his eyes wide and unfocused. A large red spatter marred his forehead and ran down his face, even as Priest could feel the tremors quaking through his arm. When he turned Arbor to face him, his lack of response and the wetness filling his vacant eyes gave Priest a start. Rage and panic warred across Arbor's face. So lost, Priest wasn't even sure if Arbor was aware of him.

He stooped low and threw Arbor over his shoulder, surprised by his weight. "C'mon, Arbor. I'm not waiting for the Station Authorities to arrive. Neither one of us needs to spend our leave in jail."

Struggling to balance, Priest lurched out the door and onto the sidewalk. Arbor was a dead weight. At this time of day, and Avers Inn being out of the way, there weren't many pedestrians about, but it was hardly desolate outside. They needed someplace to hide for a short spell. Arbor wasn't moving or protesting being hoisted around and it unnerved Priest. Taking a couple of turns, trying to stay out of sight, he pushed into a public men's room to catch his breath.

Setting Arbor on the counter was easier than the floor and put him at a more equal eye level.

"Arbor, are you okay?"

No response. The sight of the Arbor sitting stunned and lifeless alarmed him. Making sure he would support himself, Priest hurried back to the door. Peeking out, there was no sign of Rushman or the authorities, but he kept watch for several minutes, constantly checking that Arbor wouldn't fall over. Once he was felt more comfortable they wouldn't be found, Priest returned to his charge.

"Damn, Arbor. I wasn't expecting that."

Arbor's eyes were frozen and wet, a startling match to his shallow breathing. The sheen on his skin highlighted Rushman's blood spatter, an unnamed sanguine continent on the map of his face. Peeling off his shirt, Priest wet a section in the sink, thankful this part of the station still had running water and hadn't upgraded to hand sanitizers. He noticed Arbor didn't pay the slightest attention to his half-dressed state.

He dabbed at the rusty mess with the soaked edge of fabric, trying to reveal the flesh beneath. "That was quite a number you pulled on Rushman." He kept his voice quiet, like he was soothing a trapped animal, coaxing it into the open. "I probably won't be able to eat there ever again. Still, he's an ass. It would have happened someday, no matter what."

Tender strokes washed away the violent evidence while Priest stood between Arbor's legs hanging off the counter's edge, until only Arbor remained. Only the slightest discoloration could be seen on Arbor's forehead. It didn't look like there would be much of a bruise. Once he was clean, no one would ever know there had been an altercation.

As he worked, Priest laid a hand along the side of Arbor's head and neck. A subtle shift in weight pressed into his hand as a soft sigh escaped Arbor's lips. Tilting his face up for a better view, Priest couldn't help but admire the chocolate brown irises. Arbor's expressive stare gave away his every feeling. It was almost reverent, the way he studied Priest.

"He was right," Arbor spoke so soft, it was almost nothing.

Priest didn't stop even though he was elated to hear Arbor's voice. "Who was right about what?"

"That bartender. That I'm a freak."

"No, he's not. He's just a loudmouthed asshole. Rushman doesn't speak for anyone but himself." Every movement was cautious and every word was gentle as he worked. Arbor was shaken enough. There was no need to spook him.

"Everyone on the ship thinks it too."

Priest couldn't help but frown. "You keep telling yourself that and making it happen. The guys just don't like the crazy moments. I like you, and you beat my ass the first time we met. Give 'em a chance. They'll come around."

"But I'm not normal. Even you know that. You said so yourself."

Priest winced as he found a fresh portion of his shirt to work with. "Yeah, I did. But normal is boring. Normal is ordinary. I don't give a shit about normal." He wiped away a crimson blot from Arbor's cheek and studied his face. Strong cheekbones accented those soulful eyes and full lips. "You're a handsome man, Arbor."

Arbor's brow tried to knit itself together as his gaze flitted away. "No, I'm not."

"Yes, you are. And you'd believe me if you stopped hating yourself long enough to see what I see."

"How can you honestly say that? How can you like me with these little arms and legs? With this big forehead?" Arbor splayed his hands out in the air as his eyes raked over his own limbs. "There's nothing attractive about these weird, tiny proportions. How can you like this?"

Priest shrugged, his voice as calm as when he started. "Dunno. I just do. It's true, you don't come like the standard model, but I don't care about that. You may be smaller than most of us, but believe me"—Priest arched his brow as he palmed Arbor's groin—"there's nothing tiny about this."

The frightened tremors were calm, but a new shudder grazed Arbor's skin, making the corner of Priest's mouth curl. He loved the effect he had on the man. Arbor's lips parted as he sat mesmerized, finally noticing the bare chest before him. Under Priest's hand, Arbor's package hardened and lengthened as his legs opened slightly to make room for the invader. Soft wanton exhales echoed off the hard restroom walls as Priest leaned forward, leaving small bites and licks along the side of Arbor's neck.

"What are you doing?" Arbor sounded like he was going to resist, even as he ground himself into Priest's hand.

Priest worked his way up to Arbor's ear. "Making you believe me."

He knew this was hardly the right place and time, but the desire to pleasure Arbor—to make him blind with lust—overrode all good sense. He kneaded at Arbor's flesh, the growing heat radiating into his palms. The arousal was mutual. Closing in tight, Priest locked eyes with Arbor, never wavering from the connection as he unbuckled Arbor's trousers.

It took two hands to pry open the fly and heft the scalding snake from its fabric prison. The beast was trying to hide down the leg of Arbor's pants. Hot and turgid, it lurched in Priest's hands, a slick drop already forming at the head.

Leaning back, he examined the hefty prize. The foreskin was already rolled back, exposing the fat, shiny mushroom. Arbor sat transfixed as Priest ran his fingers up and down the silky hardness, tracing the fearsome veins along the length.

All the fear and loathing from Arbor's expression had dissipated into pure want. He wasn't alone. Priest wanted to touch him. Priest wanted to taste him. And he could see Arbor wanted whatever he could give him.

So he leaned forward and tasted the beautiful cock.

Arbor gasped when Priest ran his tongue under the foreskin's edge and worked his way down. The length filled his mouth and made Priest close his eyes with its hedonistic flavor. The only thought in his head was how to get more.

Wrapping his arms around Arbor's hips, he worked up and down, intent on swallowing it all. The edges of Arbor's open pants brushed his face as he delved as deep as possible, lost in the act. The sensation of his full mouth and throat left Priest rigid, but he ignored his own straining erection. This was all about worshipping Arbor and making him understand.

Priest wanted him.

It wasn't long before Arbor's thick fingers threaded into Priest's hair, his grunts becoming labored. Balls drawn up tight, tapping Priest's chin, Arbor's member swelled, signaling the oncoming orgasm. The moment Priest was waiting for was at hand. Priest pulled back, holding the bulbous tip in his mouth, as Arbor tried to stifle his own shout. Fiery gushes sprayed over Priest's taste buds, the addictive salty flavor singing a surge of energy through him, forcing a muffled cry as the world went white and he unleashed a torrent inside his own pants.

With a great deal of reluctance, Priest released his hold on Arbor, making him whimper. If they weren't in public, he would have waited until the hard member softened into slumber before giving it up. Arbor was flushed and panting with a glowing smile. The sight alone was worth a shirt turned into a bloody rag and semen-soaked pants.

"C'mon, Arbor. Let's go to your hotel room. We should stay together on this leave."

Arbor carefully stowed away his deflating cock. "Why not your hotel room?"

"I was signed in at Avers Inn and you just broke the owner's nose." Priest chuckled. "I think we should steer clear of the place. I'm gonna have to sneak in tomorrow and get my stuff."

Arbor choked down a burst of laughter as a frantic man rushed in, ran into a stall, and slammed the door closed. Grimacing, Priest reached for Arbor. The way the guy barged in, there was no way he was staying in here. Much to his surprise, Arbor allowed Priest to wrap an arm around his waist and help him down to the floor.

"Let's get the hell out of here," Arbor said.

Chapter Nine

"ARE WE ALLOWED to take this?"

The hangar had been converted into a machine shop smelling of grease and ozone. Vehicles lined the bay in various states of disrepair, their chassis wide open, with lengths of cable and engine parts spilled out on the floor in places like a mechanical abattoir. Random pieces of tech smeared with mechanical fluid sat on the shelves lining the walls, waiting to be installed. A fair amount of junk could be found among the prizes here. Everything was dirty.

Priest loved this place.

"Sure, why not? The guy who owns the shop owes me money."

He sauntered around a cycle, trailing his fingertips over the metal exterior, tracing the line of the handlebars jutting out from the center console. Several weld lines were visible, color shifts showing where obvious repairs had been completed. The windshield was relatively clean, and the long narrow seat would easily accommodate two people.

"I'm more likely to believe you owe him money, not the other way around." Arbor stood with his arms crossed, giving Priest a skeptical eye.

Priest swung a leg over, straddling the cycle. "Ha. Ha. Hop on."

With a quick touch to the center display and a few more adjustments, the cycle rumbled to life. The pad engines on the front and back awoke and the whole vehicle rose from the ground, floating less than half a meter off the shop floor.

"I don't know how to drive one of these things."

Priest shot Arbor a look, his brow arched dramatically. "I'm the pilot. You ain't driving nothing."

"It doesn't look safe."

Twisting around to the storage compartment at the rear of the vehicle, Priest pulled out a set of riding goggles and placed them on Arbor's face. A little wild and messy, the look suited Arbor. Priest didn't like him too well polished. He preferred the real man let loose.

"She just looks rough on the outside. Trust me. This baby is a fun ride." Priest offered his hand and, with a moment's dubious pause, Arbor allowed his help in pulling him onto the vehicle. Settled into position, he wrapped his arms around Priest's waist.

Priest dropped the goggles sitting atop his head over his eyes, revved the engine a few times, and tapped a control, causing the main bay door to open.

Arbor half shouted over the engine hum. "You don't see a problem with just riding off with this."

Looking over his shoulder, Priest shook his head with a Cheshire smile. "Nope. I left a note. Now let's have some fun. Hold on tight."

The fact was, the cycle was Priest's. It was a rare win in a poker game a year or two before he'd found his special deck of cards, and Lucky had agreed to store it for him. Space aboard the *Santa Claus* was limited for personal belongings. Every square centimeter of the cargo bays was calculated into a currency amount and Priest couldn't afford to store the cycle on the ship.

They visited Gamma Centauri often enough. If he gave Lucky access to the cycle, the mechanic would keep it maintained for his shore leaves. It only took a quick glance to see the fuel cells were fully charged. While en route, Priest had commed the mechanic ahead. He knew the cycle was ready and waiting for him.

But Arbor didn't need to know.

It didn't take long to find the outskirts of the city. Once they cleared the main dredge of civilization, Priest sped off along the crimson sands of the Hannoker Desert. It was a few hours from sunset, yet the harsh sun still blazed. Even so, the wind whipping across them kept them comfortable.

He gunned the engine, exhilarated by the burst of speed and excited by the tighter grip of stubby hands on his waist. The cycle vibrated underneath him, giving a pleasant reminder of how Arbor had screwed him all night and the next morning. The tender flesh shimmied and sent a constant stream of rushing tremors through his lower half. Priest made no effort to stop himself from hardening.

They cruised for hours. Arbor howled as they made sharp turns, the engine pads splitting the sands into red trails of dust. They rode for the thrill and the rush. Arbor held on tight, his excited cries urging Priest to keep going faster as he pressed himself closer.

The sun was dipping under the horizon line as they rode back to the hangar. Sweaty and covered in silt, Priest couldn't be more pleased.

Time was fading, so they hurried back to the hotel and showered together, washing one another without somehow turning the event into another moment of debauchery. Even drying each other off was affectionate without lust.

An air of glowing contentment filled Priest as they began packing. It was too bad this vacation was about to end, but knowing Arbor was boarding as well made all the negative fade out.

Arbor sifted through his belongings as he packed. "What are you going to do when we get back to the ship?"

"I need to check on Costa. He asked for some help with an errand and I want to see how that panned out."

A short pause lingered as Arbor studied the shirt in his hands. He shrugged gently, his brow arched as he commented without looking at Priest. "I still don't see what you see in him."

Priest shook his head. "He's just a friend."

"Costa McQuillen seems awfully snotty to have any real friends." While Arbor appeared cheerful, a subtle tinge of bitterness, beyond his natural sarcasm, underlined his tone.

"That's not fair." Discussing Costa with Arbor caused Priest's pulse to race, making him jam items into his duffel a little rougher than intended. Everything was going so well. Why did Arbor have to go there? Priest couldn't tell Arbor the whole story. Costa's situation wasn't his to share.

"I can't possibly imagine what you two have in common. What do you do when you hang out with him?"

Impatient with the topic, Priest blurted out his response. "I don't know. I guess we just screw around."

And as soon as the words left his mouth, Priest knew it was the wrong thing to say.

Arbor didn't stop grinning, but the light behind his smile dimmed, becoming polite and no longer intimate. Gone in an instant was the warmth and connection they'd shared for the last twenty-four hours. Priest's involvement was no secret to Arbor, but after this wonderful break, the reality didn't need to be thrown in his face.

"I didn't mean it like that."

Arbor shook his head. "You don't have to explain anything."

"But—"

He raised a hand to stop Priest. "There's no ring on this finger. Whatever reason you're friends with Costa is really none of my business. Come on, let's gather up. I think I'm ready to get back on board now." Arbor put the last of his effects into his bag. "I wanted to thank you again for keeping me out of jail after that whole thing in the bar. I really appreciate it."

The acknowledgment was perfunctory and its cool manner tugged at Priest's chest. All the excitement and closeness they shared was unraveled in loose threads on the floor and he had no idea how to weave it back together. One thoughtless comment and he'd fallen back into the state of an acquaintance. He could feel it.

"You're welcome."

"YOU CAN HOLD out a little longer."

Shivering in a cold sweat, Costa nodded into Priest's side as they lay back on the bed in Costa's quarters. With an arm around him, Priest tried to give Costa an anchor to focus through the pain and cravings wracking his body. He tried not to flinch when Costa's delicate hands twisted his shirt in knots, fisting his chest hairs inside.

The Calm dispenser sat in his hand to keep it out of Costa's reach. It felt far lighter than it should and there were another four weeks until they arrived in Omoikane. There was no way this stash was going to last, even with strict rationing.

They had fought for control of it earlier, after Costa made Priest promise not to let him have any for another four hours. Costa lasted one hour before the fight began. Priest managed not to hurt him, but he had to hold him down until Costa burst into tears.

The breakdown was so out of character, Priest almost gave in. Maintaining his composure was a source of pride and having it fall apart in tatters had to be the highest form of shame. So instead, they lay down and Priest held Costa as the withdrawal took its toll.

The hard shadows under Costa's eyes—sported when they spent time in holding—were now on his face at all times. Priest knew the craving for his meds was strong even back then. Costa simply had a better supply to keep up appearances. Now, he was crumbling.

"You may need to go see Doc Bosch. He can probably synthesize your meds."

The fierce shake of Costa's head scrubbed against his side. "No! No doctors. I don't want anyone else to know."

"He can help—"

"No, Priest! I've never met a doctor that can be trusted." A hint of panic colored Costa's voice beyond his symptoms. His hands cinched the fabric in them tighter, causing Priest to wince.

"But, Costa…"

"Please, Priest." A soft sob escaped Costa as he pressed deeper to muffle the sound. "I will be perfectly all right."

"But you're in so much pain."

Little by little, Costa's voice became wearier. "It will be worth it in the end. There's just too much muddled up inside my head right now. Once we arrive at Omoikane, I can put it all right."

"What does that mean? Costa?"

The hold on his shirt relaxed as Costa drifted away into an exhausted, fitful sleep, ending Priest's questions. As usual, Costa kept a tight hold on his secrets. His trust of normal people was limited, and it was an odd miracle Priest knew as much as he did.

The lights panels were dimmed, bathing the room in a murky haze of shadow. Every piece of tech that could reasonably be shut down without alerting Mrs. Claus was inactive, leaving only the cyber-green clock numbers on the outer wall. It marked an eerie digital silence to ease a portion of his suffering. Costa admitted the constant flow of the *Santa Claus's* systems was becoming harder to keep out of his head. What was he going to do on Omoikane, a techno-saturated planet? Priest couldn't see what good could come of it.

He couldn't leave. Costa couldn't be trusted right now with his own stash and Priest couldn't completely hide the fresh scratches on his arms he endured during the struggle for the dispenser. They would fade soon—none of them were severe—but it gave him another reason to stay right where he was. With nothing better to do than lie back and provide comfort, Priest sighed as his mind wandered in the quiet.

Things were so much better on Gamma Centauri with Arbor.

IT HAD BEEN a week since launch and Priest had barely seen or spoken to Arbor beyond pleasantries while passing in the hall. Somehow, they had both been busy with ship duties, keeping their schedules from being more compatible. Even so, when he did manage to catch Arbor for a moment, the conversation was stilted and uninspired.

Priest knew Arbor was deliberately avoiding him, and the knowledge made his world dull. Worse, he could see the hint of sadness in Arbor's eyes when they did run into each other, and it made Priest feel like complete shit.

He was the master of ruining things.

Checking the time code, he noticed a few hours had passed. Reminiscing over Gamma Centauri had eaten more time than he realized. It seemed a shame to wake Costa, nestled against him. At some point, he finally fell into a peaceful rest, probably the first he'd had in a while. But the lunch service was beginning, and Costa would need his dose before going into public, to prevent an unexplainable incident in case he lost control again.

The doses weren't lasting as long as they used to and Priest was aware Litmus had made a stronger batch than Costa had been using before. The fact didn't sit well. Costa's tolerances were going up, along with his hunger, but with the need for privacy and the ship's safety at stake, what could they do?

"Wake up, Costa. You need to eat." Priest nudged Costa, whose grimace at being disturbed was almost comical.

"Go 'way." Costa pushed away from Priest and rolled over. Priest didn't see a reason to argue. He climbed out of the bed and stretched the kinks out of his back after being in one position for so long.

"Then I'm going to the Mess Hall. I'm hungry and I have the afternoon shift. And I'm taking your meds with me."

Costa's eyes sparked awake. "The bloody hell you are."

In a flash, Costa spun and sat upright, his darkened eyes narrowed. Seeing Costa come to life over his medication brought out a wave of disappointment. The drug was becoming more important to him than his basic needs.

"I'm going to need a dose if you expect me to function properly around others." Costa wet his lips as his eyes fixated on the Calm dispenser still in Priest's hand. "I've held out long enough."

Priest sighed. "All right." He wished Costa had the strength to go without for a change. Hopefully, once he concluded his business on Omoikane, he could start reducing his dependence. It couldn't come soon enough.

Unfortunately, they had little choice. Three days ago, they tried to skip doses to conserve the supply and Costa lost control in a lift. They were nearly trapped and the emergency systems almost removed the oxygen to quell an imaginary fire it detected. That was more than a little scary. Mac was going out of his mind to determine the cause.

Keeping this secret was becoming harder to manage each day.

Costa shifted off the bed, his natural grace wearing a harsh edge, which grew with each passing day. Mesmerized by the little black cylinder, he closed the gap between them. A visible tremor cascaded through his body as he held himself still, forced to wait.

If this were a different scene or some form of roleplay, Priest would have been enjoying himself. Having this gorgeous man kneeling, supplicating himself, should have triggered any number of Priest's smuttier impulses.

Priest held up the dispenser, while Costa obediently opened his mouth, his fluttering hands surrounding Priest's wrist as if he were frightened the dose might be missed. Pressing the button, a single, careful drop landed on Costa's outstretched tongue. He immediately closed his mouth and eyes, waiting for the effect to take hold.

Long minutes passed as Priest watched closely, waiting for the dark creases marring Costa's beauty to ease. But nothing happened. In fact, the furrow between his eyes grew deeper.

With his eyes crushed shut, Costa begged. "It's not enough, Priest. I need one more."

"Are you sure? There's only so much left."

The quake in Costa's hands reached into his voice. "I need to quiet the ones and zeroes. There's so much noise, I can barely keep from lashing out, and my control has been slipping. I don't want to risk hurting anyone. The one drop simply isn't enough anymore."

"All right." Priest sighed. "But just one more."

Costa nodded, his eyes still shut, as Priest hesitantly administered a second dose, hating himself for giving in and hating himself for questioning his desire to take care of Costa.

This time the harshness in his face eventually leveled and Costa took on an appearance Priest could only describe as relief. When Costa opened his eyes, the wanton desire coming off them was palpable. Still kneeling, he grazed his fingers along Priest's thighs, a wolfish grin curling his lips.

"This is so much better. Isn't it, Priest?" The subtle touches progressed into firmer massage and Priest found himself pressing into the heat pouring off Costa's palms.

Costa licked his lips. "Since I'm already on my knees, perhaps you would be so kind as to take my confession?" A soft, lecherous chuckle issued forth. "Bless me, Father, for I am about to sin."

Priest cursed at himself as his body responded without his permission. His cock hardened as Costa kneaded the fly of his trousers, working up to his belt. It had only been a week since Gamma Centauri and he had never felt so lonely on board. The *Santa Claus* always had willing playmates to ease the tension, but this went beyond that. He needed to be touched. He needed to be pleasured. It would take nothing to snatch a fistful of Costa's hair and guide himself into that eager, moist mouth. It would be good. It would be satisfying.

But it wouldn't be with Arbor.

"Shit. Stop." Before his member could be pulled free, Priest gripped Costa's wrists and shifted his hips backward. Costa had already dismantled his belt and the buttons of his fly. "No. This isn't right."

"What?"

"I don't want to do this." He stepped out of reach and restored his clothing.

Costa's brow twisted with incredulous shock. "You can't possibly be telling me you don't find me attractive. That growth in your trousers tells a different story entirely."

"I never said that. I've always found you attractive. Problem is it doesn't go both ways. You don't really want me. You never have." Costa's face melted into some macabre blend of surprise and fear, with widened eyes and slackened mouth. "And I can't keep letting you use me that way. It's fucking with my head too much. I still want to help you, but I don't need to be seduced for that."

Costa's lower lip quivered as his eyes glistened. It was unnerving. Despite being smaller in stature, Costa was always a pillar of confidence, even when the drug cravings tested him. Now, he looked hopelessly fragile as Priest finally recognized the foreign expression haunting Costa's visage, and it had nothing to do with the Calm.

Shame.

"I'm sorry, Priest." Costa's voice broke for a moment. "I never thought you'd stay near me without the encouragement."

"Every time we've been together is just the side effect from street-made Calm, isn't it?" It was less of a question and more of a statement.

Costa nodded, leaving the room in silence. Moments later, his eyes narrowed. "How would you know about that?"

"I did some research of my own. You're not exactly giving out more info than what's on a need-to-know basis." Actually, Arbor had done the research, but there was no reason to tell Costa. He could keep a few secrets too. Since leaving Gamma Centauri, he spent his quiet evenings reading through all the data and para-human history Arbor sent him. A lot of the pieces didn't make sense yet—there was so much information to sift through—but he was sure it was only a matter of time.

Closing his eyes and clenching his fists, Costa inhaled and blew out a controlled exhale several times, settling himself. When his eyes opened again, all traces of his lust had vanished, or were hidden under his standard facade.

"I don't have much experience with trusting normal men. They tend to only want one thing." Costa stood upright, testing his balance. He smoothed his clothing as best he could, looking more like himself again. "It's not like you at all to walk away from a shag."

"Yeah, well, it surprises me too." Priest growled at himself in disbelief. He looked down. His erection was subsiding and he was nearly decent to be seen in public. "I need to head down to the Mess Hall. If I miss lunch, I'm screwed until they bring us our meal on the bridge at the end of dinner service."

"That's probably a good idea, as long as you don't mind the company. I'd like to be out of my quarters for a bit and I'm sure I could stand a bit to eat."

They walked down the corridors in relative quiet, Costa keeping a closer proximity than usual, causing him to occasionally brush against Priest. He looked more vulnerable, and Priest couldn't be sure if it was a result of the rigors of controlling his haphazard abilities or having to admit he seduced Priest for his help. Costa held his head high, but Priest had learned enough about him to see the flaw in his armor. A minor shedding of his confidence belied the inner strength he portrayed. It was subtle—a soft twitch of his jaw, the thin line of his mouth. For the first time, Priest felt needed beyond the station of a loyal serf. They were alone when the lift doors closed. Costa's shoulders sagged a fraction, and he leaned against Priest for support.

If only Costa had needed him from the beginning things might have been different, but now he wanted someone else entirely.

They exited the lift, Costa once again strong and aloof, and the pair ran into Arbor leaving the Mess Hall.

A rush of alarm and elation rushed through Priest's chest. "Hey, Arbor."

Arbor's vision darted between the two men. "Priest. Costa. I see the two of you are still getting along."

The response was cool but polite. Arbor looked well, but his eyes were dull, the spark animating them no longer shining. It pained Priest to know he was the cause. He wished he wasn't standing next to Costa.

"Yeah, well, what else is there to do?" Priest winced. What the hell was he saying? It was exactly the kind of thoughtless remark that turned off Arbor in the first place. Could his cheeks burn any hotter?

Arbor flattened his brow and looked away. "We all need our entertainment. I'd hate to think you were doing without."

The awkward stillness stretched out, with neither man willing to look the other in the eye. Priest couldn't think of what to say. He wanted to apologize, but was afraid more stupidity would fall out of his mouth and make matters worse.

Costa rolled his eyes. "I love a good juvenile drama as much as the next man, but is there a point where we can get something to eat? I'm suddenly famished."

"Please, Priest. Feed him already." Arbor scanned his eyes up and down Costa's body. "He looks like he could use a meal. I'm sure his kind burns calories faster than normals."

"Arbor!"

Costa raised his hand with a haughty sneer, dismissing the comment. "It's all right, Priest. He's simply lashing out before anyone else can make a joke out of him."

Arbor answered the jab with one of his own. "A pariah ought to know."

Priest grabbed Costa's arm and stepped between the two men. "Stop it, both of you!" Mustering the least aggressive tone he could manage, he pleaded with Arbor. "I'd like to talk sometime. Alone. Soon."

"I...I don't know. I've been really busy lately—"

"Please." Priest knew he was seconds away from shameless begging, but it would be worth it. Arbor hedged, his eyes shining and his feet shifting. His supple mouth, which Priest had become so familiar with, opened slightly as if he were ready to answer.

Mrs. Claus's synthetic voice prevented Arbor's response. "Private com for Mr. Kittering."

"Mrs. Claus, please forward it to my handheld." Arbor pulled his pad from his shoulder bag and quickly read the screen. "I need to go. It's Mac. He's going crazy with all the system anomalies we've had lately. He's very possessive of Mrs. Claus and stresses when she has problems." Arbor gave a scathing look to Costa. "I have a few theories on what's the cause." Looking around to see if anyone was nearby, Arbor returned his pad to his bag. "I'm not about to cause a scare through the ship if I'm not sure there's a real danger. Not everyone needs to know everything that goes on."

The surprise on Costa's face was unexpected. His rigid stance softened. "You haven't spoken to anyone about me?"

Arbor shrugged. "What would be the point? Then we'd both be outcasts on the ship and we'd be stuck with each other. I don't want to get to know you that well."

One would have thought Costa impervious to the dig, but he flinched at the comment. His cocky demeanor frayed and he looked completely uncomfortable as he rubbed his left arm with his right hand. Perhaps he wasn't accustomed to people not falling over themselves to get to know him.

"Even so, I would like to thank you for using your discretion in this matter."

Arbor glanced at Priest before turning on his heel and heading down the hall, giving them his back. "Trust me. I'm not doing it for your sake."

WALKING AWAY FROM Priest was excruciating. A lot of effort had gone into avoiding him and Arbor knew it couldn't last forever, but he wanted to keep contact minimal until Costa McQuillen was off the ship. The beautiful para-human was too much of a distraction for Priest, and Arbor knew he couldn't compete with his level of allure. Why would he want a dwarf when he could have the prince? The idea of the two of them naked and writhing was more than he could stand.

Priest was a free spirit. He couldn't be tied down to one man, and pretending otherwise was a source of grief. It would be best to let Priest do what he wanted with whomever he wanted, and Arbor take what affection he could get, but he couldn't bring himself to share. Not with Priest.

Once he turned the corner, Arbor stopped. With a hand pressed to the wall, he took three slow, deep breaths coupled with a mnemonic chant—his mother's technique—to quell the shaking in his chest and tried to burrow his short fingers into the unyielding hull. He had work to do and this wouldn't make him effectual in the least.

He needed to be useful. Mr. Wiggles had yet to emerge. The ransom coms had reduced in frequency, but there was no end in sight. The crew was polite yet still evasive. Conversations were still coming to a halt as he stepped into occupied rooms. It was exhausting at the best of times. He tried to smile and pretend like being isolated wasn't so painful. But in the end, he knew he'd colored their early opinions with those public scenes and it would take time to change their perceptions. For now, Mac and Priest were the only ones who actually engaged him on a regular basis.

Well...Mac did. He couldn't face Priest now.

Arbor shook his head and resumed his path. There wasn't time for self-pity and endless indulgences in life's unfair circumstances. He would be strong and find a place amongst the crew somehow. He would perform his duties and prove his value. He would learn to sleep without wondering what Priest was up to while he was alone in the dark. Arbor could learn to stop craving his caresses. He could learn to be alone. Again. No one wounds you when you're alone. It would be for the best.

Right.

Arbor headed for the databank, a subsection of engineering housing the primary computer core, which connected every system, including Mrs. Claus's AI. Mac's com asked to meet him there, hoping to help find the cause of the repeating appearances of software corruption.

There was no question Costa was responsible, but his tentative reaction told Arbor it was accidental. He couldn't imagine Priest would stand up for him if it were otherwise. Priest was many things: a scoundrel, a schemer, and a thoughtless clod at times. But he wasn't heartless. He wouldn't risk the lives of the crew. It wasn't his nature.

Mac's message was quick and to the point. No pleasantries or chatty jokes were present in the com. *I need you at the databank. Right now.* There was no question whether his frustration over the random tech failures was growing.

Voices drifted through the hall as he approached. Mac and Danverse. Mac paced the room, completely ignoring the walls of monitors and circuit boards. It was like the tech access panels found throughout the ship's hallways, but all in one location. A complete battery of the ship's knowledge and code streaming through every fiber filament cast a wave of awe over Arbor. Mac was not feeling the same.

"There has to be an answer! Events like this don't spontaneously happen!" Mac's hands flew about wildly as he threatened to wear a path into the metal flooring. His footsteps were approaching a manic circle.

Danverse stood still, yet followed Mac's every move. "Do you have any idea what could be causing it?"

"No! I don't! If I did, we wouldn't be having this conversation!"

"Mac..." Danverse growled his displeasure at Mac's tone.

Mac's pace increased as well as the rate of his speech. "It doesn't make any sense! Things like this just don't happen. I watch everything. I adjust and tweak every aspect of Mrs. Claus. There is no way this corrupt data should be appearing. There's no foreign code in the system. There's no trace of data conflict."

"What can we do?"

"I have no idea!" A crazed vibration raced through Mac as his frustration peaked. "I've been wracking my brain trying to find a solution and all I can see is the possibility of it hitting a critical system and—"

"Mac, calm down." Danverse tried to interrupt, but Mac's tirade was gaining speed.

"—killing someone and it will be all my fault because I couldn't focus enough to find a solution that could keep us all safe because that's my job that I signed up for and everyone is counting on me and if anyone gets hurt I'll never—"

"Mac."

"—forgive myself and what if something happens and a crew member is crippled and Doc Bosch can't fix it, or during the landing on Omoikane and we crash the ship and everyone dies in a giant ball of fire and—"

Danverse shouted, interrupting Mac's rant. "At ease, boy! Stand up straight! Eyes ahead!"

Mac startled and froze, his back ramrod straight, eyes fixed on a point many kilometers away. The command held such force, Arbor found himself complying in kind.

Danverse walked around him, his hands clasped behind his back as he inspected his charge with the countenance of a military official. He tapped Mac's feet apart a few millimeters with his boot and nodded in approval.

"I want you to calm down, boy. You're letting this whole thing overwhelm you. I don't like seeing you this way. It hurts me."

"But what if—?"

"Nothing. You will step back and take the help you have." The commandant pose relaxed as Danverse cupped Mac's face in his powerful hands, locking their gazes on one another. "I will help you keep your thoughts from running wild like I always do. You're too damn intelligent for your own good. And you'll have the dwarf help you. That's what he's on board for." Mac buried his face into Danverse's chest as the captain wrapped his thick arms around him and planted a gentle kiss to the crown of his head.

"Arbor." Mac's voice was muffled in the valley of Danverse's breast.

"What?"

Mac tipped his head back to look into the captain's eyes. "His name is Arbor. Don't call him 'dwarf.'"

"You're right." Danverse's shoulders softened. "I'm not the most tolerant man, but for you, I'll do better. Making you happy is all that matters to me. You're all that matters to me, Mac. You're all I have that really matters."

The two men embraced, holding onto one another like the rest of the universe didn't exist.

Arbor held back in the hall, waiting for the moment to pass. The sight of their devotion to one another dug another unfair knife into his heart. Being a voyeur was never one of his personal kinks, and the last thing he wanted was to embarrass Mac or the captain. He hated seeing Mac so distressed. He was the only real friend Arbor had on board.

Hopefully, he could find a method to manage the issue until Costa could get off the ship and be on his merry little way. Part of him wanted to tell Mac and the captain what he'd seen, but if they reacted badly to a pariah on the ship, it could splash back on Priest, and Arbor wasn't angry enough to cause that kind of chaos.

No. He would find a better way to remedy the problem. He owed Mac. It was time to start working on a proper solution to Costa McQuillen.

Chapter Ten

"WHAT DO YOU mean it's bloody empty?"

Priest shook the little black Calm dispenser near his ear, listening for any sound. "The reader says there's more doses left, but there's nothing in here. This bitch is empty."

"It can't be. You're clearly reading it wrong."

"I don't think so, Costa. I think *someone's* been using it more often than the schedule we set up." Priest's accusing stare enflamed Costa.

Costa's mouth drew a tight, thin line. How dare he suggest such a thing? It was true he had been forced to take a dose or two off-schedule, but it shouldn't have depleted the dispenser so quickly. The idea was ludicrous.

He looked around the room, refusing to acknowledge Priest. Invisible threads of binary code ran through the air, connecting every device and system in the room. Each line was a gateway his thoughts could ride into the *Santa Claus* and disconnect from the ugliness of the real world. The shimmering data bathed him in all directions, but he needed to not peer directly into it for too long. Once, the ones and zeroes were a lovely tapestry to explore, but since his power grew with all the additional terabytes stored in his head, the simple numbers were too painful. Their crystal beauty shined too bright now and burned his eyes and mind if he stared too long. He needed the Calm to dim the brightness and keep his skills manageable, bringing the constant roar in his head to a tolerable level.

The extra travel time to Omoikane was stressing his limits. The complex data in his head was becoming fragile and easy to corrupt. Years had been spent compiling all the errant fragments. He couldn't risk the loss of any portion. It was too precious a thing.

There's no way Priest, or anyone for that matter, could understand his pain, and he certainly wasn't planning on subjecting himself to his judgments, either.

"Don't be so ridiculous. Why on earth would I do such a thing? It makes no sense."

"You need to go to Doc Bosch and get set up—"

"I have already told you no, Priest! The last time I allowed a doctor to scan me I ended up on a laboratory table for days. I won't go through that again."

The only doctors he allowed to scan him since he was free were the physicians attached to the Mayflower Ark. There was no choice really, but their entire focus was making sure all the immigrants arrived alive. It was part of the contract. Casualties were worth no payment.

When Costa's para-human skills appeared, the doctors were only too excited to scan, poke, and prod him. Their medical curiosity outweighed any portion of their oath to do no harm. Even when he screamed and begged, they ignored him, treating him as something less than human. Strapped into the chair, they installed the pacifier at the base of his skull to ensure his obedience and branded the facial tattoos into his flesh, permanently marking him as an outcast. Once they finished their examination, Costa had been deemed too dangerous and a threat to global security. When he became suspicious of the whispers surrounding him, Costa found his pending extermination order in their files.

Time was critical. He sent private communiqués to several world leaders and defense contractors to prepare a bidding war. North American Continent Ambassador, Terese Dodge, had the political clout to stay the execution and place Costa in her permanent employ. As Dodge's new assistant, his skills and looks were worth more than the doctors' paranoid assessments. The scrutiny and lack of safety was over—for a time.

"Bosch isn't like that, Costa. He's a good guy. He wants to take care of us. That's why he's on board. He'll find a way to manage your powers so you don't have to be hooked on a drug."

Costa snarled, his voice twisting into something less human. "I'm not addicted to anything."

"You're a total fucking addict and too stubborn to admit it."

"I have no intention of listening to your groundless accusations. If you're not here to help, you can just fuck off." Costa didn't understand why he was lashing out at Priest. He wanted his help—needed it even. Alienating his one confidant was a poor move in the scheme of things. But the constant pain and need to control it was making him so impatient. He knew it wasn't like him, but he couldn't stop it either.

"I *am* here to help."

"Then find a new supply to keep me from imploding!"

Priest's shoulders slumped as his arms fell to his sides. "You can't get new Calm without the Doc, and I'm not stealing from him."

"Don't let the door hit you on the way out."

"Costa..."

"If you're not helping me, I don't have any use for you—hang on..." Costa froze and risked scanning around the room, reading the errant code. "The engines have stopped."

"What?"

Panic mixed with rage fueled the volume of his voice. "Why have the bloody engines stopped?"

"YOU WANT TO explain why you shut down the engines on my ship?"

Even though Danverse's question wasn't directed to Arbor, the thundering tone made his hackles rise. Arbor, Mac, and the captain were all standing in the main engine room with Sheldon, the engine specialist. Mac and Sheldon had been discussing the situation before they powered down the engine and contacted Danverse and himself. It took the captain less than five seconds to notice and demand an explanation.

Sheldon and Mac kept close to the main control access panel, away from the door. It was likely an effort to keep some distance from the irate captain.

Mac spoke first, probably figuring his relationship would be a shield of sorts. "It's about the corrupted data that keeps appearing."

"What does that have to do with delaying our arrival to Omoikane?"

Sheldon cleared his throat as his dirty hands fiddled with his suspenders. "Because it's spread to the power flow systems."

"What does that mean?"

"Until we can purge it and re-initialize the core, it's not safe to run the engines," Mac said.

"Explain." Danverse's demand flared directly to Sheldon.

"The fuel flow is really delicate. I spend a lot of time calibrating it for peak efficiency. If the random crap data imbalances the way it goes through the fuselage chambers, it could cause a number of problems."

"Like what?"

Sheldon started ticking off reasons on his fingers. "The engine could start misfiring and shut itself down. It could freeze up and not turn off at all, which would take the chance of landing down to zero percent. A power surge could imbalance the reactor and blow us all to hell. Those are the best scenarios."

Danverse scrubbed his hand over his face. "How long is this going to take to fix? Some of our cargo is time sensitive. If we don't get there on time, we don't get paid."

"We're not sure. The system is supposed to be secure and contained. This has never happened before."

"Son of a bitch!" Danverse whirled on Mac. "I thought you and Arbor were coming up with a solution to this shit."

Mac's brow creased and his back stiffened. "Don't blame me. You of all people know we've been working our asses off on this. Every time we clean up one of these fucking events, a new one sprouts from somewhere. I can't even tell what's spawning it or what the source is."

Guilt rose in Arbor's chest. He knew the source of all the data corruption, but had kept quiet since it hadn't affected a key system like this. Now, peoples' lives were at risk if the side effects of Costa's powers were left unchecked—this incident was proof. Protecting Priest's relationship with the crew was the only reason he'd kept silent. Arbor was used to being on the fringe. He didn't want Priest to know what it was like.

But now there wasn't a choice. The staff needed to know and he could only hope his knowledge wouldn't cause more trouble than it was intended to save.

Arbor gripped the shoulder strap on his bag as his breathing quickened. Danverse and Mac were still arguing out of frustration, and an anxious heat rose in his chest and face. He was about to open his mouth to interrupt the pair, when a voice down the main hall did the job for him.

"You can't go in there. You don't have clearance!"

"Take your bloody hands off me!"

Costa stormed into the room, Priest right behind him. What happened to Costa? Tired and frail, with harsh shadows under his eyes, his natural elegance was diminished to haggard tremors shaking his whole body. Costa's skin was pale and sickly, and the once pretty eyes were wide and crazed with a facial expression to match.

"I demand to know why we've stopped moving!"

Priest followed behind Costa, his slumped shoulders apologetic and chastened. "I'm sorry, Captain. I tried to stop him."

The captain didn't even look at Priest. His torso swelled in dominance as he purposely towered over his rude trespasser. Costa shook, but given his tight jaw, it had nothing to do with submission.

"Mr. McQuillen, did you happen to miss the signs and com notices that explained this area is off-limits to passengers?"

Standing shorter than the captain, Costa still managed to look down his nose at him. "I'm still waiting for an answer."

The challenge made Arbor uneasy. Danverse did not come off as a man who took insubordination lightly, and Costa was a snob. Nothing about the exchange spelled a recipe for a happy outcome. All Arbor wanted was to make himself even smaller and avoid the upcoming bloodbath.

"We're having technical difficulties. The engines will come back on once we determine it's safe to do so."

"I don't have time for this nonsense. Restart the engines this instant."

Danverse turned his back on Costa and returned to his earlier position. "I don't make a habit of bowing down to little men. So fuck off and let me figure out how to fix my ship."

"I will not be made light of by a group of military rejects with delusions of grandeur! You will start these engines and take me to Omoikane now! I will not accept any more delays from you and your incompetent crew!"

The entire crew present went silent. Arbor was afraid to speak, as a growling inhale inflated Danverse's ample chest. His thick arms went rigid at his side, fists clenching into cudgels. Every muscle in the captain's formidable body was coiled to strike. Costa had no idea how precarious his situation was. It looked like he was about to be beaten within a centimeter of his life.

Danverse let out all his air through his nose and relaxed his hands. "Mrs. Claus, contact Angus and have him come to the main engine room and escort passenger Costa McQuillen straight to the brig. I don't want to see his skinny little ass for the rest of this voyage."

"I will not be dismissed, Captain."

"You just were."

Priest closed in and placed a hand on Costa's quaking shoulder. "C'mon, Costa. Let's get out of here."

"No! Don't touch me!" Costa snatched his arm away and shoved Priest toward the others. A charge filled the air as his shoulders hunched and his brow furrowed. "We are going to Omoikane! Now!"

Everyone froze in shock as the engines powered up and the control panels began an erratic dance on the screen.

Danverse's reaction was far from pleased. "What the hell? Mac?"

"I didn't do anything." Mac looked utterly bewildered as he craned his head around the room.

Sheldon stared at Costa, awe coloring his voice. "Are you doing this? You need to stop. It's not safe right now."

Priest shouted but didn't advance. "Costa! Stop this right now!"

"What the fuck is going on?" The captain's confusion was dripping in anger.

The outer door slid open and Angus entered in full security mode, utility belt and sidearm strapped to his hip, assessing the room. Forceful and intimidating, he locked onto Costa and stalked forward.

With a panicked gasp, Costa reached out as he stumbled. "Don't touch me!"

Mrs. Claus's voice chimed in the chaos. "Fire safety protocols initiated. Engine room isolation in progress."

A series of hybrid glass walls burst upward from the floor, knocking everyone back as the room found itself divided into sections. All the exterior doors slid shut. The stats from Arbor's orientation said the transparent walls were dense enough to contain a fire on board until the ship systems could deal with the emergency. With them in place, Mac and Sheldon were trapped near the engine on the port side while everyone else was held at starboard. Costa trembled in the middle, segregated from everyone.

"Costa, what are you doing?" Priest sounded frightened.

Tremors raced through Costa's slender hand as it brushed near his manic stare. "We have to get to Omoikane. I can't afford any more delays!"

Sheldon stepped over to the erratic control panel. "Captain, the engines are pushing to full speed. If we don't shut down and recalibrate—"

"Do you hear that, McQuillen?" Danverse pounded on the safety barrier to get Costa's attention. "I don't know how you're doing this, but if you don't stop this bullshit, we may not make it at all."

"You're just lying to me." Facial twitches making his head shake, Costa's composure was unraveling. "Normals can't be trusted. I'll get there on my own."

Mac called out to the ceiling. "Mrs. Claus, Shut down and isolate all engine functions for diagnostics—"

"*Stop that!*" Costa screamed.

Mrs. Claus's calm voice appeared again. "Fire safety protocol initiated. Oxygen removal from Engine Section Alpha-Six in progress."

Costa paused, confusion clouding his eyes. "What? No...that's not right."

A ventilation hiss echoed through the engine room. Mac and Sheldon both blanched as they pressed their hands against the clear wall. A growing terror etched their faces as they both began gasping, trying to catch their breaths.

Danverse's command was rapid. "Mrs. Claus. Initialize mainframe and purge foreign datastream."

"Access denied, Captain Danverse."

"Re-initialize all command codes."

"Access denied, Captain Danverse."

Danverse turned to face across the room. "Mac?" The whites of his eyes became all too visible as the reality set in. Danverse's chest raced in quick, staccato breaths. "Mrs. Claus, shut down all fire safety protocols."

"Access denied, Captain Danverse."

"*No!*" Howling, the captain hurled himself at the wall, the desperate sound of his powerful fists beating the thick barrier reverberated a chill down Arbor's spine.

Arbor scrambled to pull his data pad out of his bag. The screen couldn't start up fast enough. His fingers shook as he pulled up the menu of his most recent side project. It wasn't complete. Most of his time had been spent figuring out how to shield his equipment from Costa's influence. The last few lines of code were still waiting to be added. It was what he was working on when he received the urgent summons to the Engine Room.

Code raced across the small screen as he typed as fast as he could, frantic to remember the last sequences. Arbor stopped and deleted a line. Shit, that wasn't right. His fingers were clumsy under the pressure and there was only one chance to do this correctly.

Mac was on his knees trying to take shallow breaths, his terror-stricken eyes locked on the captain's. His skin was taking a sheen as his eyes glistened and his body spasmed in protest. Mac's fingers tried to reach beyond the barrier to no avail. Sheldon was already thrashing on the floor, gasping for oxygen. They were both suffocating before their eyes.

Arbor pushed himself to type faster.

Costa stammered. "I...I didn't mean to do that." Fragile and quaking, he clutched his head as he winced painfully. "No. This isn't what I wanted. I...I'll stop this."

"Ship self-destruct in effect in T minus ten minutes and counting," Mrs. Claus announced.

Priest slapped the wall. "Costa, stop it!"

"No! Priest! Help me! It's not working! I can't stop it!" With both hands at his temples, Costa folded to the floor, writhing in pain. "I can't control it!"

"Mrs. Claus, contact Doc Bosch!" Priest called out.

"Engine room lockdown in progress. Communications suspended."

"Son of a bitch!" He kicked at the wall in a frenzy.

Danverse turned on Arbor. The cords in his neck were strained and the anguish in his face was unmistakable. His characteristic self-control was fraying into nonexistence as he shook Arbor by the collar. "We have to get Mac out of there! This is a coding thing! *Do something, Goddamn it! It's what we're paying you for!*"

"I'm working on it!" Arbor jerked himself free and returned to his screen. There wasn't much more left to add, but there wouldn't be an opportunity to test anything. It had to be perfect the first time. Mac was his only real friend. He'd never forgive himself if he failed.

"*Mac!*" Danverse's chilling scream was raw and broken. Mac fell over and didn't seem to be breathing.

Pulse hammering in his ears, Arbor's jaw ached from the set of his teeth. The last line of code entered, he hovered his finger over the run command as he prayed out loud. "Please let this work."

Holding his breath, he struck the start command.

Costa lurched in spasm, his hands slapping the floor as he lost control, gurgling repetitive nonsense as his eyes rolled up into his skull.

Priest's eyes were wide in shock. "What the hell are you doing to him?"

"Scrambling his thoughts so he can't affect us. I hope." Arbor adjusted the feed as his scan showed new foreign connections appearing in the sensor net. Continuously active and threaded throughout everything in the *Santa Claus*, it was the most fragile to contamination. Costa's power, conscious or not, was looking for a new way into the system. The untested schematic for the software was in

Costa's Earthgov file. Like the rest of the cataloged para-humans, a method to contain him had already been waiting in the wings in spite of the pending termination order. It took time to figure out how to implement it here, given the limitations of the ship, but Arbor was determined.

"Is it hurting him?"

Arbor's answer was quick and clipped. "I have no idea, but does it really matter at this point?" He tweaked his algorithm to lock Costa's access out of another vulnerable feed. If there had been the time, he would have built the program to do this automatically. Instead, he would have to monitor Costa directly until they had him under control.

Danverse grabbed Arbor's shoulder. "Arbor, what's going on?"

"I'm trying to save us! Mrs. Claus, reset all command functions! Shut down engines and all safety protocols for diagnostics." He spun out of Danverse's hold. "Help Mac!"

He'd never been happier to hear Mrs. Claus. "Command functions reset. Safety protocols shutting down. Powering down main engines, Mr. Kittering." A loud hiss of air escaped as the clear walls lowered into the floor. The engine's hum drifted away as the power was cut.

Danverse yelled at the top of his lungs. "*Shut down self-destruct. Now!*"

"Self-destruct sequence terminated, Captain Danverse."

Danverse was climbing over the hybrid walls before they'd completely receded into the deck. Passing Costa in the center, he snarled and kicked him in the face, flipping him onto his back. Without another pause, he raced to Mac, sliding into a kneeling position.

"Mac? Mac? Fuck me, he's not breathing." The panic in his tone was far worse than the captain screaming. "Angus! Get Sheldon!" Rolling Mac onto his back, Danverse placed his mouth over his boy's and breathed into him. Angus wasted no time doing the same for Sheldon.

Priest wasted no time. "Mrs. Claus, contact Doc Bosch. Medical emergency! Main engine room. Two men down—oxygen deprivation. Make sure he brings his med synthesizer!"

Rubbing his face, Priest kneeled near Costa. His troubled expression brought a keen of jealousy behind Arbor's eyes. Costa continued to roll around in a languid state with drowsy eyes, and fresh blood spatter stained the tattoos on his cheek. A large bruise was already forming across his pretty face.

The immediate threat might have been calmed, Arbor couldn't stem the disquiet. Another tweak to the datapad program was necessary. Even half-conscious, Costa's power was reaching out for a new link with Mrs. Claus. Until they could decide what to do, he would have to manually keep the scrambled feed of garbage binary streaming into Costa's head.

"I didn't think it could get this bad." Running his hands through his short hair, Priest's lower lip trembled as he tried to keep calm. "I never thought..."

Arbor's pulse had yet to quiet as he listened to the patterns of rhythmic breaths being performed on Mac and Sheldon. With Priest distraught over Costa and Danverse's urgent gasps between breaths, everyone present was teetering on a knife's edge. Dr. Bosch couldn't get here fast enough.

Short minutes lasted an eternity. The door slid open and Dr. Bosch rushed into the room with his burly medical aide, Carson, in tight formation. Carson sprinted over to the downed crewmen. When Bosch paused as he passed Costa's half-conscious body, Priest latched onto his forearm.

"Doc! Can you make Calm?"

The doctor's forehead twisted. "Of course I can. Why would I do such a thing? Do you even know what it's for?"

"Of course I do. It's for him." Priest pointed at Costa's dazed body. "He needs to be dosed so we can get his powers under control before he accidentally kills us all."

Dr. Bosch looked down at Costa with his analyzing stare, assessing the immediate situation. Less than a second later, the doctor straightened, his razor-sharp gaze more dominant than one would expect from someone his size.

"Are you telling me we have a sick para-human on board and no one informed me?"

Priest withered at the inquisition, embarrassment staining his cheeks.

"Doctor! Now's not the time." Arbor made another adjustment on his pad. "He's not at risk. I have this under control. Go take care of Mac and Sheldon. They need you more."

"Priest..." Costa moaned, his voice was weak and thready. "We have to save Poll."

"What?"

"He's all that matters." Costa's voice drifted into incoherence as Arbor calibrated his program once again.

"Doc, hurry! Mac's still not breathing!" Danverse's voice was fracturing.

Dr. Bosch rushed over to Mac, stiff-arming the captain to one side. Working quickly, he pulled out several devices Arbor didn't recognize. Danverse stood, his footsteps in a shiftless disarray. Arbor had never seen the captain like this. He continued to hyperventilate as he circled the scene, lost and aimless, his natural strength bleeding out, leaving him bleary-eyed. The sight made Arbor's chest ache.

Haunted breaths became angry snarls as Danverse's stare flitted back and forth between Mac and the one responsible. A new sense of dread filled Arbor as the captain's stance grew more impatient and hostile.

An inhuman snarl escaped the captain as he snatched Angus's gun from its holster. The power cell hummed loud as he thumbed the control, increasing the phase pistol's strength. He strode over to Costa, weapon poised.

"Priest! Look out!"

Priest turned and leaped. "Captain, no!" Pushing the gun toward the ceiling, Priest wrapped himself around the captain.

"Let go of me!" Danverse was enraged. Priest wrestled with the captain, trying to keep a grip on his wrist and prevent him from aiming. They twisted and turned as Priest quickly lost ground. Danverse was larger and stronger, and Priest didn't have his mad intentions.

Priest begged through his teeth. "Don't do this!"

Angus rushed over and added to the pile, lifting the captain's hand as he attempted to aim at the addled man on the floor.

"Get off me!" Danverse elbowed Angus in the face, causing him to stagger back, blood pouring out of his nose and mouth. With a shove, Priest wrapped his leg behind Danverse's, holding on as they capsized.

Both men landed on the deck with a grunt and the weapon discharged, showering them with white-hot sparks as the flash struck the hull. The particle beam burned and scarred the metal as it arced across the ceiling, down the wall, and across Arbor's face and chest.

Chapter Eleven

EACH FRACTION OF a second stretched itself into an endless nightmare.

Arbor's body lurched, his limbs flailing even as the phaser beam faded. His personal datapad flipped end over end in the air. Embers flared and extinguished themselves across his clothing and skin as he slumped backward like a discarded rag doll. The handheld struck the deck, shattering the screen into tiny splinters.

Priest couldn't stop himself from screaming. *"Arbor!"* His arms and legs were still wrapped with the captain's, but the struggle for the gun was over. Angus held his face, continuing to bleed profusely from his nose. Dr. Bosch and Carson had paused treating the men, covering the unconscious bodies with their own after the gunshot.

Fear swelled into purpose, and Priest wrenched himself free of the tangle with Danverse.

"Priest..." Costa's moans bore little more weight than a feather. "Please help me...help me save Poll..."

Torn between the two men, the soft entreaty stilled Priest's progress even as the sound inflated into a harrowing wail. Costa arched, his scream pitching off the walls as the whole room went insane.

The doors slammed shut and the main engine roared to life in uneven surges. The illumination strobed in white hot bursts. Every control panel and monitor went into seizure, flashing uncontrolled streams of data. Layers of cacophonous noise erupted from the audio array, forcing every man to the ground against the onslaught.

Hands crushed over his ears, Priest could barely hear himself as he tried to scream over the volume. *"Costa, stop! I have your meds!"*

The room went silent.

The engine reduced to a rumbling hum and every screen calmed to a single point of information aimed at Priest. An eerie sensation of being watched washed over him. Costa's consciousness could be felt everywhere, threaded into every system. And he had its complete attention.

Priest spun and roused Dr. Bosch, beckoning with his outstretched hand. With the unspoken request, Dr. Bosch tightened, his mouth a thin line. He knew the doctor hated what Priest was asking of him, but what choice did they have? Dr. Bosch reached into his medical bag and drew out his medication synthesizer. Tapping out a quick series on the device's small control panel, he set the dosage and slid it over to Priest.

Having been on the receiving end of Dr. Bosch's care, Priest knew to place the transdermal aperture against Costa's neck, near the shoulder, and pressed the pad. A gentle hiss escaped, followed by an instantaneous gasp of ecstasy from Costa's lips. His slender body relaxed and he drifted away. The doctor had dosed him hard. All the commandeered tech reset itself, and the room fell back to normal in short order.

Dr. Bosch sprang forward and snatched the synthesizer from Priest's hand. "Mrs. Claus, medical emergency! Direct all crew with medical training to main engine room!" He slid to his knees next to Arbor's side. "Four men down. One critical for immediate evac to sick bay. Sterilize Bed One and activate surgical theatre. Prepare protocols for massive phaser burns and system shock."

As Dr. Bosch shouted his orders, the reality weighed Priest down. The immediate world blurred and slowed. His rapid pulse and harsh breaths echoed with the other voices, overlapping into a droning dirge. Mired in the pandemonium, he could only bear witness as crew members flooded the room.

Dr. Bosch directed everyone, assigning men to injured parties with an unbroken focus on Arbor. Everything happened as if Priest wasn't on the same plane of existence. Crew members flew about the room ignoring him, their focal point on other men with greater need.

Carson pulled out the portable gurney, placing the long cylinder on the floor at Arbor's feet. Pressing the main control, a flexible, hyper-thin sheet scrolled out and slid itself under the unmoving dwarf. Touching another tab caused the sheeting's surface to harden. Grabbing the new edge, they lifted Arbor off the ground and rushed him out of the room. The rest of the injured were either carried out over someone's shoulder or left the room under their own power.

It barely registered when Priest found himself alone in the vast room.

Why couldn't he grasp a handhold to climb out of this haze? He'd seen tragic events play out in front of him before. Why did this one affect him so much more? He ambled forward with his muddy thinking to where Arbor fell. Something brushed against his boot, making him look down.

Arbor's shoulder bag lay on the floor, the strap in two pieces where the phaser had cut it free, a fine char on each severed edge. Priest stooped down and picked up the satchel. The durable leather was softened with wear, but the bag contained everything Arbor needed to make his day-to-day life easier. He wanted to be part of that too. A few salty drops darkened the leather as he clutched the bag to his chest.

He needed to be there for Arbor. He needed Arbor. The fog snapped away and Priest bolted out the door. He couldn't get to sick bay fast enough.

The infirmary was abuzz with activity when Priest stormed into the room. Mac and Sheldon were lying down and awake, being tended to by separate crew members. Danverse, pale and shaken, hovered over Mac. One crew member was cleaning up Angus as he sat still with a small device resting along his cheek and nose, apparently repairing the damage.

Costa lay alone, sleeping peacefully, unaffected by the bustle of men and machines around him. In spite of the blood and bruising along the side of his face, with the dark circles under his eyes abated, he looked somehow angelic.

One bed was obscured from view. A flexible screen was drawn, segregating it from the rest of the beds. Was that the surgical station? Where were Dr. Bosch and Carson? A new layer of fear bled in from the fringes. Where was Arbor?

Dr. Bosch stepped out from behind the screen wearing a stark white surgical gown and clear safety goggles. "Sterilize the wound tract and I'll be right back." Stripping off his latex gloves, Dr. Bosch went to each triage station and wasted no time assessing each injured man. In less than a minute, he was satisfied enough to raise his voice above the activity.

"Thank you for all your help, gentlemen, but now I need fewer people in sick bay and I have to ask everyone to leave." He motioned his hands, ushering the extra crew outside. Priest didn't want to leave—he'd just arrived—but found himself swept along with the herd into the hallway. "The automated medical sensors can take over from this point. Mac and Sheldon will be staying overnight. Strictly for observation. Otherwise, I need it quiet to work. That goes for you, too, Captain."

"But, Mac—"

"Will be perfectly fine." The doctor had to practically shove Danverse out the door. "You can coddle him tomorrow."

"What about McQuillen?"

"A stasis field is in place and he's medicated so heavily he won't wake up for hours."

Danverse pointed at Costa. "I want that man under control, Doctor." His hand trembled with rage, blunting the force of his command.

"I think you've done enough for one day, Captain." Dr. Bosch's words were edged with venom, mirroring the intensity of his stare. A professional decorum was likely the only thing keeping him from exploding.

Before Dr. Bosch could turn and leave, Priest pushed forward from the crowd. "Doc, how's Arbor?"

Dr. Bosch flashed a disdainful glance at the captain. "He's fortunate to not have been cut in half." Priest's stomach rolled. "Even still, he's barely stable and there's a lot of damage to regenerate, even after we remove all the burned tissues."

"Is he going to be all right?" Priest's lungs stilled, unwilling to continue in the silence.

Dr. Bosch paused for a moment, uncertainty flickering across his eyes. "I'll do my best, Priest."

The sick bay doors slid closed as the doctor hurried back to the surgical suite. Priest's breath rushed out, taking his strength with it. He leaned forward, splaying his fingertips on the hard surface as if he could reach Arbor through the metal. The touch didn't cause the door to open. Dr. Bosch had locked them all out.

"How long have you known McQuillen was para-human?"

Priest turned and faced the captain, finding his worried expression covered by the alpha mask he wore. Natural charisma made Danverse the leader and influenced others to follow. This time, however, it was a frayed facade with little tremors of mania along the edges.

"I didn't find out until after we left Alpha Centauri."

"Why didn't you report him?"

"Because he didn't do anything wrong." Most of the men excused from sick bay had halted and were watching the exchange. Their curious gazes only fed the growing anxiety, dark and ugly, slicing through Priest.

Danverse edged closer, his formidable size eclipsing Priest. "You didn't realize he was crazy?"

"He's not crazy. Costa's a manipulative dick sometimes, but he's not trying to kill us. He could have found a way to do that weeks ago. All he wants is to get to Omoikane. His powers were getting out of control and he ran out of Calm. He wasn't prepared for a trip this long. His supply ran out."

"You should have told me the second you found out. You put all our lives at risk."

Priest wilted at the captain's domineering pose and venom. "I didn't realize any of this was possible. I was trying to convince him to go to Doc Bosch when the engines stopped. Then all hell broke loose."

Apparently the answer was insufficient, because Danverse grabbed Priest by the collar and pinned him against the sick bay doors. He grunted at how the molding edges dug into his back, and dropped Arbor's satchel.

Danverse loomed forward, his fierce snarl making his fury unmistakable. "I'm holding you personally responsible for the danger you put all of us in, Priest. Every crew member could have died today because of you. Five people ended up in sick bay."

It wasn't anger bubbling up in Priest, rising to the surface. It wasn't even the guilt singing its tawdry verses in his ear about his hand in this debacle. It was fear. Fear for the future of the wounded man behind the medical screen. Fear for a future he might never know. Fear cutting like poisoned blades under his skin, demanding a reaction.

Priest slapped Danverse's hand away and shoved him backward. "And *you* put two of them in there!" A sick tremor paired itself in a chilled rush of sweat as he glared at the captain. "You're so full of shit. The only person you gave a damn about today was Mac, and you're trying to justify how you tried to execute an unconscious man."

"I was protecting the crew—"

"*You fucked up and shot an innocent bystander! The man who saved us all!* Costa may have lost control and people got hurt, but he tried to stop it! He was in so much pain and he begged me to help him, but I didn't know how!" Priest inhaled sharply to hold back the shame threatening to spill over into tears. "Arbor figured it out. He saved Mac's life and turned Costa off. So what did you do? Tried to kill one and probably ended up killing the other. Your own crewman. As long as the ship is safe, what's a little collateral damage, right?"

All the vitriol bled out of him as the swelling in his eyes made it hard to see. Danverse rose taller, an impenetrable wall of force. The seething flowed off his body in a tangible wave.

A shudder wracked Priest as the words, coarse with sadness, continued. "Congratulations. You've saved us all. You should be so proud of yourself. I hope you're happy. Mac is going to be fine. You'll have your happy ever after." Priest gasped. The words were becoming harder to speak. "*Your* man will walk out of here."

"This is *not* about Mac." Danverse's quiet menace could be felt as well as heard. "This is about how your holding back information nearly cost the lives of everyone on board. Your keeping secrets ultimately led to every one of these injuries, no matter how they happened. Give me one good reason not to throw you in the brig and forget you're in there."

"Arbor knew. How do you think he figured out how to shut Costa down?" Priest's eyes burned and his voice became hoarse. "Maybe you should punish him for not narcing out Costa too. No, wait, you already did." A single tear raced down his cheek, his vision blurring as his body shook. "And since you need to punish someone, you might as well punish me too. Go ahead! Protect the crew! *Go on, Captain! Do it! Right here in front of everyone! Put a gun to my fucking head and punish me already!*"

Startled by the raw outburst, Danverse's mouth hung open, a response refusing to form. Priest slumped back against the door, the sturdy barrier preventing him from becoming a pile on the floor. Nausea twisted inside him as haunted silence filled the corridor with its suffocating aura. Shoulders listing, the heat in Danverse's eyes faded as he regarded Priest. Every man stood as if in unspoken prayer, unwilling to overpower even the most marginal sound.

The awkward hush dragged until Mrs. Claus finally broke through, her pleasant mood shocking in its contrast. "Corporal Jones. Your automated reminder. Your flight shift begins in fifteen minutes."

"*Your* man? Arbor?" Danverse's brow furrowed as he focused. "I thought I heard it was you and McQuillen that were..."

Priest's shoulders were almost too heavy to move, but he forced a shrug. "I was still figuring out how I fucked things up and how to undo it. Now it may not matter."

"Priest..." Danverse looked lost, as if somehow trying to conjure an apology his instincts didn't allow. It didn't make Priest feel any better. He wasn't sure he wanted to. The gravity of the situation dulled his ability to love or hate any of the men in front of him. Whether they pitied him or judged him, their stares were too penetrating, too deep into feelings he couldn't manage.

It took a massive effort to push away from the wall. Priest rubbed the back of his hand across his nose and mouth, trying to sober himself. Without looking a single man in the eye, he walked forward, every step a slow burden. The miniature crowd parted, letting him pass.

Priest's voice was as flat as his soul crushed under the invisible weight. "I have to go. I have a work shift."

"Take it off. We'll manage."

Stopping in the hall, Priest turned, his weary eyes locked on the captain, barely able to utter more than a whisper. "What else am I supposed to do?"

With the engines down, there wasn't anywhere for the ship to go, but no one stopped him as he ambled away.

PRIEST MISSED THE last meal service, but hunger never visited him on the bridge. The engines were eventually brought online and his shift's last few hours were uneventful. Only once did he have to divert due to random debris in the flight path. A moment of activity within hours of nothing. Staring out into the blackness and counting the stars made the time pass. So far, the navigator, Micah, had been blissfully quiet. Priest wasn't in the mood for conversation.

Captain Danverse hadn't come to the bridge, and that was fine as far as Priest was concerned. The captain's presence would make it much harder to stay sane, to keep the events he couldn't change from eating him alive. His flight shift gave him something to pour himself into, rather than reliving the memory of Arbor falling to the engine room floor over and over.

It wasn't as if Priest hated the captain. He didn't. In all honesty, he admired the man, even with his blatant flaws. The memory of confronting him felt surreal. Priest would have never done anything so stupid in the past, but this time Danverse deserved every hard word. The crew would be outraged if and when the details of the incident became news, but in the end, they would forgive. Danverse gave each and every one a new life and took care of his crew. It was difficult to just forget such a thing. This was the first time the captain's actions spun into the realm of dangerous. But Priest knew, in the end, the crew would understand why it happened.

Danverse's love for Mac was inescapable and all-consuming. Losing him would be the one thing to bring the captain to madness.

Priest was in the Mess Hall the night everyone first discovered Danverse finally got off his ass and approached Mac. It was about time. The fireplug tech had to wait over a year. The pair was eating in the hall and every man in the room looked proud and somewhat jealous of the connection they were sharing.

An argument broke out when Mac found out Danverse had ordered all the men away from him. A year of avoidance from the crew had isolated Mac, but no one wanted to interfere with the captain's claim. Mac stormed out, leaving Danverse behind. The crushed look on his face wrote the story of how lost the captain was without Mac.

Ultimately, they reconciled, and Danverse stopped fucking the crew as a method of punishment or recreation. The two men were devoted to each other—the proof in their fleeting touches and lack of personal space. Watching them together left Priest with a subtle craving for that kind of passion, but the idea never swamped him as a requirement to breathe.

Not until now. Not until Arbor.

And he needed Arbor. He needed to see his crooked smile and hear the snark in his voice. He needed to find the man in his bed and spend mornings and nights ruining the sheets. Now that he knew the difference, life without Arbor would be unbearable. It made him understand what kind of devotion could bring the captain to such depths.

It was awful something so terrible was necessary to make those thoughts and feelings crystallize.

The chance Arbor might not survive was a rusty spike in his chest he needed to ignore, no matter how deep the wound might be. He needed to be strong. Arbor's enormous life in a small body was in the hands of someone with far more talents than he possessed. It could be hours before anyone got word, and sitting outside of sick bay was a complete waste of time. Even if they let him in, he would only be in the way.

No matter how powerful the urge to run back and hover, Priest would trust in Dr. Bosch's skills. The man was practically a miracle worker. Arbor was safest in the infirmary. And so was Costa.

It was hard to believe how his interest in Costa could run so far off course. Priest was still attracted to the slender man, but deep down he knew Costa had no real interest in him and their affair was nothing more than entertainment on both sides. Somewhere, the realization crept around in the back of his mind even when he lied to himself Arbor's attentions were purely casual.

So much time wasted. Would he have done things differently had he seen the future? Probably not. At least in the aftermath, Priest could be honest with himself. He still would have tried to bed Costa. Now Costa was unconscious, restrained in his bed back in sick bay.

Hopefully Dr. Bosch could help Costa. There had to be a way to manage both his addiction and his power. If anyone could find that way, it would be the doc. The man was brilliant. But did he have all the information he needed?

Priest pulled up his personal logs on the side monitor. It didn't take long to find the horde of files Arbor had sent him regarding Earth and its para-human history. Nothing had been deleted. Priest had reviewed the com multiple times while he tried to understand the mystery surrounding Costa McQuillen. Would these details be of use to the doctor? There was only one way to find out. One touch to the screen and everything was forwarded to Dr. Bosch's office. The minor effort made him feel a bit less useless, but not by much.

"Priest?" Micah's rough voice nearly startled Priest. He'd been so quiet for so long.

Taking a deep breath, he turned to his navigator. "Yeah?"

"I read the emergency logs. Is Arbor going to be all right?" Micah squirmed in his seat while his gaze rested anywhere but directly on Priest.

"I don't know."

"Are you okay?"

A long, weak exhale deflated Priest as he turned back to the black void, full of distant stars. "No. No, I'm not."

AFTER THE KITCHEN closed, Erron brought a meal up to the bridge, but Priest couldn't find his appetite. Erron squeezed his shoulder with his unsteady hand, eyes brimming with sympathy, and left the covered dish on the dashboard. An hour later, it sat untouched until he came back to retrieve the offering. Now, with Priest's shift at an end, the thought of food was still nothing more than a distant interest.

Without a coherent thought, Priest found himself standing in front of the sick bay doors. He hovered short of the entrance, the fear of what he might find an invisible ward against him. A jagged sensation kept his weight shifting between his feet, standing still proving impossible. The effort to touch the doors was exhausting.

He pressed his hand to the surface and the doors remained closed. Red text scrolled onto the black com panel next to the door.

No Admittance. Surgery in Progress.

It had been at least nine hours and they were still in surgery? An unseen hand squeezed Priest's heart in its relentless grip. He stumbled back against the wall and slid to the floor. The gasping shudders wracking his shoulders were only held in check by laying his head in his hands.

"PRIEST? HOW LONG have you been out here?"

Priest's head snapped up at Carson's voice. The nurse knelt over him, weary lines in his unshaven face. Angry muscles screamed their protest as Priest attempted to raise himself off the hallway floor. Somehow, in the aftermath of everything, he'd fallen asleep against his will.

"I don't know. I must have gone down a while ago." He wiped the spittle from the corner of his mouth with a clumsy hand. Nothing functioned as intended, the soreness and fatigue working their curses upon him.

Carson reached up and placed two fingers to Priest's neck before holding Priest's eye open with his thumb, peering into the depths. "You look like shit. Are you all right?"

Priest shrugged off Carson's hand, nearly slapping him away. "Fuck off! Stop touching me." The physical contact garnered an unaccustomed wave of revulsion. Carson and Priest had played together on a lonely night or two in the past, but the touch made him scuttle back along the wall out of reach.

"I'm only trying to examine you."

Priest's voice was rough. "I know!" He held up his hands to keep Carson at bay, even though he wasn't advancing. Priest knew he was only doing his job, but he had no wish for medical attention. The only contact he wanted now was hidden behind the medical screen deep inside sick bay.

"What is all the commotion?" Dr. Bosch strode through the infirmary entrance. "I have patients resting in here."

Rolling forward, Priest scrambled to stand, his twisted and disheveled shirt biting the soft skin under his arm. He fell hard to the floor once as he found his footing. A new rush of dread came over him as he tried to order the thoughts racing in his head.

The doctor took one look at Priest's rumpled appearance and frowned. The expression was harsher given his visible weariness. "Priest. Do you know what time it is?"

Priest gave a feeble shake of his head. He felt like a pitiful child past his bedtime. There was as much a chance he'd be scolded and sent to his room, given all the turmoil he was in the middle of, but he couldn't stand not knowing Arbor's fate. His mouth started and stopped, the seizure in his chest stalling his words. His eyes filled, making his vision waver. In the end, he could only bring himself to utter one word.

"Arbor?"

Dr. Bosch nodded. "He coded twice, but he's stable for now."

A violent rush of air burst free as Priest lurched forward and grasped the doctor in a crushing hug. Relief flooded him as he began laughing, only it sounded much more like wounded sobs to his ears. He held on tight, refusing to let go as Dr. Bosch recovered from the sudden gesture and returned the embrace.

"Oh, Priest. I had no idea." Dr. Bosch whispered at Priest's temple, the severity vanishing from his voice. He stroked Priest's head with a gentle hand. "I'm so sorry. If I'd known I would have commed you sooner."

On the edge of hysterics, Priest took a long time to bring himself under control. His bleary eyes stung and his face was streaked by a waterfall of tears. Once he could speak again without humiliating himself further, he pulled away from the doctor. Carson was still there as well, keeping politely quiet.

"Can I see him?" Priest wiped him eyes but the effort was futile.

Bosch shook his head. "Not yet. Believe me, it's for the best. It's not a pretty sight. You don't want to see him like this."

"What do you mean?"

"Arbor's stable but there's still a great deal of danger. I'm keeping him unconscious and in stasis while we regenerate the muscular and skeletal tissues that had to be removed. I saved his eye, but there might be residual effects to the left side of his vision I can't diagnose at this point. I can't risk any interference with the bio-field keeping his wounds sterile."

Hearing the description raised the bile in Priest's stomach. A shaky breath rattled into the air. "But he's going to be okay?"

"I think so. It's early yet, but he's responding well. You need to be patient another week. There was a lot of damage."

Arbor should live. The knowledge made Priest want to celebrate and weep. Not sure what to do, he took a step forward only to be caught by Dr. Bosch when his foot lacked the strength to hold him upright.

"Whoa! You're looking a little pale. Carson, help me set Priest down inside."

"I'll be okay." Priest tried to shake off the doctor and nurse to no avail as they ushered him into sick bay and sat him on an empty bed.

"I'm the doctor, thank you very much. When I start piloting the ship, I'll be sure to ask your advice. Carson, why don't you get some rest? I'll com you if I need you."

"You need some sleep, too, Doc."

"You can relieve me later. I'd like to talk to Priest privately."

Carson nodded. "I'll be back soon, Doc."

It didn't take the doctor long to note how dehydrated Priest was. Thinking back, he realized he hadn't eaten or drank anything since before the whole debacle in the engine room. Adding in the stress he was under, it was no surprise why he was so haggard.

While Dr. Bosch continued to gather a few additional medical tools, Priest looked around. Mac and Sheldon were no longer in sick bay. The medical privacy screen was still up around the first table and the thought of Arbor lying wounded behind it sent a chilled shudder through his bones. Costa lay unmoving in his bed, unconscious to the point of morbid.

"Is Costa okay?"

"He's riding a heavy dose of Calm right now. I'd rather not keep him sedated for the rest of the flight, but the story of what happened has already gotten around the ship and the crew is uncomfortable, to say the least. I can't monitor his condition in the brig, so I have to keep him here. I also wanted to thank you for the information you passed along. I think it will be a lot of help."

Priest winced as Dr. Bosch shined a light back and forth into his eyes one at a time. "Arbor found all of it. I just forwarded it."

"Clever man."

"Yeah, he is." He blinked rapidly to restore his vision as his gaze drifted back over to Costa. "Is keeping him doped up helping him?"

"I didn't have a choice. He woke earlier and I started asking him questions. Even with the truth compelling effects of the Calm, he gave me nothing. He didn't lie, but he evaded all the answers." Dr. Bosch activated a small device against Priest's shoulder. "This will add vitamins and fluids until you can get a proper meal in you."

"Costa's not exactly a sharing kind of guy. He doesn't trust doctors either. They've treated him pretty shitty in the past. I've been trying to get him up here to see you since his supply went low and he was having a hard time coping."

The doctor put away his medical tools. "He started to panic and the med-scanners malfunctioned. It looked like he was trying to override them. I activated the stasis field to keep him under control, but his abilities still reached out to commandeer the equipment. There are too many sensitive devices in here and I couldn't risk another outburst like in the engine room. Arbor's condition is too fragile. He didn't give me any choice but to sedate him."

"I can't blame you there."

"I need to know how bad his addiction is."

Knowing Costa's grip on his secrets, it felt like a breach of confidence, but Priest had to do what he could. Keeping this information hidden nearly killed them all. The proof was lying in bed, barely alive behind the privacy screen.

"It's pretty bad, Doc. It was working less and less each time and he was shaking really bad when he wasn't using for too long. He was getting lots of headaches and he'd lose control. The Calm let him get a grip on it."

"Calm is supposed to suppress his powers."

"He told me he was too strong for that to happen and the Calm made it manageable."

Dr. Bosch scratched his chin as he paced and pondered. "I don't have a lot of experience with Calm, but it's not supposed to cause this kind of dependence. But if he's using street level drugs, there's no way to determine how potent or how severe the side effects would be. I'm going to have to synthesize a cleaner version until we can manage his symptoms better."

The doctor paused, the circle he trod on the floor no longer important. Stepping over to the monitor closest to Priest, he called up a file showing a wavering image of what looked like the inside of a man's head. Another panel showed a waveform pattern. It shifted and fluctuated in a way that was almost difficult to look at.

"You were talking about his headaches. Do you know what this is?"

"No."

"It's a scan of Mr. McQuillen's brain. I was trying to understand how his powers work so I could treat him better."

Priest couldn't help but squint at the image. "Why is it out of focus?"

"That's what I was wondering. It wouldn't settle no matter what I did, and I've already verified the scanner is calibrated correctly. At first I thought it was just the unique qualities of how his mind deciphers and transmits data. But now I'm thinking it's something altogether different."

Priest turned to the doctor, who had yet to pry his attention away from the screen. "Like what?"

"I'd swear it looks like he's carrying a massive overload of data in his head."

Chapter Twelve

CAREFULLY...CAREFULLY...PRIEST guided the razor down his cheek. It was an unfamiliar task. Normally he kept a heavy five o'clock shadow rather than shave. He prayed he could finish without drawing blood—that would be awkward. An ultraviolet razor would have been more efficient, but the device would also keep the hair from growing back for weeks, and he couldn't commit to changing his look for so long.

He stood over the middle of the sink row, a towel cinched around his waist, freshly showered. The lather was cool by the time he was complete, but it was worth it. Priest couldn't remember the last time he'd looked so clean cut. Even his hair was groomed, tidy and neat. He leaned in close to the mirror to check for unexpected blemishes. Nothing worth noting could be seen.

Back in his quarters, he gathered his clothes, finding the nicest shirt and pants he owned. Newly pressed and laundered this morning, the matching vest made for a smart outfit. His boots were still scuffed, but it would have to do. He didn't own nice shoes. Hopefully, no one would notice. Once dressed, he fussed and smoothed his clothes multiple times, obsessed with his appearance in a way he'd never been before. Checking his hair one last time, he went out into the hall.

An anxious excitement had kept his appetite at bay since he woke. Stepping down the corridor, he gave polite nods and tried not to blush at the positive comments other crew members gave him about his appearance. Pulse racing, he paused outside the sick bay doors, encouraging himself to go inside.

The doors slid open to find Dr. Bosch examining Costa. Both men paused, taking more than a stunned second glance, adding to the nervous charge running down his spine. Dr. Bosch set down his scanner as Priest rocked on his heels, hoping they wouldn't look at his shoes.

"Is Arbor awake?" Priest felt like an adolescent asking a father's permission.

Dr. Bosch nodded with a pleasant smile. "He's been asking for you. He's still healing, so don't disturb the tech. He's still weak, so don't overexcite him." The doctor's eyes narrowed and he pointed a finger at Priest. "No funny business."

Priest's vision shook, he nodded so hard in agreement.

Chest tight, his eyes misted as he approached the privacy screen. It had been over a week of sleepless nights. How many times he had wished and prayed for this moment—and now that it was here, he could barely handle it. The walk across the room took ages, even though it was only a matter of meters. When he brushed his fingers along the edge of the screen, he stopped, took a ragged breath, and entered the enclosure.

As soon as he caught sight of Priest, Arbor gave him a weak smile. He barely took up half the bed, the sheets tucked up to his chest. Several pieces of medical tech were attached to his body: two small pieces to the side of his face and three larger items to his shoulder and chest.

He looked tired but well. Dr. Bosch had done an amazing job. The only oddity was from the crown of his head down his face and chest. A five-centimeter-wide line of skin was a different shade, fresher than the rest. Unblemished and new, the areas crossing his jaw and reaching above his hairline were free of stubble.

Priest's voice shook even with one small word. "Hi."

"Hi, yourself." Even as frail as he was, Arbor beamed.

"How are you feeling?"

"Better now that you're here."

A wave of relief battled the fear seizing his chest. "Really?"

"Yes, really."

Priest's shaky grin fought against a week's worth of uncertainty and dread. Even with Arbor's acceptance, doubt tainted his thoughts. He edged closer to the bed, his hand hovering over the newly healed areas, the skin having a sheen like a newborn's.

"Does it hurt?"

Arbor gave a minimal shrug. "Some, but not too bad. Bosch is taking good care of me. My vision's a little fuzzy on the left side, but he said that's to be expected."

"I would have been here more, but he told me not to."

Arbor reached over and twined his unsteady fingers with Priest's. "It's okay. He told me I was kind of a mess. I wasn't even conscious until this morning. No one would have wanted to see me."

"I wanted to." Priest fixated on Arbor's hand in his own, the warmth making his tenuous self-control ready to fracture. He told himself he would be strong.

"You're here now. That's good enough." Arbor's weary eyes still twinkled as they scanned over Priest. "You look really good. Did you dress up just for me?"

Priest flushed as he barked aloud, an equal mix of whimper and laugh. "Yeah. I did."

"I'm going to be okay, Priest."

"I know." Tears streaked down Priest's face against his best efforts. "But I was so scared. I haven't stopped seeing the whole thing in my head since it happened. I haven't stopped being scared you wouldn't make it. I don't know what I would have done."

"You'd have moved on."

Priest hissed as he choked down a sob. "I don't think so. I need you, Arbor. Please don't leave me."

"I promise, Priest. I won't." Arbor's eyes glossed as he shifted himself to one side and patted the bed. "Get up here."

Priest shook his head. "I don't want to hurt you."

"You won't."

With a quick scan to make sure no one was watching, Priest sniffled as he carefully climbed in alongside Arbor, making sure to stay above the covers. Arbor rolled closer and feathered a kiss onto Priest's lips. The touch was so sweet and affirming, it took all of Priest's will not to give in and make it something more than Arbor was ready for. Being sure not to disturb any of the medical devices, he wrapped himself around his man. Priest couldn't look into his eyes, so he buried his face into Arbor's shoulder.

Priest's words were whispers between staggered breaths. "I fucked up so much, and thought I had all the time in the world to make it up. I almost didn't get the chance."

Arbor pressed his lips above Priest's temple. "I made mistakes too. It's not all your fault."

Buried in the embrace, Priest broke down, endless days of despair spilling out over Arbor's chest and shoulder. And through it all, even with his feeble strength, Arbor held him tight and murmured along his head how everything would be all right. He continued until Priest began to believe it.

Sometime later, Priest calmed down, but refused to let go of Arbor. Now that he had him, Priest wasn't willing to give him up. He'd waited long enough for his touch. Nuzzling into Arbor, Priest felt something like himself again. There was a good chance his world would be so much better now.

Arbor's voice teased as he ran his fingers curled through Priest's hair. "Does this mean you love me?"

"Let's not go getting crazy now."

Both men burst out laughing. Priest snuggled closer, his head nestled against Arbor's chest. He traced lazy circles on Arbor's skin with his fingers as he whispered without raising his head. "I do, you know."

A soft kiss brushed the top of Priest's head. "I know. Me too."

Lost in bliss within a hospital bed, Priest's eyes drifted closed. The sound of Arbor's gentle breathing lulled him down into the first restful sleep in days.

A MILD TAPPING brought Priest out of his slumber.

"I hope I'm not interrupting." Danverse's knuckle posed on the frame of the privacy screen.

Arbor shook his head. "No, Captain."

Danverse rounded the screen, his once-proud shoulders lacking their usual power. Normally commanding, he approached with caution. Barely able to look Arbor in the eye, Danverse nodded to both men.

Priest shifted and wiped the sleep from his eyes. "How long have I been asleep?"

"A few hours. It's been really nice."

Those words made Danverse's presence unwelcome. These first moments of true peace he'd shared after all the chaos were interrupted. Was it too much to ask to lie quietly, curled up with the feel of Arbor in his arms? There had been enough animosity brewing amid the terror for the last week. Priest could do without the reminder of how Arbor ended up in sick bay in the first place.

"Bosch told me you were awake and I wanted to see how you were doing."

"I'm doing all right." Arbor squeezed Priest's hand and kissed his forehead. "Better than all right."

"I found this on my doorstep. I believe it belongs to you." In the captain's outstretched hand sat Mr. Wiggles, in no worse condition than when he first disappeared from Arbor's quarters. Danverse handed the sock monkey to Arbor, whose eyes came alive as the broad grin split his face.

Arbor pulled Mr. Wiggles close and inhaled deeply. "Thank you, Captain."

"I can't take any credit. Priest put out the ship-wide com days ago, telling the crew how you saved us all, and asking that your property be returned. All I did was bring him here. And Mac told me to give you this." Danverse pulled Arbor's private handheld from his pocket and passed it over. The screen was flawless and no one would know any damage had occurred. "It's all repaired and ready to go."

The return of Arbor's stuff was good and all, but Priest was still waiting for an apology. "It hardly makes up for what happened."

"Priest!"

Danverse held up his hand, a sad weariness evident in his eyes. "No, Arbor, Priest's right. I can't tell you how sorry I am. You saved us all and this is how I said thank you."

"It was an accident—"

"That never should have happened." Priest wanted Danverse to know, he hadn't forgiven. Not yet.

Arbor opened his mouth to speak, but Danverse, slumping his posture and ducking his head stopped him.

Even Priest was taken aback by the gesture. Danverse willingly submitted to no one.

"He's right." Danverse scrubbed his large hand through his tight, dirty-blond hair. "Mac could have died and it was happening in front of me and there wasn't anything I could do to save him. It made me a little psychotic. My boy's everything to me and I almost lost him. I'd do anything for him."

"He knows," Arbor said.

Danverse frowned, shaking his head. "But that doesn't make it right and doesn't excuse what happened."

"You're damn right it doesn't." Priest's temper simmered and seared.

Arbor placed a hand on Priest's chest. "Please, stop. I don't want to do this."

Rolling slightly, he faced Arbor, his brow twisted in disbelief. "You're not angry?"

"No. Believe it or not, I'm not."

"How can you not be?"

Arbor sighed as he stroked Priest's cheek. "It was a stupid accident. That's all. I've spent too much time taking everything that happens to me like a personal attack, and none of it had anything to do with me being a dwarf. I stopped Costa. I saved the ship. I got shot. Being little didn't matter. It didn't help or hinder me. I've always been oversensitive about being different and it's been ramped up to maximum since all the crap that landed me in prison as well as the stuff that happened there. It won't be easy, but I need to let it go. Almost dying kind of changes your perspective."

"Really?" The anger in his chest dissipated as Arbor searched deep into his eyes.

"Besides, if it were you on the floor dying, and I had the gun, I'd have done the same thing."

Priest's voice went soft and pleading. "You would? Over me?"

"Without a second thought."

No one had ever spoken to Priest before with such honesty and devotion. It intensified all the emotions swirling in his chest. The piercing brown of Arbor's eyes never looked so rich. Priest felt he could get lost in them with half a chance. His breathing hitched as he pulled Arbor closer. "You're amazing."

"I know."

Arbor closed the gap, sealing his mouth over Priest's. He hardened instantly as Arbor's tongue demanded entrance and slid along his own. Despite Arbor's eagerness, Priest forced himself to pull away. Arbor almost whined at the separation.

"When Bosch gives you the thumbs up, we're going to ruin a bed for a few days. I promise."

Arbor's eyes traced the line of Priest's mouth as he grinned. "You're damn right we will. And see? Being a dwarf didn't get me you either."

"No, it didn't. That was all you."

An awkward clearing of the captain's throat reminded them they weren't alone. As if Danverse hadn't been chastised enough when he arrived, now he looked downright uncomfortable. Making a deliberate act to stand tall, he schooled his features into some semblance of dignity.

"I can't thank you enough for saving Mac, Arbor. Whatever you need, just let me know."

Priest grinned with a sly inspiration. "You could give him a raise."

The captain paused, a blank stare erasing his expression. "I suppose that could be arranged."

A sudden tension could be felt through Arbor's hands as a thready gasp escaped. However, he didn't say a word.

"And a hazard pay bonus." Priest tried not to smile too broadly. If Arbor could forgive Danverse, he could do the same, but it would cost. Big. It wasn't often anyone had one over on the captain. He couldn't pass up the easy opportunity.

Danverse's brow flattened and he grumbled. "I'm starting to approve of you two together less and less."

A conspiratorial chuckle escaped from Arbor. "I think it's a little late for that now, Captain."

EVENTUALLY, DR. BOSCH made Priest go back to his quarters. The sick bay was not a hotel, and Arbor needed real rest. Enough visitors had come through for one day. Despite his protests, Dr. Bosch ordered Priest out and prescribed him a proper meal. It was the first time in days he'd found himself wanting to eat.

His next work shift was a dual task of maintaining the flight path and watching the clock. Priest was heading back to sick bay at his earliest opportunity.

After the fastest shower in *Santa Claus* history, Priest dressed and hurried to the infirmary.

The privacy screen was gone, making Arbor part of the room. Hopefully, it meant he'd be well enough to come back to the real world soon. Arbor smiled wide as Priest caught his eye. Bosch administered an injection to Costa, who reclined casually in bed, causing him to flush and exhale. Priest walked by the scene and greeted Arbor.

"You look good." It was true. The weariness around Arbor's eyes was reduced and he looked even healthier than yesterday.

Arbor grinned, locking his gaze on Priest. "I had a really good night's sleep."

"I'd bring you some hooch to celebrate, but Bosch would kill me."

Dr. Bosch chided as he walked past to his office. "No, I wouldn't. Paralyzing your spinal column would be more entertaining."

Cupping Arbor's cheek in his hand, Priest place a chaste kiss to his lips. Soon, Arbor would be home. He could wait a little longer for something more. Until then, he would be content with stolen morsels like these. So caught up in Arbor's smile, he didn't notice the soft footsteps closing in on them.

Costa stood at the foot of the bed, his head bowed. "I really am sorry for all of this madness and what happened to you, Mr. Kittering. My intention was to just travel along quietly and be on my way."

Arbor gave Costa a polite gesture of thanks. "I appreciate it."

"I'll only be on board a short time more. After that, I will no longer be a concern to you."

"I'm sorry I haven't visited you sooner." Given the severity of Arbor's injuries, Priest hadn't come to sick bay until Bosch told him Arbor was awake. In the process, he'd neglected the man at the center of the crisis. In part, Priest wasn't sure he could face him.

Costa's smile was sad as his gaze flickered to their joined hands. "You had a good reason."

"How are you feeling, Costa?"

Costa nodded but the elegance of his movement was blunted and his eyes were somewhat lidded. "Much better, thank you. Dr. Bosch has formulated a clean version of Calm and it's working far better for me, with far fewer side effects."

"You still look high."

"I require a strong dosage."

It didn't take long to realize Dr. Bosch had administered Costa's dose of Calm when he first walked in. From what he'd read, even the clean version used by the Earth Government caused para-humans to be truthful and compliant. Costa was being more forthcoming than usual. Perhaps the drug was working as intended.

"Can I ask you something?"

"Of course."

"Why did you latch on to me?"

Costa's brow furrowed and he looked away. "I thought I might need some assistance. I'm not familiar with the cluster and you seemed worldly enough, in spite of what I saw as your shortcomings. You were attracted to me, and I knew I could use that."

"You could have just asked. I would have helped."

"I was born on a world that imprisoned my kind for being something less than human. I'm not accustomed to trusting people. By the time I realized you might actually be a decent person, I'd gone too far." Costa continued to look between Priest and Arbor, his expression filled with longing. Was that regret?

Priest decided not to continue this line of questioning. Reminding Arbor of his indiscretions with Costa might not be a good idea.

The week of waiting to hear word of Arbor's recovery was hell, but left Priest with inordinate amounts of time to fathom his thoughts. So much had happened, and he was in part responsible. He needed to catalog the chain of events to keep him sane. It wasn't enough to simply cover the details of the engine room fiasco and what happened to Arbor. He also scoured over everyone else's part in how they arrived at this point.

A great many pieces were missing in those events and only one person could complete the timeline. It would be a matter of asking the right questions. Costa was clearly under the influence and it made Priest feel like shit to use his weakness, but all the introspection in the cluster wouldn't give him the answers he wanted. It was Costa's nature to withhold information and keep secrets. Without the Calm, he'd get nothing. He would have to make use of the chance before it disappeared.

"I've been thinking a lot about the night we met."

Costa snorted and grinned. "I would rather not remember my time spent being assaulted by security and ending up in jail."

"You told me about your plans in Omoikane."

The grin on Costa's face evaporated. "I suppose I did."

Priest released Arbor's hand and took a step closer to Costa. Placing a hand on his shoulder, he wasn't so surprised when Costa at first tensed, then relaxed into the touch. Using as soothing and nonconfrontational a tone as he could muster, Priest continued.

"Bosch says your brain scan is overloaded with data."

"Like most doctors, he's very thorough." Costa stiffened under Priest's hand. His fear of physicians was still valid, regardless of Dr. Bosch's good care. The medical information could be held off for now. They could get back to that. It was time to take another avenue.

"When everything went to hell in the engine room, you begged me to save Poll. He's your twin brother, right?"

Creases formed around Costa's eyes and his mouth tightened. "Yes."

"Poll's dead. Isn't he, Costa?"

"Yes." Costa wrapped his slender arms around himself.

"Your last name is Gilliard. Isn't it?"

"Yes."

"You're supposed to be dead too. Aren't you?"

Costa paused. "Yes." He dipped his head, making his long hair fall forward, partially hiding his face.

"Why did you meet with Swaden in the parking garage?"

"He told me that he had found a way to organize a meeting between Poll and me. It was illegal for us to meet, given our positions, but it had been so long since we'd laid eyes on one another I was willing to believe him."

"What happened?"

"He lied." A snarl formed and the familiar scathing tone returned. "The sodding bastard had no intention of ever bringing us together, and I was livid. I made a few pedophile comments about him I probably should've kept to myself. He didn't appreciate my link to Poll and wanted it broken. So he severed it."

"How did you survive?"

Costa's fingers dug into his skin as a haunted pall washed over his face. "I didn't."

"I don't understand."

Taking a shaky breath, Costa pulled away and turned his back on them. Priest worried he'd pushed too far and Costa would stop talking. There was so much more he needed to know.

With a haggard inhale, Costa wiped at his eyes. "I woke up in the crematorium in Quarantine. The smell and smoke of burning meat stained the walls. You never really forget the place once you've been there. Karesh, the para-human working the furnace, thought I was pretty and resurrected me." A mirthless laugh issued forth. "How bloody ironic that the world's most powerful healer was put to work in an abattoir. I would be willing to bet they didn't want him helping anyone. When he brought me back, he altered my DNA enough to remove me from the world systems. I helped him forge my incineration documentation and I disappeared."

"He changed the ID tattoos too."

"He couldn't erase them, but turned them into something more interesting." Costa caressed the colorful designs across his right cheek.

"What happened then?"

Costa took an achingly slow breath and released it in equal fashion. "The world imploded."

"The para-human revolt?" Arbor asked.

Costa nodded. "Karesh hid me for a time but was killed during the skirmish when an automated drone tracked him down. He had no ability to heal himself. My DNA ID was no longer on file, so the system didn't recognize me. I was spared."

"What did you do when it ended?"

"I continued to hide and tried to find Poll." Costa's voice faltered. "You have no idea how defeating it was to find he was already dead. It was like I had failed him. When I discovered that he was responsible for the revolt, killing himself in the process, I was shocked. I never believed he had that kind of rage in him. He was always such a gentle soul. It's why I tried to place us somewhere safe from the very beginning."

The puzzle piece formed in Priest's head. "He found out Swaden had killed you."

A grim smile came over Costa. "Yes, and I'm strangely flattered by that."

"There's no mention of what happened afterward. You were off the grid and free."

"That was its own punishment, I suppose. You simply can't be an illegal in a fascist world like Earth. I had no choice but to hide for my life. I fabricated a new ID for myself, but humans couldn't be trusted anymore. They wiped us all out."

"The revolt happened a long time ago. Why didn't you migrate sooner?"

"I found something I wasn't expecting and it compelled me to stay."

"Like what?" Arbor had been listening so quietly and intently, Priest almost forgot he was in the room.

A wistful smile graced Costa's face. "Poll."

Priest could tell he was on to something important here, but he had no idea what it was. He needed more. Guiding Costa into an honest answer would require careful phrasing. He didn't want him dodging his question like he did with the doctor.

"But Poll was dead. You found his body?"

"No, that was disposed of long before I knew what happened."

"I don't understand. What did you find?"

"I found an echo of his consciousness on the Link."

Arbor sounded awed and confused. "How is that possible?"

"Poll reached out across the entire planet at once." The pride in Costa's voice couldn't be fabricated. "He took control of the entire system of para-human enslavement in every country and dismantled it all like a bloody house of cards. I never would have believed him capable of such a feat. Such a thing was unheard of. It left an indelible imprint on the Link that was uniquely his."

This was the missing piece keeping Priest up at night. The sliver of information that made everything make sense. All of the secrecy, all of the intrigue distilled into one fact.

"The extra data in your head. You collected him."

"I couldn't risk doing it all at once and lose myself the way Poll did. It took nine years, but I sifted through the Link and collected every whisper, every shade, every fragment of who he was I could find."

Arbor's voice peaked in shock. "He's in your head?"

"There's two of us in here now. It's crowded and sometimes very painful." Costa absentmindedly rubbed his temple.

"That's insane. How can you do that?"

"Karesh made me stronger when he brought me back, but even I can't do this forever." Costa's brow creased. "It's taken far too long. Every day I can't get to Omoikane, the more I lose. His data is starting to degrade and his memories will become rubbish. After all the hell we've survived, I may end up losing him before I can save him."

Priest tried to keep calm. "That's why you're dosing so hard. Can you talk to him?"

"I wish I could." A mistiness crept into Costa's lidded eyes. "Poll was the foil for all my hard edges. Waking up to find him gone after all we had been through was like the worst kind of nightmare. I have him, but he's not real yet. His data is so compressed it isn't even a real mind right now. It needs a vessel."

Priest's whisper was a revelation. "The android."

"The what?" Arbor asked.

"I've gone over everything I can think of, but I just remembered. When we first met and talked in the bar, you mentioned Omoikane had the most advanced android ever made with an intellect capacity rivaling a human being."

Costa's brow quirked in surprise. "You actually remember that?"

"I've had a lot of time to think recently." Priest reached over and grasped Arbor's hand. He wanted to make sure there were no misunderstandings. "About a lot of things."

Arbor smiled and squeezed Priest's hand in return. The world was good. Nothing would make him happier than to steal Arbor away and lounge together in private, but the conversation wasn't finished. While still holding Arbor's hand, Priest focused his complete attention on Costa.

"You were going to steal the android."

Costa looked up at Priest, his eyes wide and lost. "It's my only chance."

Chapter Thirteen

MAC GATHERED UP a few of the jockstraps Danverse insisted he wear and packed them in his bag. He looked over and found the captain stuffing a pair of leather manacles into his own luggage. A heated shiver rushed through his limbs, radiating from his groin. This was going to be a fun leave. Packing their bags would usually have been done before they landed, but they had plenty of time to spare for a change.

"Why are we staying on Omoikane for ten days? We don't need that kind of time to be ready for the next shipment."

Danverse shrugged. "I thought it would be a nice break for the crew."

Double checking he had all his incidentals, Mac buckled his duffel. He tested the weight on his shoulder. It was full but manageable.

"Well, yeah, but we've never been on shore leave for so long. We're not exactly in a tourist area, either. I checked the local guides. There's not a whole lot to do around here."

"If we need to launch sooner than expected, I can pull everyone back. They won't go too far."

Mac paused. Even though he'd never been witness to it, the only protocol for ending shore leave early was in an emergency. All crew members had an alarm built into their personal coms for such an occasion. Mac had never seen it implemented, but why would it be on the captain's mind?

Questions in Mac's head always demanded answers. It was the nature of his overactive thinking. He analyzed everything to the point of burying himself. The only things out of the ordinary on this trip were the incident with Costa McQuillen, Arbor's accident, and the captain's retreat from the crew.

Since the mess in the engine room, Danverse spent most of his free time in seclusion with Mac, the shame in wounding Arbor having cut him deep. The captain brushed off the implication when Mac confronted him, but he knew his man well enough to know when he was lying. He even lied when Mac found him watching a restricted feed of McQuillen, Arbor, and Priest talking in sick bay during Arbor's recovery—plotting.

"Does this have anything to do with that restricted security vid from sick bay?"

The captain continued to pack without looking up. "I didn't say that."

Mac dropped his bag to the floor and circled over to Danverse. "Holy shit. They're really going to do it."

"We don't know that. I'm just giving the crew enough time to do whatever they need to do."

"I read McQuillen's medical report Bosch sent you. Can he still pull this off?"

"You shouldn't have been reading over my shoulder."

Mac felt guilty. He wasn't sure what he was seeing when he looked, but once he did, it was too late to unsee. Passenger and crew confidentiality was something he tried to be mindful of, given how small their community was. Everyone knew a little too much about each other as it was on the *Santa Claus*.

"Marc, this isn't small. This is serious. What do we do if this all goes tits up?"

"Pray that it doesn't." Danverse placed the last item in his bag and fastened it. "Mrs. Claus, delete all forms of data, security, and otherwise linked to passenger Costa McQuillen. Captain's privilege."

"Do you wish to include restricted feeds in this initialization, Captain Danverse?"

Mac froze. Deleting files and documentation was highly illegal in the face of a government security audit. If the group's escapade blew up, it could be traced back to the ship, and Mac didn't want to think what would happen then. If the captain was willing to go to this extent, he must have some kind of premonition on how this might end. The thought alone left him cold.

Danverse took a deep breath and answered. "Yes, Mrs. Claus. Costa McQuillen was never on board. Authorization code Omega-376-Gamma."

"ARE YOU SURE it's him?"

Costa sighed. He hated repeating himself. "Yes, Priest. He's the only employee in that part of the lab whose personnel file marks him as non-hetero and single."

Priest dipped the grilled meat strip into the sauce on the left—it was the only one making the dish edible. If he weren't keeping his eye on the man eating across the dining room, he wouldn't touch this poor excuse for bar food. The sloppy man munched alone on a plate of pasta, sauce stains gone unnoticed on his poor fitting shirt buttoned up to his throat. His hair was wild with unkempt dark curls. Patches of unshaven growth did nothing to enhance his rounded, ruddy face.

"He looks like a scientist."

"That would be because he *is* a scientist. There are times when people live out their own stereotypes, even in this age. So which one of us do you think he'll respond to?"

"I'm not sure yet. I'll let you know when he goes to the bathroom."

Costa sat close to give the impression the two of them were together. They spent a great deal of time having a drink at the bar to burn time until the nerdy guy arrived. Now they were having a quiet dinner of dubious food in this cheap restaurant, simply waiting. At least Costa managed to not balk at the quality of the cuisine.

"How were you so sure you could lure him here?"

Priest took a swig of his ale—the only palatable item he'd found so far. "Arbor went through his personal data accounts. He's signed up for a bunch of restaurants' promotional programs, including this one. With the number of places he's signed up for, he's a cheap ass looking for a deal. I had Arbor com him a forged gift certificate for a free meal that expires tonight."

"You really do surprise me sometimes. You can be quite devious when you put your mind to it."

"I've run a scam or two in my time."

"Do they usually succeed?"

"Sometimes. If they're well planned out."

"I wouldn't have expected you being capable of such subterfuge."

Priest shrugged. "I guess I'm not as stupid as you say I look." Costa averted his eyes. "It's okay. You're not the first person to say it. Stop looking so down. We're supposed to look like we're on a date."

"I can imagine Arbor isn't overly thrilled by this charade. It is a charade, isn't it?" Costa's brow arched as he placed his hand on Priest's forearm.

Not wanting to break the facade of a happy couple, Priest didn't move his arm as he leaned forward to whisper in Costa's ear. "Believe it or not, it is a charade."

Shifting back in his seat, Priest took another bite of his heavily sauced meat stick, trying not to grimace. Costa's shoulders shifted subtly and his smile leveled a small amount. He looked somehow...disappointed?

Even if it were the case, he would simply have to deal with it. Once upon a time, Priest imagined what fun could be had with Costa and Arbor in the same bed together, and he'd be lying if the idea didn't flash through his thoughts from time to time. But now, it wasn't the goal. Sex with Costa came with a price. It would cost him Arbor. The risk wasn't worth it anymore.

"Tell me, Priest, and I don't mean to be rude, but what exactly do you see in that little man?"

The scientist was working through a second helping of his all-you-can-eat meat basket. Maybe they shouldn't have given the guy the best deal this place had to offer, but they needed the enticement. This would take longer than Priest wanted, but they had no choice.

"You don't really want to hear this."

Costa rubbed his temple, signaling the start of a headache. The circles under his eyes, as well as his facial tattoos, were barely hidden by cosmetics. "I must be completely mental for saying so, but yes, yes I do."

"Arbor's smart as hell, but he's never looked down at me. He treats me like a treasure. He makes me feel special. Even when we argue, we're waiting to make up. And when he almost died, it was like someone up there was telling me I didn't deserve him. I make a lot of mistakes and say the wrong thing when I don't think. I need to do better by him. So now all I want to do is spend my time making him feel as special as he makes me."

"But here you are with me right now."

"Don't be a bitch. This isn't a real date, Costa. You know that. That part of you and me is over. I'm helping my friend, because he needs it and because I feel like part of all of this is my fault. I don't walk out on my people just because some shit went down between us."

The aristocratic stiffness in Costa's frame disarmed itself as a ghost of a pleasant smile graced his lips. He settled back in his chair and regarded Priest, vaguely awestruck. Could that be possible? It seemed unlikely, but here they were.

"I think for the very first time, I'm actually finding myself somewhat jealous of the little sod." Costa's eyes narrowed a touch as he leaned forward. "If you tell him I said anything of the sort, I'll deny it even as I beat you to death in front of your entire crew."

"It wouldn't be the first time someone's beat my ass in front of them."

They waited patiently as the scientist sucked down a third complimentary drink. Priest chose a table in line to the restroom for a reason. It would all be a waste if the guy didn't wash up after his meal.

Their food was almost cold when the scientist swiped the panel embedded in the table to signal the end of his meal, stood, and walked toward the restroom. The cheap little shit didn't even tip the server. Priest gave Costa a quiet signal and both men glanced at the guy as he walked past. As he entered the restroom, the scientist's gaze roamed over Priest and barely acknowledged Costa.

"It would appear the next act of this play is in your hands." Costa didn't appear pleased. Being dismissed didn't sit well with him.

Priest snickered as he stood and brushed off his hands. "I guess he's not into twinks. Don't wait too long."

With a strengthening inhale, Priest entered the washroom. Thankfully, no one else was inside, making everything much easier. He rounded the stalls and found the scientist at one of the pair of urinals. He stiffened in surprise when Priest took the spot next to him. Unzipping his pants, Priest made sure the guy got a good look, gave him a polite nod, and relieved himself. The ale he had earlier helped.

"How you doing?" Priest looked the guy over.

"I'm okay." The guy kept taking surreptitious glances in Priest's direction and didn't seem to be in a hurry to leave when he finished.

Priest made a show of shaking off and hefting himself back into his pants when he finished. The scientist was skittish and mesmerized. The pair washed their hands, taking their time as Priest made a point to stand just a tad too close. The scientist was beginning to breathe harder, and it wasn't from fear.

When the guy turned—perhaps to leave—Priest made a point to press against him, molding his torso against the man who looked starved for attention. The scientist froze, unwilling to leave, as he locked his eyes on Priest. Brushing the back of his knuckles over the guy's chest, Priest felt the nipple harden under his shirt.

This guy was overheating fast, and Priest felt like a shit for doing this to him. Arbor didn't like this part of the plan either, but mugging the guy was out of the question. Violence was not Priest's method and would only stir up trouble with the authorities. He hoped Costa wouldn't wait too long.

Priest aligned his larger body over the guy, causing a needy gasp to fill the empty restroom. Tremors filled the scientist as Priest began running his hands over the man's torso and arms. The telltale erection poking him in the hip couldn't be missed.

"What the fuck are you doing, Spaniard?" Costa shouted as he burst into the restroom.

Priest jumped back and put up his hands. "We weren't doing nothing, baby."

Costa rushed forward and slapped Priest—hard. The scientist squirmed to get past, but Costa blocked his path and pressed himself close. "And just where do you think you're going, you fucking tart?"

The scientist was trembling so hard, he wasn't aware of Costa's hands zipping through his pockets.

"Leave him alone, baby." Priest laid his hand on Costa's shoulder as if to restrain him.

Costa slapped his hand away. "Don't you, *baby* me, you slag. How many times do I have to find you with your cock in some low life twat?" Snarling, Costa gave the scientist a small shove. "I don't know who you think you are, but if I ever find you near him again, I'll remove your bollocks."

Grabbing Priest by the collar, Costa directed them out of the restroom. Without missing a step, they gathered up, the scientist not looking at either of them as he made a hasty exit.

"I didn't tell you to slap me." Priest hoped the burn on his cheek wasn't bright red. If Costa never slapped him again it would be too soon.

"I improvised to add a moment of authenticity to my performance."

Priest helped Costa put on his jacket. "It felt very authentic. You're better at this than I would have expected."

"You're not the only one who's been forced to do what's necessary to survive."

"Did you get it?"

Costa leaned into Priest, making an appropriate show of his hand in his pocket. "Of course I did."

Priest placed his hand at the small of Costa's back and led him toward the door. "Then let's get out of here."

THE VEHICLE PARK was well lit, but Arbor was still apprehensive. He was well healed, but anxiety left an odd tension in a line down his face and chest. He'd been cleared for duty, but it would be some time before he felt what passed for normal once again.

Thankfully the vehicle only used handheld controls to drive, because his feet wouldn't reach the floor and having the modifications added to the rental would have drawn too much attention. Costa had forged the identification—he was very skilled—so the craft should be untraceable in the end. Even so, the seat was pushed as far forward as it could be to accommodate him. It was annoying but manageable.

The capital city of Omoikane was filled with buildings more industrial than beautiful in an artistic sense, but they had a charm for their functionality. Everything was sleek and tall with a floor plan like a circuit grid. In one of Costa's rare moments of excitement, he told them the streets were composed of a honeycomb of durable, programmable panels, allowing the pavement to be rewritten as necessary with high visibility lines and directionals.

What he wouldn't give for a closer look, but the impending excursion ruined the sightseeing. Waiting the last two hours was excruciating and nerve-racking. If he found out Priest and Costa were sitting in the restaurant having a good time while he was stuck out here, he'd kill them both.

Arbor knew Priest chose him over the beautiful para-human. He knew it. But some doubts were harder to quash than others. Why else would he have offered his help?

A chime emitted from his handheld sitting in the passenger seat. It was time to pick up the boys. He wished he could have gone in with them, but they needed to be less obvious. Priest protested when Arbor pointed out how a dwarf stands out in a crowd and they didn't need everyone's eyes on them. It made him feel good that Priest wanted to keep him close, but a small amount of anonymity was necessary.

The craft started and Arbor guided it with a smooth glide to the lot next to the restaurant where Priest and Costa waited, looking as nonchalant as possible. It looked like they were on a date. Arbor hated it. He set the transport down and Costa immediately disengaged and jumped into the back.

Arbor shifted over to the passenger side, as Priest grunted trying to get into the driver's seat. Keeping his mouth tight to contain the impending laughter, Arbor watched him adjust the seat and climb in.

The door slid shut and Priest leaned over and placed an affirming kiss on his lips. "How are you feeling?"

The feel of Priest's hand stroking the back of his head washed out the jealousy and made Arbor almost giggle. "Fine. Bosch gave me a clean bill of health over a week ago. Stop fussing."

A loving smirk curled Priest's lips. "I can't help it."

With a few effortless touches of Priest's hands, the rented craft rose from the street level and shifted into traffic.

Arbor looked at Costa over his shoulder. "You snatched the ID pieces you need?"

Costa examined the scientist's stolen security card in his fingers bearing the logo of Forethought Industries. "Once I've read his key, I can fool the palm scanner into reading his DNA ID that's encoded on it."

"How can you remember that kind of complex information?"

"A photographic memory is a byproduct of my abilities. The skill has saved me on more than one occasion."

City lights played their games inside and out of the vehicle, casting their garish marks in patterned lines and twisting the shadows into something alive. If their itinerary wasn't so serious, they might have been able to enjoy the spectacle.

"We can get into the lab, but how are we going to keep from being spotted by security systems?" Priest caught Costa's eye using the mirror. "The setup in that place is no joke."

"I have that covered." Arbor raised his handheld pad. "I'm using Swaden's trick to make the systems ignore us once we're inside. It's a kind of digital camouflage. It should keep from drawing any attention to us better than directly hacking sensitive software." Arbor noticed the narrowed eyes Costa directed at him. "Sorry. Swaden may have been a totally deranged Nazi, but he was fucking brilliant. Normally I wouldn't stoop to his tactics, but we need it."

"You used his information and tactics to incapacitate me in the engine room quickly enough. Although I have to admit, it was very clever and underhanded."

"You didn't exactly leave me with much choice."

Costa nodded and shrugged in some silent form of acceptance. "After everything that's happened, I have to admit I'm surprised you're willing to assist me, Arbor."

"Yeah, well, I've spent a lot of time bitching about my crappy life, but yours was way worse than mine could ever be. You've done some shitty things, but once you spilled your guts I knew your motives were honest. I can forgive some things."

"And the fact that once this is done, I'll be off the ship and away from Priest wouldn't be influencing your decision at all?"

Arbor grinned. "That's a bonus."

Costa leaned forward and gave Priest a rough poke in the shoulder. "And with regards to what you refer to so colorfully as *spilling of my guts*. I'm not particularly thrilled that you interrogated me while under the influence."

"Please. You evaded all of Bosch's questions when he tried. You were begging to confess and needed an excuse. Suck it up."

Wrapping his arms around his chest, Costa pouted and slumped back in his seat. Even the shadows moving about the car in the night couldn't hide the severity of the lines in Costa's face. Was he unhappy, or was the stress of his burden taking more of a toll than he was letting on? Could it be both?

WHENEVER PRIEST IMAGINED being involved in a deal of this scale, he thought it would be a grand affair. It would be daring and exciting, and the payoff would be so sweet.

Unnerved and guilty were the emotions plaguing him now.

Acquiring the key card worked exactly as expected—too well in fact. Once upon a time, hitting on the scientist to gain something wouldn't have fazed him. It would have been fun. But now all he felt was dirty.

Before he found himself on the *Santa Claus*, money became thin when the military downsized after the Civil War. Work was in short supply, with an influx of unemployed soldiers. Priest was forced to do a few unsavory things to afford food and the cheap accommodations he could manage. Sometimes it didn't work out, but that was the challenge and the rush.

Everything was so different now he'd found Arbor. The risk in this paled in comparison to how he felt when they were together. The excitement that used to charge the color in his world from such antics was now a dull gray. When this was all over, he was washing his hands of all of it. No more scams and schemes. He would even get rid of the Luxorian deck of cards.

Well, maybe not the deck of cards. They were worth a lot of currency—but the rest of it...for Arbor, yes.

Standing outside of the Forethought Industries building, he checked the time to make sure the night shift was in place. This site was closer to the city than he would like. Why had Costa insisted this business was the only one? Arbor's research found three companies in the vicinity with similar android manufacture in progress, one of which was on the outskirts of everything. It was a much better target, but Costa required this particular laboratory. The risk was higher. If he hadn't promised to help, Priest would walk away.

Costa talked a good game, but Priest could see the edge in his movements. The clean dosages of Calm Dr. Bosch gave him were doing a better job of keeping him under control, but there was no way Costa was cured. Nothing would make him happier than not having Arbor involved, but it became clear Costa wouldn't be able to camouflage them and finish his task at the same time.

The sooner this was over, the better off they would all be. Costa would move on, and he and Arbor could figure out where they were going.

He walked up to the front door and rapped on the glass until the lone guard left his station and opened the door.

"Is there something I can help you with?" The heavy-set man looked suspicious as he laid eyes on Priest.

"I hope so, man. I'm so fucking lost."

Priest pulled out the holo map he'd picked up from the station when they landed and activated it. The grid of the city expanded out, covering way more than it should, blocking the guard's view.

"I know these things are supposed to be user-friendly"—Priest spun the map, the graphics a dizzying display—"but I can't even figure out where I am on this thing."

"Sir, I can't see—"

"I know! See what I mean?"

Talking fast and frantic, Priest barely allowed the guard a chance to speak, let alone think. Three-dimensional versions of streets and avenues filled his vision, swirling at Priest's slightest movement. It was enough to cause motion sickness in the strongest stomach.

From the corner of his eye, Priest watched Costa and Arbor override the lock on the side lobby door and sneak inside. He didn't have to watch to know what would happen next. Arbor would go to the security guard's terminal and hack the security feeds to go into an endless loop and show nothing going on, while his camouflage program kept the pair of them invisible from any scan.

It was a mite frightening how quickly Arbor did his part before he and Costa headed down the hallway behind the guard station. His man was a little too good at his task. As quick as it began, they disappeared from sight.

"Oh wait! I feel so stupid. I get it now." Slapping his forehead with the butt of his hand, Priest collapsed the hologram and threw it into his backpack, and shook the guard's hand. "Sorry to bug you. Thanks for your help!"

The guard snorted, looking baffled and a bit stunned. "I don't know what I did, but you're welcome. Have a good night."

Waving to the guard, Priest went around the block, only to double back to a poorly lit rear entrance. The door slid open on cue, Costa and Arbor on the other side.

A flash of anxiety lit up Priest's chest. "Lab's on the top floor. Let's do this."

Chapter Fourteen

"YOU'RE SURE THEY won't notice the lab being opened?" Priest peeked down the small corridor. A single set of dual doors were the only items of interest existing on the top floor. Heavy and reinforced, they were far beyond what one would think would be necessary on a nonmilitary installation.

Arbor nervously scanned his personal pad. "No. Everything is blind at the station right now. We're clear. Can we get moving?"

"Unless you can recall the DNA ID off this man's card, this would be much easier with quiet." Costa sounded as impatient as Arbor.

Inserting the stolen key in the slot, the palm pad brightened. Priest and Arbor both held their breaths as Costa placed his hand on the panel. The status screen fluctuated as his brow creased. Priest crossed his fingers. The plan required Costa to manipulate the tech without alerting the system. It didn't appear he was having an easy time of it.

"Access granted."

Costa's hands trembled as he released his breath and stepped back. The massive doors hissed open, breaking an airtight seal. Everyone exchanged glances as they inhaled and entered the darkened lab.

As the main doors closed, a series of light panels spontaneously charged to life. Banks of monitors booted up, and various manufacturing devices hummed in startup. The glow from a miniature reactor caught Priest's attention from behind a thick Plexiglas safety door. What could the lab be doing where they required their own power source?

A row of workstations lined one side of the lab, containing the kind of tech Mac would wet himself over if he could get this close. Stacks of equipment and inventory formed hallways in the vast open space. The whole floor seemed dedicated to the laboratory. One of the workstations connected to the wall where an assembly line could be seen. There was something about this specific tech drawing everyone's attention.

Above the keyboard and control panels, an expansive monitor held a schematic of what looked like the internal structure of a human body. Overlapping layers of random biological systems were highlighted in various colors for definition. In a side window, a pointer segregated the head on the body diagram. The callout held the specifications for a small circular device to be implanted at the base of the skull. The tag read, Pacifier Implant.

Arbor stepped close to the monitor, fixated on the display. "Why does this tech look so familiar?" After a long pause, he spun towards Costa. "Who owns Forethought Industries?"

Costa's voice was cold and edged with venom. "A man by the name of Arthur Swaden, formerly of Earth."

Arbor's voice flattened. "Swaden. As in Anthony Swaden, architect of para-human containment?"

"His brother."

"You knew this?" Priest couldn't believe what he was hearing.

"I did a great deal of research before placing Poll with Swaden. His brother, Arthur, migrated to the cluster after he couldn't compete with Anthony's success. It appears he stole copies of his brother's designs to start his own version of the family business."

This didn't make any sense to Priest. "But the cluster doesn't have a para-human problem."

Arbor answered, saving Costa the explanation. "But if they decide they have one, Swaden is already in position to corner the market."

A collective silence came over the trio as Costa stood tall, his regal posture humming with anger. "History always finds a curious way to repeat itself."

Resisting the urge to scream, Priest raked his hand over his face. Costa's agenda was bigger than he imagined when he signed on. Arbor stood frozen, his eyes wide and mouth agape, shock and disbelief etching their way across his face.

Priest was outraged. "Why didn't you tell us about this when we asked you what was going on in sick bay?"

"I suppose while you fished information from me while I was compelled to answer you, you neglected to ask the right questions." The haughty veneer Costa was famous for was back in abundance. All Priest wanted to do was smack it off his face as he stalked forward, crowding Costa.

"You were afraid we wouldn't agree if we knew."

"Other than an amount of extra knowledge, nothing has actually changed. You've come this far, you may as well see it through to the end."

A quiet panic laced Arbor's voice. "What do you mean *to the end*?"

"We're going to destroy this facility. Everything I've learned points to all copies of the data and blueprints being here in this building. We're going to finish what Poll started and ensure that what happened on Earth does not happen here as well."

Priest didn't even try to disguise his contempt. "No, Costa. You can't expect us to follow through on that."

Costa howled in return. "Oh, I see. *Now* you find your moral compass. Where was that conveniently located when my people were being slaughtered?"

"That's not fair! I've only read about what happened on Earth. I grew up in the cluster."

Costa snarled and poked Priest in the chest. "This bastard and his family enslaved and murdered tens of thousands of people because it was easier than living alongside them. Swaden will prepare his equipment and, when the time is right, he'll sell these ghastly inventions to the World Governments. How can you sit back and do nothing when you can stop the horror from happening again?"

Priest slapped Costa's hand away. "If you'd been honest with us from the start, I'd be on board. But you weren't. I don't know what you've been through, not really. I'm fine with helping you with Poll, but this is too much to ask." Incensed, Priest walked in circles. In the back of his mind, he'd known there was some additional agenda for Costa, but he'd refused to admit it to himself. Now that he knew, he wished he'd never agreed to any part of this deal.

"This is called terrorist activity, Costa! If we help you and this whole thing goes to hell, we end up in prison! Forever! I'm not going to risk Arbor being sent back. Maybe you don't care about that, but we do! You can't ask that from either of us. You had your choices taken away from you a long time ago. How can you do the same thing to us? It doesn't make you any better than Swaden and the rest of them. Or worse, it makes you look like you think you're better than us regular people because you were born that way. And that's pretty much what starts the whole thing, isn't it? One side proving who's stronger?"

Costa's voice pitched into a roar. "You will help me!"

"Or what?" Priest shouted. "You'll stick a pacifier on the back of my neck and tattoo my face to make me know my place? Just because you're doing this for the greater good doesn't make it right! I bet Swaden said exactly the same thing to himself when he put two bullets in you!"

Costa started and looked away. Both men stood unmoving, the tension eventually deflating as Costa's posture lost its intensity. A twisted line crossed his brow and he chewed his lower lip. When he finally spoke, it was much softer and defeated.

"That was a cheap tactic, but I suppose you're right." Costa ground his teeth as he continued. The admission had to be grating. "It is a bit much to ask to put yourself at that level of risk. You've both helped me more than anyone else would have done in the same position. I hope you're willing to forgive me."

"I'm sorry too." If Costa could admit his fault, Priest could at least throw him a rope. He stepped forward and laid a gentle hand on Costa's shoulder. "Let's do what we came here for and get the hell out of this place."

Arbor looked only too eager to agree. "I have the lab pulled up. I think it's down this way."

With a hurried step, Arbor headed down the makeshift corridor along the workstations. They passed a few darkened offices, rounding a corner to an enclosure mounted onto the far wall of the building. A short platform sat walled into the alcove, surrounded by a series of monitors and hard-wired computers. On top of the platform, in its niche, was the android treasure they sought.

The height of an average man, the generic figure stood. Its skin was pink and waxy, the body devoid of gender. Small, colorless nipples stuck out from the flat chest and the groin was smooth. Not male, not female. There was something unnatural about how still it perched, a rubbery statue of sexless, synthetic flesh. Carefully, Priest stepped closer. The eyes were closed, and he prayed they wouldn't snap open as he tried to hold down his revulsion. This was the breakthrough tech Costa was so excited about?

"This is kind of nasty."

Costa strode over to the bank of monitors and read the display. "The appearance subroutines and synth-flesh are installed but not activated. This is the raw body template prior to features being established. We're in luck they also haven't had the opportunity to upload the AI. It's a blank canvas waiting for programming."

Priest brow wrinkled as he poked the pink doll. "This thing can't be hidden easily."

"Once we're finished, we'll need to wrap him until we can find a safer place to begin the startup sequence. You brought the container, correct?"

"Yeah, I got it." Priest reached into Arbor's bag and pulled out a flat, quarter-meter metal square. Tapping a few buttons, he unfolded the panel, reshaping it until it formed a long box. A shiver iced Priest's spine at the sight of a metal coffin.

Arbor sidled close to Priest. "Your box is too tall to hide. How is that going to work?"

"It has a built-in anti-grav and it's shielded to block scans. I've used it to bring a few things on board that weren't on the manifest in the past."

Arbor looked aghast. "You've smuggled things on board the ship?"

"Not anymore." Priest winced at Arbor's disapproval—just one more reason to get this over with and walk away. "Besides, now's not the time to discuss this."

Costa huffed. "Could the two of you take your juvenile nonsense elsewhere? We have important work to do and I am trying to concentrate."

Priest cringed when Costa stepped up on the platform and placed his hands flat on the android's chest. The weird skin creeped him right out. A tense quiet fell over the trio as the monitors flickered and Costa crushed his eyes closed. Sharp lines dug trenches along his features and a sheen burst out along his temples. Stamping down the urge to make sure Costa was all right was difficult. He didn't need the distraction. The alcove hummed as the lights increased.

Priest wanted to hurl when the android's skin rippled.

The pink flesh swelled, urging shapes to push from underneath, filling out the frame with a natural musculature. The synth-flesh color darkened with all the subtle undertones, making it indistinguishable from the real thing. Genitals sprouted from the groin and the face lost its indistinct quality, sharpening and narrowing the cheek lines and features. Dark hair sprouted on the head and groin and, once it stopped, a beautiful, nude replica of Costa stood in its place.

The monitors calmed and Costa stepped back. The tremors in his hands and unsteady footing were pronounced.

"You're struggling. Are you okay?"

"I'm perfectly fine. I just need to gather myself before I take the next step." Costa's eyes glistened as he looked up at his doppelganger. "He's exactly as I remember him, but taller."

Even though Priest had seen Costa undressed on a number of occasions, there was something creepy about the unconscious naked male in front of him. He was compelled to avert his eyes. The fact the nerds programmed the android to be capable of having genitals was disturbing enough. Now it looked like a dead version—or even a sex-doll version—of Costa. They needed to finish.

"Are you sure you have the strength to do this?"

Costa's trembling fingers graced the inert android's cheek. "Strength was never the issue between Poll and me. I was always the stronger of us. Delicacy was always Poll's forte. His skills had the finesse of a ballet dancer."

Arbor's eyes widened. "But Poll reached across the whole planet at once. How powerful are you?"

"I may be stronger than I once was, but currently I need a great deal more focus to keep from smashing my way through the door. Uploading Poll's data into this artificial brain is not going to be a simple task in the least."

"Maybe you should rest first."

"I seriously doubt we have that kind of time." Costa's voice softened as he whispered to the android. "Please show me I've done the right thing, Poll."

With a slow inhale, Costa's back straightened and his eyes closed. The monitors flickered as he once again placed his hands on the android body. The minutes passed in an eternity as Priest was forced to sit back and watch. Sweat broke out, soaking Costa's skin in a wave strong enough to erode the cosmetics covering his tattoos. The creases in his forehead were alarming as they grew in relation to the quake in his arms and legs. He stumbled as his skin paled and a line of blood spilled down his chin from his nose.

Something was wrong. Priest had seen Costa through withdrawal, watched his anguish mar his beauty. This was worse. He stepped forward and placed his hand on Costa's back. The clothing was wet with perspiration, and the tremors under his hand were out of control.

"Costa! You have to stop this!"

Teeth gnashed tight, Costa hissed. "Don't... not... bloody... finished..."

Priest jumped back when one of the monitors exploded in a bloom of sparks. The lights in the lab were beginning to strobe. The sounds of the manufacturing lab were becoming louder than what was safe. Nothing good ever came from these moments in Costa's presence.

Shifting his foot, Costa tried to steady himself as he refused to quit. Hard-pulsing veins appeared along his temple and his hair clung to his face. A sick keen came from him, causing Priest to shudder. Tears and sweat lines were indistinguishable from one another on Costa's face.

Without warning, Costa exhaled, and the room's discord abated. The noise retreated and the light and monitors stabilized. Costa's shoulders sagged in relief and he panted.

"There... Poll's saved." There was nothing level about Costa's thready voice.

Arbor checked the monitors next to the sleeping statue. "The AI's installed. He's in there."

Costa shifted his weight and his legs crumbled beneath him. Sprawled upon the stage before the perfect copy of himself, he coughed, sending a spray of crimson across his cheek and jaw. Priest rushed in, kneeling and pulling Costa into his lap.

"Costa, what's happening?"

His raspy weakness scared Priest. "Your Dr. Bosch...warned me my body was...becoming far too fragile...after using my power constantly for...so long. He was very kind...for a physician." Costa's arms and legs sat where they landed, unmoving since he collapsed. Only his head lolled about, his bloodshot eyes barely focused. His breathing was shallow and his speech was forced, nearly slurred.

Priest's pulse raced. "Don't worry. We'll get you out of here." Caressing Costa's face, Priest's words held little conviction. The skin under his palm was clammy and cool.

"That's very...sweet of you, but an utter...waste of time. I've done what I came for...and it appears I'm done as well. I was hoping...to see Poll open his eyes one last time."

A choking gasp escaped Priest. "Don't talk like that."

Costa's eyes drifted closed and Priest nearly screamed in denial. Arbor stepped near and knelt beside them both, the shock in his face a mirror of them all.

The lights brightened, a new spray of sparks burst from the charred monitor, and the machinery noise returned, growing louder than before. Both men craned their heads around, frightened and confused.

Priest wasn't sure who he was asking. "What's happening?"

Arbor pulled up his personal pad, his eyes narrowing as he scrolled through the screens. "The mini-reactor has started up in the assembly. It's on full and all the safety overrides are blocked."

Another flow of blood rushed from Costa's nose as his eyes opened halfway. "I...win."

Priest looked down at the bloody, fragile man in his arms. A wave of realization hit him dead center and his internal shriek of hysteria was stronger than everything that came before.

"It's like the engine room! He's going to blow this place! Son of a bitch!"

Over the sound of the machines, he could barely be heard. "You need to leave...me behind. I'll only...slow you down." Costa coughed again, dark sanguine further staining his beauty as his lidded eyes found Priest. "There...isn't time. Save Poll... You promised..."

Priest held Costa's head steady and forced him to look in his eyes. "Stay with me, Costa! We're not leaving you behind!"

"I can stall...the final moment long enough...to get you to a safe distance. But not...if you drag me out of here. And since my arms and legs...refuse to move, you will...have to drag me."

"Then we'll drag you too."

"Then...no one will survive it."

"Shut down the reactor!"

Costa's eyes rolled without direction, but his wavering voice held firm in its intent. "No."

"Please!"

A new anguish wracked Costa's words. "Take Poll with you...and activate him somewhere...safe. He deserves better...than this sad existence." Tears streaked lines through the blood and salt on Costa's cheeks. "I promised him...I would make his life better...when I arranged his sponsorship to Swaden. I need that promise...to not be a lie. Please. Go. Don't make all of this...end in vain."

"It's not supposed to be like this!" It took every iota of self-control to keep Priest from bursting into heaving sobs. Even so, he swallowed and gasped through every one of Costa's fractured sentences.

"It wasn't supposed...to be like this for any of us. Now you have the chance...to undo some of the horror we've lived with."

Priest's head snapped toward Arbor. "How much time do we have?"

The room's volume was deafening as Arbor checked his pad, telling Priest what he already knew. "Not nearly enough."

"*Damn it!*"

Trying to control himself, Priest pulled Costa close to his chest. Costa didn't even begin to return the gesture, his smaller body a limp rag doll. Accepting Costa was right was an ache in his chest. He pressed a kiss to Costa's forehead, an errant tear dripping down on his face.

"You see, Priest? I told you...I'm not the man to fall for..."

Priest chuckled in a sick, sad way. "Then everything's fine, 'cause in the end, I didn't. But that doesn't mean I wanted this to happen either. Fuck." He hissed back a sob. "We won't forget you, Costa."

"Arbor is far luckier...than he deserves." Costa's head lolled to the side allowing him to see Arbor. "You'd better take...very good care of Priest or I'll haunt you...and erase your handheld."

Arbor sniffed and stroked the wet hair from Costa's face. "I'll do my best. For him and for Poll."

"You both...should hurry. I'm not sure how much...longer I can delay the inevitable. There's far less of me now...than there used to be and it's becoming...quite cold in here."

Now that the moment was upon them, Priest froze. Walking away from the sagging man in his arms was more than he could manage. The guilt stilled his body. Every memory from their first meeting in the bar crashed in on him. Could this whole scenario have been avoided if he'd just ignored Costa in the first place?

Arbor grabbed a fistful of Priest's sleeve. "Come on!" The unmistakable terror in Arbor's eyes broke his stupor. "Please, I can't run very fast."

He could barely hear the plea, but it broke Priest's recriminations. Arbor needed him. There were enough risks in this escapade and he couldn't bear the thought of losing anyone else. Priest gently laid Costa down and placed a goodbye kiss on his lips. One by one, the lights in the lab were beginning to blow out from the overload. If they didn't hurry, they wouldn't be able to see their way out.

With a grunt, he lifted the unmoving android and scrambled to the container. Putting Poll inside and locking the lid was too disquieting to focus on. Heartbeat in a frenzy, Priest activated the box from the handle's control, causing it to hover off the floor. He snatched Arbor's hand, gave Costa one last farewell glance, and raced for the lift.

Thankfully, the lift was working. It was dangerous, but the stairs would take too long and Arbor would never be able to keep up. The floor display counted down and Priest's foot couldn't stop its restless tapping. A million things could go wrong at this juncture.

"Arbor, can you set off the fire alarms? We need to make sure no one's in the building."

Arbor scrolled through a few windows on his pad. His composure was fraying. "Costa's already done it. Suppression teams are on their way!"

The doors opened as they reached the ground floor. "Shit! Is your camouflage program still running?"

"Yes! Move faster! We have to get the fuck out of here!" Arbor pulled Priest toward the rear exit.

If suppression teams were on their way, the authorities wouldn't be far behind. They couldn't be found near the building. Priest pushed faster, nearly dragging Arbor behind. His smaller legs were sprinting and barely keeping up with Priest's longer strides.

Priest gripped the outer door's edge as it slid open, trying to shove it faster. They bolted out the back with the box in tow, running down the alleyway between the line of buildings. Stones flew under their feet as they rounded the corner behind the neighboring building.

The night sky went white and the thunderous concussion slammed them into the ground. The explosion could be felt and seen through everything around them. Priest managed to cover Arbor with his body as debris rained through the alley.

When the initial roar subsided, Priest rolled over. A sharp pain lanced through his ankle and shoulder from the fall, but he hazarded a look. The crate was intact and still hovering nearby against the wall, and Arbor was gasping heavily, but still breathing. There was far less charred rubble and silt covering the ground than there should be. The blast must have atomized a great deal of it. He crawled back around the corner to see.

The top half of the Forethought Industries skyscraper was gone, and what was left was a charred tower of useless material. Every window was shattered and blackened, and the metal structure didn't stand as straight as it should. Fire suppression units hovered around, firing foam into the burning husk even as pieces continued to collapse inward. Priest prayed everyone had gotten to a safe distance before the detonation, and he didn't want to watch if the whole building came down. Nothing inside could possibly be recovered.

Costa succeeded—in all of it. And that thought didn't make Priest want to cheer in triumph. It just left him numb at the loss of his friend.

Not a single word was uttered as Priest helped Arbor to his feet and dusted himself off. The ringing in his ears muffled the approaching sirens. The crate was still floating, so, with Arbor's hand in his, they limped back the way they came.

The rental sat exactly where they left it, several blocks away. The box fit inside the boot and the door closing held a finality resonating with grief. Priest slumped against the vehicle, the weight of reality a burden, leaving him small and lost in the world.

Swallowing back the tears, he scrubbed his face in his hands until he felt Arbor's hands on his waist. Arbor was shaking, his pleading eyes wet and glossy. The heat of his small palms was a lifeline Priest needed more than anything.

He stooped down, wrapped his arms around Arbor, and hoisted him off the ground in a crushing hug. No protest was made, Arbor simply clutched tighter as Priest absorbed the strength to not let the whole evening bury him.

Arbor didn't move a centimeter, his ragged voice buried against Priest's neck and shoulder. "Take me home."

All Priest could do was nod in silence.

Chapter Fifteen

THERE WAS ONLY one other person in the shower room with Arbor, and he managed to stay calm. He focused on the hot spray against his skin, feeling the rush of water pooling and trailing over his body. The other man had said hello, making small chatter, and went about his business. He didn't work his way closer and he didn't do anything to invade Arbor's personal space.

Priest had started bringing him into the shower with him during more populated times to break his reactions. So far it was working. The alarm he felt with others in the room was diminishing in small doses, but a bit of the old nightmare taunted him at inopportune moments. Experiences in prison could be difficult to unlearn.

He reached high for the soap dispenser and went through the ritual. Soaping his body with his stubby fingers, he repeated the mantra. The *Santa Claus* is a safe place. The *Santa Claus* is a safe place.

Each day was easier than the last.

He'd taken to showering alone over the last week, proud of himself for overcoming at least part of his jitters. Bit by bit, he convinced himself, those fears would be nothing but bad memories and could be ignored. Hopefully, sooner rather than later.

A graveled voice sparked a new frisson of apprehension down his spine. "There's the man I was looking for."

Arbor turned to see the mechanic, Dante, entering the shower room. Normally, Arbor was fine in the large man's presence, but the sight of him naked and coming his way was testing his rehabilitation.

Maybe it was the sight of broad muscles straining under Dante's dark complexion or the jet-black hair shaved into a thick stripe down his scalp. Maybe it was the devilish goatee or the dozen or so tattoos over his chest and shoulders he wore like badges of honor. Maybe it was the bullring in his nose or the matching rings in his nipples, or the last one glinting off the lights from the head of his swinging, veined cock. Maybe it was how everything about the man was fierce and imposing.

Arbor froze as Dante walked toward him, his fearsome body blocking the only escape from the room. The other bather was gone, and Arbor hadn't noticed the man's exit. There was no one else to witness what might happen next.

Dante took the shower next to Arbor and started the water.

"Do you think you can help me sync my tools? A couple of the scanners are giving me a problem, man. Pretty sure it's a software thing." Pressing his hands to the wall, Dante ran his head under the spray, causing his mohawk to flatten to his head in heavy strands. There was nothing threatening about his posture or attitude.

Arbor wanted to kick himself for being so paranoid.

"Yeah. I can help with that. It should be pretty easy." Taking a quiet breath to settle himself, Arbor went back to his shower. He forced his face into the center of the spray, trying to wash away the stupid.

Dante peeked over in Arbor's direction. "You're looking a little skittish. I make you nervous?"

"It's not you. I just have a lot of baggage."

"Everyone's got baggage. It's just how you carry it."

Arbor thought for a moment. "It's getting lighter." It was becoming easier to keep his anxieties from completely taking over. He only needed to be more sensible and think before reacting.

"Well, if it helps, I'm the scariest dude on this ship, and you got nothing to worry about."

Arbor chuckled as the panic began to disarm itself. "It does, thanks. I never got the chance to thank you for the work you did on my quarters."

"No sweat, brother. A man's home should be comfortable. When Priest asked for help, I jumped on board. It was something that should've been done a long time ago."

"I really appreciate it. We can go over your tools tomorrow morning. It shouldn't take long."

"Muchas gracias. I've been having trouble with them since that passenger McQuillen freaked out and nearly killed us all."

Arbor could only nod as Dante all but growled out the last part. Costa's presence had created a lasting ripple in Mrs. Claus's data and a great deal of his time was spent tracking down and cleaning up the disruption. Re-initializing the whole system wasn't an option while the ship was en route. It wasn't surprising the effect could be felt in other random areas on the ship as well.

The worry was abating but a wave of sadness filled its place. They were deep into a voyage back to Alpha Centauri and it had been several weeks since the catastrophe on Omoikane. Arbor had no doubt Costa planned how his end would come, but the man deserved better. A lifetime's worth of personal hell was at the core of all Costa's problems. Even with all the games and manipulations, Arbor couldn't help but sympathize with the turns his life took.

All of his resentment and jealousy dissipated with the destruction of Forethought Industries.

Still shaken and covered with debris, Arbor and Priest had gone back to the *Santa Claus* that night and never left the vessel's safety for the rest of their leave. Standing in this very spot, they shared the shower, rinsing away the grime and horror of the evening's events. Tending to each other, they were never out of contact. It wasn't a sensual act, rather their need to be tethered. They clung to each other in the dark, flinching at every noise, and waited for the backlash that never came.

No authorities came knocking on the door. No one questioned them afterward. The suffocating tension lasted until the ship launched two days later. For some reason, the captain brought everyone back early. Neither he nor Priest spent much time discussing it. They wanted to move on.

"That's all done now," Arbor said.

Now thoroughly wet, Dante began washing himself with two overflowing handfuls of soap. "That's good. The crew wasn't happy to have him on board after that messed up shit that got you hurt. Yeah, I know the captain was involved, too, but McQuillen was in the middle of it. There'd have been a problem if he came back after we landed in Omoikane."

Dante's hands went straight down his chest and into his groin, bringing forth heaps of suds over the mounds of muscle. Was he putting on a show or was this his usual bathing routine? Not wanting to give him any ideas by staying too long, Arbor finished his rinse off and shut down the water.

"I better get going. The captain gave me permission to hang out with Priest on the bridge tonight. I haven't been up there since I came on board."

Dante nodded without looking, focused on his personal hygiene. "You have a good time. You deserve it."

Water poured off Arbor's body, leaving a trail as his wet footsteps slapped the tile floor. Arbor almost stumbled into the wall as he collected his towel from the hook on the wall next to the entrance. It was a relief to bury his face in the thick fabric. He could barely see with the water running into his eyes.

Dante called out. "Arbor?" Every word the man said bore a vibration akin to an animal's snarl.

Pulling his face from the towel, Arbor turned back. Facing the wall, Dante was still lathering, rivers of white foam outlining the valleys of his back and haunches. "Yes?"

"Make sure Priest is treating you right."

Arbor's brow arched with an odd sort of confusion. "Okay...I will." He stared at the wide shoulders of the mechanic as if trying to read the man's thoughts. Why would Dante be saying that?

Dante peered over his shoulder, his dark gaze roaming over Arbor's dripping wet body. "'Cause if he don't, brother, I'll be knocking on your door."

A new kind of shiver raced over Arbor's body, and it wasn't fear. "Really?" But the sensation wasn't arousal either.

"Go have fun." Dante turned back to his shower like he hadn't said a word. "Come find me in the morning when you have the time."

In a mild daze, Arbor headed into the locker room and retrieved his clothing. Had Dante really made a pass at him? The idea was absurd, yet there it was in front of him.

How many years had Arbor seen himself as someone unworthy of love and affection? How many years were wasted believing no one would see something worthwhile inside him due to a fluke of nature? Priest proved him wrong, even when he resisted the concept.

Arbor wasn't actually interested. Dante proved to be a good-natured man, but his fetishes were too extreme for Arbor, if the other crew members' rumors could be believed. Arbor didn't do kinks. Someone else would have to make Dante happy. It was, however, flattering beyond measure.

Dante had a magnificent body men would kill for, but nothing trumped the charge in Arbor's chest and quickening of his breath whenever he set eyes on Priest. When Priest smiled back, his feet threatened to resist gravity. Showering with Priest lately had been an exercise in self-control. There had been others in the room at the same time. No. Priest was all Arbor needed.

Arbor buckled his pants and slipped on his sandals, striding out of the locker room with an energized step. Walking down the hallway to his quarters, several crew members smiled and greeted him as he passed without shying away or giving a cursory nod. For the first time in so long, he felt welcome. It all began after the incident in the engine room and the return of Mr. Wiggles. The shift of attitude among the crew was subtle at first, but sowed itself, grew, and flourished.

After a lifetime of chaos, Arbor felt confident, desirable, and part of a community—no longer an outcast.

THE VAST NOTHING of space rarely looked so inviting.

Priest sat back in the pilot's chair with Arbor wedged between his thighs and pressed back against his chest. They were deep into the flight path, with little to do, and it felt right to have one arm belted around Arbor's torso, holding him tight. He could still reach all the controls and steer the

Santa Claus on the rare chance the sensors picked up anything.

"How's the view, Arbor?"

Danverse stood at his bridge console watching over the pair. He seemed all right with them sharing the chair. When Arbor climbed in, Priest's breath caught, anticipating the loud command to cease and desist. If anything, Danverse looked almost pleased. Priest would take it. There was no telling how long the captain's approval could last.

"It doesn't get any better than this. Thank you for allowing me on the bridge, Captain."

Priest stage-whispered into Arbor's ear. "Ass kisser."

"You could stand to take a few lessons from your man, Priest."

"And ruin my well-earned reputation, sir?"

Danverse snorted, a genuine rumble of laughter rolling his words. "Just don't crash us into anything."

Arbor squeezed the arm around him. "Don't worry. I'll keep a watch out."

A permanent grin blessed Priest's face. Arbor was right. It didn't get any better than this.

Priest looked down at the man who had settled into his chair and his life. The small patch of skin at his scalp was visible where the hair didn't grow properly yet. Dr. Bosch said the newly regenerated skin would have to catch up to the rest. Arbor spent a lot of time trying to cover it up, and kept himself clean-shaven to hide the similar area on his jawline. When Priest told him, "Chicks dig scars," Arbor punched him in the balls.

Priest had to sleep alone that night. The scars were never brought up again, even though he liked them. They were proof Arbor was alive and Lady Luck smiled on him— on them both.

The only unfair thing right now was the furrow of Arbor's buttocks molding around his groin. It was still unfamiliar territory and he wanted to play there, but he didn't pressure his man. The sensation, however, was a merciless tease. If Priest popped a chubby now—and he was already halfway there—there would be nothing he could do about it. How ironic Arbor would have to sit there to hide his hard-on, although he was the source of the problem.

How much longer was it until his shift ended?

Priest and Arbor both turned at the sound of the bridge main door sliding open.

"Hey, Mac." Arbor waved.

Nodding to them both, Mac stepped in and approached Danverse at his station.

"Hey, boy."

Mac pressed in, wedging himself so close Danverse was forced to turn away from his console. He shifted back a step, trying to read Mac's face. Staring down at his boy, Danverse waited patiently for Mac to speak.

With his head lowered, Mac looked up through his lashes. "I've been bad, sir."

The confused expression dissolved into something stoic with an undertone of deviance. "You have, boy?"

"Yes, sir." Mac stood with his hands behind his back and his shoulders dropped in penitence.

Danverse slid his hand over Mac's neck and fingered the dark hairs at the base of his skull. "Are you asking to be properly disciplined?"

"If you think it's what I need, sir."

The hint of a lusty grin came over the captain as his chest swelled and his grip on Mac firmed. "Priest, I'm going to the Day Cabin for a while to discuss a situation with Mac. We don't wish to be disturbed. For at least twenty minutes."

Licking his lips, Danverse's gaze roamed over Mac. "Make it thirty."

Priest nearly rolled his eyes. It was like watching the opening for bad porn unfolding before him. "Sure thing, Captain."

"Arbor's in charge of the bridge."

Arbor saluted. "Aye, aye, Captain."

"Wait a minute! Arbor's not even a ranked officer!"

"Do not disturb, Corporal." Danverse placed an arm around Mac's waist and ushered him toward the adjoining door which led to the Day Cabin. Before they entered, Priest caught Mac and Arbor sharing an identical smirk and glance. What the hell was that?

The door slid shut and the lock engaged. Arbor settled back into the seat against Priest and let out a breath. "Do they do that very often?"

"A little more often than I'd like in front of me, but it's his ship."

"So they'll be gone for thirty minutes at least."

"Definitely."

Arbor hopped out of the seat and faced Priest. "Good."

Rubbing up the length of Priest's thighs, the heat of Arbor's palms was making quick work of finishing the erection begging to be born. Kneading and squeezing the muscles of Priest's legs, Arbor leaned forward, nuzzling his face against the trapped hardness straining the fabric underneath. With both hands, Priest held on to the welcome head in his lap.

Grabbing Priest's wrists, Arbor redirected them to the active pads on his armrests. "Keep your hands on the flight controls, Corporal Jones."

"What are you doing?"

"Quiet. You heard the captain. I'm in charge here."

Priest gave Arbor a compliant, yet dirty smirk. "If you say so, sir."

The look between Mac and Arbor: the two of them planned this. Mac distracts Danverse and Arbor gets to play on the bridge. Was there a reason to complain or call out the deception? Hell no. Priest was riding this game out to its conclusion.

Arbor's hands worked their way to the buttons of Priest's fly and wasted no time releasing him into the air. The feel of those small but sturdy hands was magic. They glided over his shaft and cupped his balls as he sat back and enjoyed the attention. If Arbor wanted to service him, why would he object?

It was difficult not to cry out when Arbor leaned forward and ran his thick wet tongue over every centimeter of Priest's obscenely exposed organ. Holding himself still was a challenge, but he kept his hands in position and touched nothing he wasn't supposed to. There would be no benefit if Arbor stopped because he didn't follow orders.

It was becoming hard to focus as the heat and lust blurred his senses. An observant lover, Arbor had wasted no time learning what kind of suction and friction made Priest a speechless idiot. When the wet heat stopped, he wanted to whimper at the loss.

Holding firm to Priest's cock with one hand, Arbor dismantled his own pants with the other and kicked them to the side. If it was possible, the sight made Priest's aching pillar even harder. A small vial sat in the palm of Arbor's free hand. With his thumb, he flipped it open and squeezed a fine line of clear liquid over the head of Priest's cock. He nearly screamed when Arbor slid his hand over the rigid length, spreading the slick fluid.

Arbor kept stroking, making Priest's struggle to stay seated more and more difficult. He arched each time Arbor reached the base.

With a twist of Arbor's fist, a hard shiver bulleted to the tips of Priest's every extremity, making him slam his head back against the seat. "Oh fuck, that's so good."

"It gets better."

When Arbor stopped this time, he climbed up and straddled Priest's hips.

"What are you doing?" The gorgeous sight of Arbor's leaking hardness was only matched by the soft brushing of his bare bottom against Priest's swollen member. Arbor reached back and planted the slippery glans between his silky cheeks.

"Just shut up and pilot the ship, Corporal. Daddy's working here."

Priest was afraid to move as he felt himself sliding inside. The grasping heat enveloped the head and swallowed down the shaft. He could feel the ring of muscle tightening and releasing as it worked. The sensation left Priest gasping for air.

Arbor moved up and down, making the gradual descent. When the globes of his ass finally met Priest's balls, both men let out their breaths.

Air rushed out of Priest in a sweet rush. "Oh god, you're tight."

"I'm sorry I waited so long." Arbor was breathing hard and a sheen of sweat glossed his forehead. Priest worried he was hurting him, but one glance down at Arbor's hard dick changed everything. A thread of slick arousal left its evidence from the exposed tip, over the foreskin, down to the base and beyond. Arbor was fine.

Locking eyes with Priest, Arbor rose and settled back down again, eliciting a pleasured cry from both men. It wasn't long before the slow, deliberate action became a desperate ride of craving.

With both hands on Priest's shoulders to steady himself, Arbor bounced at a wild pace. Grunting and snarling, he rode in a frenzy, finally giving Priest something he'd adamantly refused until now. Priest sat with a death grip on the armrest, holding back his wish to grab Arbor by the hips and start pounding like a beast. Each thrust was a sign of the trust placed into his hands. He let Arbor give in to his needs.

If only he could last forever in this perfect moment of hedonism. But the pleasure was peaking and Priest couldn't hold out as the tight channel wrung the orgasm out of him. His head slammed back as each pulse shot deep into his partner, his mouth wordless and frozen in ecstasy.

Even as Priest's body was suffering the aftershocks, Arbor continued his ride until he stood and shoved his thick cock into Priest's open mouth. Holding onto each side of his head, Arbor started a reckless plunge in and out. Priest suckled as hard as he could for his reward.

Arbor's balls were pulled tight as the flesh swelled and surged, filling Priest's mouth with his release. Sharp pains blossomed along his scalp as Arbor's fists tightened, but he sucked and licked, refusing to stop until Arbor couldn't take any more. Priest tried to follow as Arbor pried himself out from between Priest's lips. Cock shiny and softening, Arbor slumped down into Priest's lap.

"That was fucking incredible." Priest murmured his awe because speaking too loud seemed wrong in the sanctity of the moment. The sticky wetness cooling on his lips and chin was a mix of what escaped during Arbor's finish, but he made no quick effort to clean himself. Anything he could do to prolong the event was worth it. Arbor leaned forward, wrapping himself around Priest, his chest heaving as they calmed.

"I've been dying to do this."

"Does Danverse know you planned this?" Priest stroked Arbor's hair with a gentle touch, trying to share the floating sensation.

Arbor snorted and shook his head. "No. But Mac was happy to run interference. Everyone gets what they want, even the captain."

Priest raised Arbor's head with his hand and peered deep into his eyes. "You didn't have to do that for me."

"I know."

"But I'm really glad you did. It means a lot to me that you're willing." He placed a deep kiss on Arbor's mouth, their tongues dancing along each other in lazy harmony. When Priest pulled back, both men were grinning like idiots. "I still expect you to fuck me regularly though."

Not having lost their lusty haze, Arbor shifted forward and ran his tongue over Priest's chin, taking his time to clean the mess he'd left behind. With one hand, he tilted Priest's head back to catch a line running down into the valley of his neck.

"Oh, I will. You don't ever have to worry. That ass of yours is too sweet to give up on."

Priest cupped Arbor's bare bottom in his hands, the silky firmness sending new surges of heat into him. "I hate to say this, but we'd better get dressed. The captain'll be in a good mood when he comes out, but he'll only deal with so much." Priest chuckled as he brushed his lips over Arbor's. "But as soon as I'm off shift, it's my turn."

PRIEST TRIED TO sound offended as they entered Arbor's quarters. "What do you mean Dante hit on you?"

While he wasn't exactly worried, he wasn't thrilled either. A possessiveness was welling up inside him over the idea of Arbor with other men. What a startling new development. Arbor's over-the-top chiding wasn't helping matters. Was it possible to be annoyed and entertained at the same time? The little snot was looking awfully pleased with himself.

"I'm pretty sure he'll challenge you to a duel if you don't treat me right."

Chuckling, Priest knelt and placed a playful bite at the junction of Arbor's neck and shoulder. "If I didn't want to treat you right, do you think I would have gotten him to help me with all of this?"

Arbor's quarters had undergone a severe overhaul. The furniture had all been shortened to accommodate his stature. There would be no more awkward climbing into the chair to sit in front of the newly lowered desk. Mr. Wiggles sat proudly on one of the shelves, which had been relocated to the lower half of the walls. Only long-term storage rested on ledges out of reach, but since storage bays in the walls couldn't be realistically altered, a series of movable ladders had been installed. The bed was surrounded by a two-tier platform, effectively creating a series of stairs. Everything in Arbor's room was refitted to accommodate his size.

"I still can't believe you went to all this trouble."

Arbor leaned back into Priest, who wrapped his arm around him without thinking. Leaning his head against Priest, Arbor let out a contented sigh—the kind he only made when he was happy and smiling.

Priest brushed a kiss along Arbor's temple. "You deserve to finally have a home that fits you for a change. I kind of feel like a giant in here, but I like it."

"If I haven't told you enough, I love it."

"Good. Although I'm starting to rethink having Dante help. Even if he is our best maintenance tech."

After he petitioned Danverse to modify Arbor's quarters, Priest worried Dante wouldn't be interested in helping. Now he understood why Dante was only too thrilled to be involved. Without him, it would have taken Priest weeks to figure out the best method to accomplish everything. Dante took every suggestion Priest had and even improved on it, making it all a reality in less than seven days. The look on Arbor's face when it was finished was worth burning every free period he had for a week.

Arbor swiveled his head to look Priest in the face. "You don't think he'd actually try anything, do you?"

"No. That's not Dante's style. He doesn't play with the partnered crew members. For all his intensity, he's way too honorable to be a home-wrecker." Priest knew it was true, and had nothing to worry about the hulking tech, but it still itched at him.

"Then why did he say something today?"

Priest shrugged. "Probably to let you know you have friends you didn't think you had and make sure you were good with me. He may be honorable, but my reputation ain't nowhere near so clean." A flash of doubt hit Priest and the question came out without thinking. "Unless you want to try him out."

Arbor turned with an odd look that quickly sobered. Climbing up the steps of his bed, he stood on the mattress and grabbed Priest's collar, pulling him close. Priest couldn't help but stare into those deep eyes, and what he saw there wasn't the annoyed reaction expected when he said something stupid.

"Your reputation is perfectly good with me." The shine in Arbor's eyes graced the buoyant smile on his lips. "And you don't ever need to worry. I don't want to share."

A laughing exhale of relief blew out of Priest. "Me neither."

Hearing those words meant so much. After so many years of bouncing from bed to bed and short-term partners, Priest had never heard such devotion in another man's voice aimed his way. It made his world brighter and encouraged him to be a better man. Not a total nerdy chump, but better. The warmth he felt made him ignore Arbor's impish smirk.

"But if you fuck me over, I'm gonna have Dante kick your ass."

Priest pulled Arbor so close his breath puffed against his mouth. "Never. Gonna. Happen."

With radiant smiles, they shared a soft caress of lips filled with unspoken potential. It was short and potent, leaving Priest drifting on a sea of calm waters. Life was good.

Arbor pulled back, his face growing serious. "Not that I want to break the moment, but I need to check the cargo."

The moment calmed and Priest nodded, making way for Arbor to step down and head for the tallest closet storage. Arbor typed his password into the adjoining keypad and Priest suppressed a cringe—like he always did—as the door opened.

Inside stood the metal crate, untouched and unseen by anyone other than the two of them. Arbor checked the container's edges for flaws or issues, but Priest believed opening it made Arbor equally uneasy. A few quick touches to the controls and the lid swung open, a mannequin named Poll its only inhabitant.

The whole thing was eerie. It was like having a corpse hidden under the cupboards. Weeks ago, they managed to find a few pieces of clothing to make Poll decent. There was something unsettling about his state of undress, which neither one wanted to comment on.

Priest couldn't help but crack jokes to ease the tension. "See, this is why you can't leave me. You're an accomplice. A studly accomplice, but an accomplice. How's he doing?"

Arbor looked over the readout on his handheld. "Shut down, but all systems are green. No significant activity. Tell me again why he's stashed in my closet?"

"Because if someone sees the crate in mine, they'll think I'm smuggling and start asking questions. With you, not so much."

"There better not be any smuggling in the future, Priest. I don't want to lose you over a prison sentence. For either of us."

Priest leaned forward and resisted the urge to touch the sleeping android. "Then we stay clean and don't do anything stupid."

"This kind of qualifies."

"Yeah. Kind of."

It was bizarre how lifelike Poll's body was—aside from not breathing. The synth-flesh was indistinguishable from the real thing and, other than being taller and lacking the facial tattoos, was a dead-on copy of Costa. Knowing Costa was gone didn't make Poll's presence any easier.

It should have helped knowing they might have saved Poll in this extraordinary way, but his face was a reminder of a friend lost. Priest wondered what would have happened if Costa could have survived. It seemed an unfair gambit for the twins to trade places. But Costa was the dominant one. It would be in his nature to sacrifice himself to set his brother free.

At least there was honor, if not comfort, in the thought.

Arbor leaned in, examining Poll's hands and arms without touching. "The tech in me wants to boot him up and test the transfer. We have no way of being sure it worked until we do. Sometimes it feels really creepy knowing he's in here."

"I promised to take care of him."

Arbor stepped backward and his shoulders dropped. "I know. I wish we could activate him on board, but from what Dante said earlier, it sounds like the crew is still really touchy over what happened with Costa in the engine room. A taller, android version of him isn't going to go over well. They aren't ready for that."

"As soon as we can find a safe place to start him up and get him settled, we will. Maybe on Alpha Centauri."

Priest closed the lid, activated the lock on the crate, and shut the closet. It was easier when Poll wasn't visible.

"He's stolen property. We can't cut him loose just anywhere."

"I know. As soon as we can, we'll figure something out. Until then, we keep him boxed and out of sight."

Walking forward, Arbor wrapped his arms around Priest's hips and pressed his face into his abdomen. "It still seems wrong."

"Because it is." Priest returned the embrace and hunched over so he could kiss the top of Arbor's head. "But we didn't go through all of this to have him impounded. What happened to them was all kinds of fucked up. No one deserved the life they lived through. It's too late for Costa, but one way or another we'll find a happy ending for Poll."

"All right." Arbor nodded into Priest. "We can do this."

Priest stroked a feather-light touch through Arbor's hair. "So you're with me until the happy ending?"

"Even beyond that."

Acknowledgements

A special heartfelt thanks to NineStar Press for giving this book & series new life. I love the care it's received in this new edition.

Thank you members, friends, & staff at Gay Authors.org. Without you all I might never have had the courage to take this ride.

And a special thanks and love for Tom, who may not have understood my muses (yes, plural) and creative needs, but put up with me and them anyway.

About the Author

While spending years more focused on visual arts, J. Alan Veerkamp never let go of his innate passion for storytelling, wanting to write and draw comic books when he grew up. Once he discovered M/M fiction, a whole new world opened filled with possibilities. Why couldn't you have fantastic and dynamic sexy tales with an M/M cast? He started reading the online tales of authors like, Night Tempest, Rob Colton, and Alicia Nordwell, which only fueled his need to create. Eventually he found GayAuthors.org, and with a little coercive nudge, started sharing his tales with an unexpected level of positive response. The experience and support gave him the courage to cross his fingers and aim for the world of M/M publishing.

Born and raised in Michigan, J. Alan continues to type away, wishing it was practical to use an noisy, old fashioned keyboard that clacks with each strike, if just to annoy his loving partner and spoiled miniature dachshund.

Facebook: www.facebook.com/jalanveerkamp

Twitter: @jalanveerkamp

Website: www.jalanveerkamp.wordpress.com

Other books by this author

The Luxorian Fugitive
A Cook's Tale

Also Available from NineStar Press

Connect with NineStar Press

Website: NineStarPress.com

Facebook: NineStarPress

Facebook Reader Group: NineStarNiche

Twitter: @ninestarpress

Tumblr: NineStarPress

Costa McQuillen has escaped from Earth, where being para-human—a Pariah—with tech empathic abilities is illegal, and marks him for extermination. Arrogant and standoffish, Costa is unable to trust anyone but is willing to risk everyone's safety in his desperate effort to reach the planet Omoikane. His best solution, gaining passage on board the *Santa Claus*.

Arbor Kittering is the crew's newest coding tech. Having spent a short time in prison for data hacking and falsifying government files, the *Santa Claus* is his last chance at a new start—if he can decipher the strange malfunctions plaguing the ship.

Eugene "Priest" Jones, the *Santa Claus*'s Head Pilot, is a bit of a scoundrel. Perpetually single, Priest is attracted to Costa *and* Arbor. In truth, he'd like to have both, but it's clear even his grifting and gambling skills can't make that happen.

Now as they all travel together, it appears Priest needs to make a choice before it's too late as each of their lives intertwine with potentially dangerous and deadly consequences.